# THE DEMON HUNTER'S WIFE

## C J POWELL

For L and E.

I have fun with you every day!

xxx

# Meet Cute

Mum crawls upon the ceiling.

Her pyjamas are on backwards.

Both facts.

Both unusual.

Also unusual is the book that lies on the floor of the living room. Leather-bound, with aged cream pages covered in strange glyphs bordered by columns of hand-drawn skulls. Next to the book is a small bell. Next to that, a picture of Dad in his uniform.

Flickering scented candles, the big Yankee ones that come in jars, sit arranged in a pentagram around the picture. Between them are lines drawn in what looks like salt.

The room smells lovely. Cinnamon, a hint of nutmeg, and something else festive. Bergamot? It's often bergamot with Mum. She says it makes her feel like she's at a day spa in the comfort of her own home.

"Mum? What are you doing up there?"

"Mum?" slavers Mum from up high, her voice several octaves lower than it should be. "Your mother is gone." She spins 180 degrees on her hands and feet and scampers like a spider to the centre of the room, stopping just short of the hanging wicker lampshade.

Sadie's hand goes to her head to steady it. It's been a messy night on the Winchester tiles, and the room is spinning like a merry-go-round. With the back of her mouth as dry as sand, and her head throbbing like a penis in a romance novel, all she's dreamed about on the short taxi ride home is a big pint of water and to finish her kebab, whilst watching a terrible monster movie on Netflix.

"How did you get up there?"

"I do not know how I came to be here, but you will be my first sacrifice."

Mum drops from the ceiling, lands on her haunches, and shimmies forwards with a jerky, boneless movement more commonly associated with those inflatable air dancers that are sometimes found outside of car sales showrooms.

Sadie's danger sense isn't that well-honed — whose is at twenty-one when you've never lived away from your quiet leafy suburb in Hampshire? — so she steps further into the living room. Perhaps Mum's just having an unusually erratic sleepwalking episode. She's not been sleeping that well since Dad passed. Sadie sometimes hears her crying through the walls.

Something strange draws her attention to the floor. Mum's feet look weird.

Ah! It finally comes together. Synapses spring to life inside her work-shy student brain. Pieces of evidence collide to form an unexpected whole. Her heart rate skyrockets. She's made a mistake.

A big one.

Mum's pyjamas aren't on backwards.

Ooooh noooo!

It's her head that's on the wrong way round.

"Er, Mum?" Sadie takes a tentative step back.

Mum's face lights up as she stalks closer. Not metaphorically, with caring and motherly love: her eyes actually light up, shining a glacial blue with menacing hunger. She gropes forwards with threatening hands outstretched.

Ah, shit! Sadie falls back and raises her kebab in doner defence.

Just as Mum grips her arm with ice-cold fingers, the lounge window explodes inwards, showering the room with deadly shards.

Through it, he came. Landing in a diving roll and springing up to his feet.

He says something, and judging by his smug expression, it seems he is proud of whatever it was. For his benefit, she assumes it was witty and cool. Something that might have created a good first impression. That might have tickled a part of her that had hitherto remained untickled. But, telling the truth, she hadn't heard him over the slavering of her mother.

He draws a shining sword from a sheath on his back and races across the room. Says something dashing like, "Why'd you guys always feel the need to spin the head around? It really gives you away."

Mum vomits in his general direction, dousing him from head to toe in a gout of black gunge.

"Herp," says Sadie, trying not to throw up herself.

He and Mum circle one another, preparing for battle as if they had done it a thousand times. Mum moves in a way Sadie has never seen, scratching out with clawed fingers. He swings the sword in retaliation, but Mum is too quick. She scrapes a red gouge from his bare forearm with long, jagged fingernails. Sadie could have sworn Mum's nails had been short when she'd left for the pub. Perhaps she's been taking a potent biotin supplement?

"Don't hurt her. She's my mother!" shouts Sadie. But she's too confused, or perhaps afraid, to do anything to help either party. Instead she waits, hopping from foot to foot in anguish.

Despite her mother's head being the wrong way round, and what appears to be the continuation of an age-old battle between the forces of light and dark going on in the living room, Sadie can't help but notice that this man is rather attractive in an odd, magician-y sort of way. Short brown hair. Piercing blue eyes. Just the right amount of stubble to bring out the square of his jaw without making him look too scraggy. Black jeans, black denim jacket over a black hoody. A brown leather satchel thrown over his shoulder. Even the addition of her mother's inky vomit gives him a smooth, oiled-up, Chippendale-like charm. Not that he's overly muscled. She's never been a fan of the overly muscled man.

He doesn't appear much older than her. Maybe a year or two?

His eyes widen as he spots her. "Where'd you come from?"

"The pub."

He dodges another blow from Mum's swiping claws. "If I can't hurt it, what else would you suggest I do?"

"Well, you can stop referring to my mother as an 'it' for a start."

He scoffs with minor annoyance and sheaths his sword, then gropes for something in the front pocket of his satchel. He removes a green cloth, holding it in a cupped hand, stands his ground, chooses his moment, then pounces and wraps the cloth around Mum's mouth.

Sadie blinks. What is this? A kidnapping? She should do something. She scans the room for a weapon. Her eyes fall on Dad's old service rifle hung up over the fireplace. It no longer works. Instead, with her eyes trained on the rucking pair, she slips to the side and removes a large novel from the bookcase.

Mum's lids droop, and with a little more erratic flailing and spinning, she passes out. When the man turns his back to ease her to the floor, Sadie smacks him over the head as hard as she can.

"Leave her alone," she says, swinging it again.

"Oi, what?" He raises an arm to protect himself. "Why'd you do that?"

She lifts the book threateningly, and he flinches back.

"Bloody flip—!" he exclaims, and rubs the back of his head with a frown. "That the thanks I get for saving literally everyone's life from eternal damnation?"

"What are you on about? It's only a paperback." She jabs it at him, wobbling a bit thanks to all the rum and coke in her blood. "It was this or the kebab. And I sure as hell can't eat...um...hold on." She holds up a finger and steadies the book before her eyes, getting a good look at the title, then brandishes it again, ready for fighting. "I sure as hell can't eat Danielle flippin' Steel's *Five Days In Paris* as a post-drunken-night-out greasy appeasement while I watch a shit movie on Netflix, can I, you mum-kidnapping twat?"

He snorts. "I'm not kidnapping your mum." Then lets out a heavy sigh. "But, bit of advice—" He eases himself away towards the pentagram of sweet-smelling candles and picks up the open book in the centre — the one with the skulls and strange writing. When he snaps it shut, the candles snuff out as if by an unseen force. Trails of wispy grey smoke rise from their smouldering wicks. "—next time you're faced with a possible kidnapper, and the only thing you can think to grab is a book, make it something substantial like this one."

He scrutinises the book for a moment, holding it at arm's length so he can see the cover. He thumbs the pages with a worried eye before glancing up at her and giving it a shake.

"Actually, come to think of it, never hit someone with this book. It's a ritual book. Hit someone with this book, and their skin'll peel directly from their bones and their eyes'll turn to wine. See?"

He points at two symbols on the cover as if she should know what they mean. One shows a wide-mouthed skull with a wine glass beneath its chin. The other could perhaps be a pile of skin.

"Seems like an accident waiting to happen..."

"It does." He stuffs the book into his satchel. 'I better keep hold of it."

Her brows knit together in a frown. "Hold on, who are you?"

"The name's Kilmore. Dirk Kilmore." He removes a slightly curved and polished stick from a holster on his belt — part of her wants to call it a wand, but that's ridiculous — and holds it up to her face. The tip glows white as he looks deep into her eyes. "You're not hearing any voices? Other than mine."

He smells sweaty. Kind of dirty, but not in a bad way. More the way her father used to after working in the garden.

She shakes her head. Holds her breath inside. Can't speak as his ice-blue eyes search hers.

"You're alright," he says, when satisfied whatever he's looking for either is or isn't there. The light on the stick dims, and he puts it away.

He jabs a thumb at Mum. "I'm afraid your mother has been possessed by a greater demon." He places his hands on his hips and shakes his head like a cowboy plumber pricing up for the '*worst leak he's ever seen*'. "Real nasty one, too."

"Oh, shit." She glances past him to Mum, who is now asleep with her head at the correct rotation. Sadie squints, unsure. "Is that an 'oh, shit' thing?"

"Yeah!" says Dirk, impressing the point with a quick nod and a blow of air from his nose. "Well, kind of. It's actually quite good for me." He gives an encouraging thumbs up. "Means it's not out there, and I can keep it contained." He waves a hand towards the shattered window. He tenses and opens his mouth as if to say more, then looks at her and shakes his head. "I won't bore you with the details of my night. Let's just say—" he nods towards Mum's sleeping body,

"—this is better than the alternative. I'll figure out the rest." His gaze returns to the window. He taps his fingers together distractedly. "Um..."

"Should I be expecting another visitor?" she says.

He shakes himself. "No. No, don't worry."

"Oh, OK." Sadie shakes her head, not feeling fully in the loop. But he seems nice enough. And those eyes— Wait! "Hold on a minute...did you say a greater demon?"

He nods. "Uh huh. Come on, help me get her on the sofa."

He moves to grab Mum's arms. Sadie's legs don't seem to want to carry her any closer.

"Hurry! Before the sleeper potion wears off."

As if in a dream — or, more accurately, a drunken stupor — Sadie drops the Danielle Steel, grabs Mum's legs, and helps him heave her onto the sofa.

"There," he says, wiping his hands together as if he's about to say all in a day's work. "All in a day's work. Oh, and—"

He opens his satchel and brings out a long, thin blue candle. Using a spark from the stick he'd examined her eyes with, he lights it, then slides it into an empty, wide-necked vase on the coffee table.

"Keep this burning in the room with her. It'll suppress the beast. I'll have more sent to you. You'll have to burn two or three a week, but do that and everything should be right as rain." He glances around the living room, then points at the shattered window. "Someone will be over to fix that. Other than that, you should be good to go." From somewhere, maybe his satchel again, he draws a pad and a pen. "What address is this?"

"42 Abbey's Hill."

"Ah, yes." He writes it down, then taps the end of the pen on his chin. "Whoever comes over tomorrow to fix the window — it might be me — will do a bit of a spell for your mum so that she'll remember to burn those candles herself, but won't remember why. Probably safest."

He makes another note, then glances up at her over his pad. Something seems to surprise him and his face softens. He smiles. A tiny flame ignites in her chest.

A match struck in the darkness. He swallows and wets his lips nervously with his tongue.

There's a little shake in his voice as he asks, "And just for my records, what's your name?" Those blue eyes twinkle. "And what's your number?"

# REALITY

"Oh, that's so romantic," says Jane, with a semi-conscious swoon.

Yeah, and entirely fictional.

Telling the story of how she and Dirk met puts Sadie on edge. She always feels like she might get caught in the lie.

A chance encounter on a train. Two twenty-somethings catch each other's eye whilst reading the same book (not the one she'd whacked him with — something a little more hip hop happening). A brief discussion about the intricacies of the character development and the underlying themes. He invites her for a drink. Cocktails turn to dinner, to dancing. A whirlwind romance. A total slush-fest.

Swoon away, Jane; swoon away.

She'd come up with it one Saturday night while Dirk had been out working and she'd been, once more, left at home alone. It was basically a mash-up of the various rom-coms that had been out at the time. Over the years, she'd added to it, and had so far made up their whole first week together sans possessed mother.

It wasn't like she could tell anyone the truth.

She wrinkles her nose and nods. "Isn't it?"

"I wish Stan and me had a story like that."

Jane stares wistfully out over her plated panini as they sit with coffees and snacks in the local play cafe: a long, thin eatery with tables and chairs for parents on one side and little sectioned-off shops and services for the kids on the other. The chaotic clamour of kids careering, playing, and generally trashing the place fills the air. It's a bit like being in the centre of a whirlwind tearing through a toy factory discharging hungry little goblins.

"Stan just told me I looked fit while he was smashed at the pub." Jane hugs her new-born daughter to her shoulder and gives her a reassuring pat as she vomits an excess of breast milk over a muslin.

"Looks like that worked out OK for him," says Sadie. She cranes her neck to see where Ellie is and catches sight of her in the miniature vet's office, listening intently to the leg of a fluffy bunny with a Fisher-Price stethoscope. Oh God, she's adorable.

Jane laughs. "Sure did."

Sadie sips her coffee. Black. Two shots. More sugars. Closes her eyes. She'll need another after this. Last night had been rough.

She watches Ellie. She hasn't sat down since they arrived. Moving from car garage, to supermarket, to hairdressers, to vets, leaving a trail of destruction in her wake. Where does she get the energy? Sadie knows. The little poppet saps it straight from her mother.

It's been just over two years since Sadie's had a proper night's sleep. And at least two and a half since she's had a comfortable one. She rubs her dry eyes and chews the corner of her mouth. Watches that cute little face mouth 'bu-dum, bu-dum' as she listens to the make-believe heart in the bunny's right knee. The joy is sometimes overwhelming.

It's worth every waking moment.

And every moment is waking.

"I'm starting back at work again soon," says Jane, expertly taking her panini one-handed, keeping the contents exactly where they're supposed to be, and managing a bite without getting any pesto on her face or little Anna's back. She's dignified like that.

They'd met during baby swimming classes, and had managed, before Jane became pregnant with her second, to become good friends. Though, despite meeting every other week, Sadie still feels a strange awkwardness between them. Like they're only friends because they're trying to make sure their kids have someone to play with regularly. Dirk tells Sadie that feeling is just her mind playing tricks on her. And most of the time she's able to stuff it down where it belongs in the dark recesses of her subconscious, where it can thrive as deep-seated anxiety waiting to re-emerge whenever she plans a play date.

At Jane's words of returning to work, a bitter pang hits Sadie in the chest. It's fear. Fear at how reliant she is on outside forces. Fear of being left behind. Fear of not doing what others expect of her.

She realises she's scowling, so hides it with a quick bite of coffee and walnut cake. Once upon a time, she'd been so courageous. She'd never wanted for much, but she at least wanted to have made whatever she had for herself. When did that change? When did she become so worried about what other people thought?

Before Dirk had come along, she'd studied English, hoping to become a teacher. Her aim had been to help kids who'd been denied a good start in life. She'd always loved children. But, instead of going away to continue her studies once uni had finished, she'd stayed in Winchester to be with him. Not because he'd asked her to, but because she'd wanted to see how far it might go. And his work meant he couldn't move away, what with the Bureau being based in town. So while she waited to see if the relationship might work out, she got a temporary job running admin at a warehouse that filled trucks with food ready to head out to supermarkets.

He'd been a keeper. And in those early days, his "job" hadn't paid much, so her temporary job had become permanent.

She'd been good at it as well. Worked hard. Got promoted. She'd always been organised. Her father had drilled into her from a young age that an organised house, body, and mind were the cornerstones of a good life.

By the time they married, Dirk was earning more, so they made an unspoken agreement. Actually, not so much an agreement. More that they'd fallen into a groove well-worn by many married couples before them. Her job wasn't paying loads, and she didn't love it. His was, and he did. With him working most weekends, and her working weeks, they saw little of each other, so she quit.

From then on, he'd do what he was good at — kill the demons, earn the money — and she'd do what she was good at — cook, clean, organise, and make their home beautiful. It was all very 1950s, but the same thing had worked for her parents, so why not them?

With her new free time, she busied herself with readying the house for the pitter patter of little feet, which for a long time, and still, for the most part, she loved.

But sometimes that pitter patter takes a while to arrive.

Before Ellie, Sadie tried to use her extra free time to give back to the community. A fundraiser for Help The Heroes in memory of Dad; a reading group for underprivileged kids that no one came to; volunteering at the library and a charity shop until she was "made redundant". Winchester wasn't exactly a hotbed of impoverished children. Except perhaps the Hanley council estate. And while Dirk was supportive on almost every level, even he drew a line at her going up there. She tried as hard as she could to give her time to a good cause, as a hobby as much as anything, but nothing had ever picked up any traction.

She'd even tried a few crafty business ideas for herself — knitting hats, drawing birthday cards, and coming up with slogans for T-shirts and mugs. But nothing ever stuck.

Now she worries that maybe she always moved on to the next shiny idea too quickly, never quite sure if she was doing the right thing.

Dirk always offered encouragement. He was good like that. Always said when she was feeling low that, "It's not worth climbing a ladder unless you've checked it's against the right wall first."

So, she kept moving her ladder from wall to wall until she'd become a master of no trades. And then, when they were finally blessed, she'd become stuck fast. Stuck with the baby. Stuck with mountains of washable nappies in her bid to do something for the environment. Stuck with cooking and cleaning and coffee with friends who would someday go back to their jobs and leave her.

Friends she's not sure if she's really friends with, or if they just put up with her because they happened to have kids at similar times. Friends who she latches on to because she doesn't have anyone else. Friend, singular, because her old school friends had left home to go to uni and had never come back, and her old uni friends had left uni to go back home. Winchester was lovely, but it was hardly somewhere the youth of the country came to make their fortunes.

Friend, who she should really be talking to, instead of sitting here feeling sorry for herself and staring mindlessly at a pair of two-year-olds fighting over the use of a miniature shopping trolley.

"Oh, really?" she says.

What had Jane been saying? Something about work that had sent Sadie down a depressing path.

"Do you think you'll be OK to go back?"

Jane's little boy Teddy whizzes past on a balance bike wearing an Elsa-style blue ballgown.

"Not too fast!" Jane calls, and Teddy slows down immediately.

"Hmm," says Sadie, impressed at the power of a mother who clearly knows what she's doing. Ellie would have sped up, crashed the bike through the cafe's front window, and kept right on, defiantly screaming, "Too. Fast. For. Eveeer!"

"Yeah, it'll be fine," continues Jane. "Teddy's got nursery all sorted, and this one—" she says, patting little Anna on the back, "—is going to spend a few days a week with my mum. They need me back at the clinic. It's three days. I can manage."

Two little kids and already going back to work. Jane was ever so capable.

"I'd love to start working again," says Sadie, realising in that moment that she would. Anything to break up the monotony. "But..."

She doesn't really have a proper excuse. Except maybe she could never leave Ellie with her mum. Dirk assures her that the candles keep whatever it is inside her locked up, but she'd been acting increasingly strangely in recent years. Forgetful. Occasionally zoning out. Saying odd things. You couldn't leave a baby with her. It wasn't worth the risk.

Imagine if that thing inside her bubbled to the surface while she was alone with Ellie.

"It's not for everyone," says Jane, clearly spotting a drop in Sadie's mood. "But I can't wait to get back."

Ellie appears from nowhere and drops a bundle of toy babies onto the floor next to their table, then downs her babycino in a style reminiscent of her mother, aged twenty, doing shots in Vodka Bar on any student night.

Her top lip comes away with a Mario moustache of milky cocoa powder. Sadie bends to retrieve the toys from the floor, for what the small of her aching back tells her is the one hundredth time that day. That little, pudgy, squishable hand reaches out as she passes a baby back.

Sadie gazes into those beautiful blue eyes. Dirk's eyes.

Ellie smiles. "Thank you, Mummy."

And once again, it is all worth it.

# THE LAST BREAKFAST

Thursday morning. Sadie spins around the kitchen as she does every Thursday. She likes to get Dirk filled up on pancakes, orange juice, and coffee before he leaves for his weekly work trips. Loves the hour-long breakfasts they have before he goes away. Good food eaten slowly over calming, easy conversation. Nothing beats that.

Those moments before he heads out are the ones she works hardest towards. She wants to make sure those precious hours before he leaves are happy ones; lasting memories. Doesn't like to think that maybe it's because they could be their last.

So, while Dirk bumps around upstairs, packing his bag and prepping for his trip, she flips, and juices, and brews. And washes, and cleans, and dances with Ellie to her dad's old record player while it spins Fleetwood Mac or David Bowie. A whirling domestic deity.

She couldn't do a lot, but making breakfast fit for a king while entertaining a two-year-old is one of her specialities.

The day is warm and bright. A perfect spring morning. A cool breeze blows through the open patio doors carrying the smell of cut grass and flowers. It takes the edge off the warmth from the rays of sun shining through the kitchen windows, and the heat from the burning gas hob. Sadie takes a long, relaxed breath, filling her lungs. If this isn't Heaven, it's certainly close.

Ellie giggles as she climbs up on to her little wooden tower, which gives her the height to stand upright next to the kitchen surface.

"Can you chop the strawberries nicely for Daddy's breakfast?" Sadie passes over the blunt toddler knife. The fruit always ends up squashed flat, but she likes to involve her daughter and it can save a meltdown.

Ellie mashes with a little too much enthusiasm, almost immediately catching one of her fingers hard.

"Ooh," she says, and her eyes gleam with tears.

"Oh, honey." Sadie watches her, not wanting to dive directly in with the gasping mum routine that often makes mountains of molehills. "Are you OK?" She lifts Ellie's hand and kisses her finger. She doesn't cry.

"I am brave and strong," Ellie says, lifting her chin. Something Sadie's own mother had said back when she had hurt herself as a child, and something she uses now.

"You are." Sadie's chest swells.

"Hide!" shouts Ellie at the sound of the familiar creak caused by Dirk at the top of the stairs. She dives from the tower and buries herself beneath the kitchen table, pulling the seat cushion over her face.

He drops his bag by the kitchen door as he enters. "Has anyone seen my Ellie?" He walks straight up to Sadie, places his hands on her hips and plants a moist kiss on her cheek.

He smells clean. Not an aftershave man, but there's a scent to him she craves. His musk, he'd called it in one of his more self-aware moments.

She wipes the wetness of his kiss from her cheek as he turns and looks around the room, hands on his hips. "Ellie, where are you? Is she behind the curtain, Mummy?" He tip-toes across the room and pulls it back. "Nope."

It's one of those games that never gets old for either of them.

While they play, Sadie pushes the last of the round American-style pancakes from the pan into equal stacks on her and Dirk's plates. Pours over the golden maple syrup. Scrapes Ellie's squashed strawberries next to each.

"Is she behind here?" says Dirk, shifting the fridge from its position by the wall. He always takes their games to the extremes.

Ellie giggles from beneath the table. "Nooo, Daddy."

He looks up with over-dramatised puzzlement, like a startled meerkat. Sadie laughs. He has one of those flexible faces that can move any feature with expert precision.

"Did you hear something, Mummy?" he says.

She holds up her hands. "I don't know, Daddy. Did you definitely check behind the curtain?"

"I'm here," says Ellie impatiently, crawling like a four-legged spider from beneath the table.

Dirk lets out a shocked gasp. "Have you been under there the whole time?" He lifts her up. The muscles in his strong forearms stand out like cords beneath his skin. He twirls her overhead. Ellie shrieks with glee.

Sadie's heart leaps. It always does when he throws their daughter around, though she doesn't say. Their joy at having found each other blows any shadows away. Perhaps it is just a case of nature meeting nurture, perhaps as simple as a chemical reaction in her brain brought on by maternal hormones, but whenever she sees them together like this, she feels it's as if two souls have battled the perils and breadths of time and space just to be together for the short time a father and daughter can have.

She blinks. Sniffs.

Because that time is never enough. One always ends up without the other.

She prays Ellie will remember how much she means to them as she grows older. And, if possible, how much they had meant to her.

"Alright, you two: breakfast's ready." Sadie looks away, runs a finger under her eye, then carries the plates to the table while Dirk spins Ellie into her high chair.

She sits too.

"Oh, I forgot the coffee."

She moves to stand.

"I'll get it."

He leaps across the room. How does he always have so much energy? More so when he's going away to work. Like the thought of being out of the house, of doing something useful, of escaping them, fills him with a powerful charge.

He grabs the mugs and the glasses of orange juice she'd also left on the side. His long fingers wrap right around them as he carries them to the table.

When Mum was more herself, she had always likened him to a dog. A yes man with sporadic, wild energy who could also fall asleep at the drop of a hat. One minute chasing the kids around at family get-togethers, the next snoring on the sofa opposite her uncle.

"This is great," he says, gathering up his cutlery.

It was always great.

"So, what's the gig this weekend?" She watches him tuck in whilst sipping her coffee. "Werewolves? Goblins?"

"Nah, nothing too strenuous. We have a hot tip that a couple of bogeymen have been…" He glances at Ellie, who is happily dipping her little pancake into her stewed fruit compote. He mouths the next words, "… eating people," then continues talking as normal, "… down in the New Forest. Me and Burty are heading over there. Give 'em the old—" he flashes a finger across his neck, and makes a clicking sound, "—find where they've crawled up from, close it up, and, if there's no traffic, I'll be back in time for dinner on Saturday." He forks in a headful of pancakes.

"How do you—" she runs a finger across her throat and makes a clicking sound, "—a bogeyman?"

"Vicks VapoRub," he says with the straightest face going.

She laughs. "You're kidding?"

He shakes his head. "Dries them all up. That or a salt grenade." He mimics biting a pin and spins his arm over his head in a throwing gesture.

She doesn't know if she believes him.

He strokes his beard. He's let it grow out again. "What are you two up to while I'm away?"

"Maybe the park. Might take her to check in on Mum. She's been forgetting stuff again." She throws him a meaningful look that he sees but doesn't catch, so continues. "We've already seen Jane and the kids this week, so that's out." She holds her coffee in front of her lips in both hands. Breathes in the vapour.

"Jane's thinking of starting back at work," she adds, watching his eyes for his immediate reaction.

He wrinkles his nose. "What does she do?" He picks up his mug too, takes a sip. He hums and his forehead lines in quiet, grateful delight. A smile touches her lips. She likes it when he enjoys her food.

"Gynaecologist. Three days a week away from the kids."

He must sense something in her tone because he says, "Have you ever thought about giving teaching another go? I could cut down on some work stuff. After the bogeymen I've got one thing I'm looking into for a friend, and then I could maybe reduce my hours. I'd love to take Ellie for more time."

Has he been thinking about it already? Does he want her to start working again? Does he think she's not pulling her weight?

"Would the Bureau be OK with that?" she asks, putting her mug next to her untouched breakfast with a clonk. "Don't they need you?"

"Yeah, but you need me too, and pretty soon we might be able to leave Ellie with—"

"Not with Mum," she snaps. Ellie looks up from her pancake berry dip-a-thon. A look she gives if ever she senses Mummy and Daddy bickering at the dining table. She's aware like that. Blood red covers her little fingers. Sadie shudders.

"The candles work, hun. She's had one episode."

Sadie leans forward. Tries to keep her tone even so Ellie doesn't think they are fighting — not that they are; not yet. "She ate her neighbour's dog, hun."

He'd had to perform a memory wipe spell on several witnesses.

She didn't want to know what might happen if the demon rose to the surface while Ellie was with Mum.

"The candles work if she remembers to burn them."

"But it's not like her memory is that fresh anymore. She nearly burnt the house down last week leaving the hob on."

"I know." Dirk pats her on the hand, then his eyebrows jump with cocky assurance. "So I finally heard back from one of my guys, and I think I may have found something that could solve the problem."

"Really?" She leans back. Doesn't want to get her hopes up.

He waggles his hand from side to side. "I don't want to make any promises, but it could help."

"What is it?"

"Imagine a leech that could suck out someone's consciousness."

"I will not imagine that. Sounds disgusting."

"Some call it a demon leech. Might be getting one delivered from the Amazon."

She blows a raspberry. "Sell everything now, don't they?" She forks in a piece of pancake, delighted to discover it's mainly maple syrup.

He laughs. "No, *the* Amazon." Then holds up a palm. "Like I said: no promises. Please don't get excited, yet."

"I'll try not to." She smiles. This is good news. Mum might finally be free.

"If you left Ellie with her, that'd mean you could start something like Jane," he says. His face is open, honest. Him trying to solve the unsolvable. "I think it could work."

"Thank you. But I don't know. What would be the point?" She gives him her best 'I'm fine, honest' smile. "I've been out of it so long. Who would hire me? I'm past it. Jane actually studied for her job. Rose up the ranks. It's a proper job. Not like figuring out which Tesco superstore a crate of beans needs to go to." She rubs her eyes. Takes another sip of coffee. "I'm just venting—"

He bats a hand and screws up his face. "Pfft! Gynaecology can't be that hard..." He gives a cheeky smile.

She sighs. He's made the follow-up joke before...

"I'm pretty sure fifty percent of the people I know would love a job like that."

She rolls her eyes, then sticks out her tongue. "It's not what you think it is." She lets out a tired sigh. "I just always wanted to make an impact, you know? Like you. I think I've missed my chance."

She doesn't want to sound ungrateful. Everyone likes to believe they've got something to offer. And everyone hopes they will get their moment to offer it. Sometimes she worries that if she were in any way brilliant, it is a slow sort of brilliance. A brilliance that requires nurturing. A fire that might take more than a lifetime to warm up and get roaring. Now, she has so little time to herself to feed that spark, she worries she might never burn as brightly as she can.

He places his fork by the side of his plate and reaches across the table, taking her hand in his. "I know you. I know you're someone that needs time to stretch and wake and sit there for a bit with a coffee to think about what exactly you're going to do. I know you don't really get that time to yourself anymore. But you need to know, you make a massive impact to me, to Ellie, to everything we have here. We wouldn't be anything without you." He lowers his head to look up into her down-turned eyes. Despite everything that changes about him as he gets older, those blue eyes always remain. "But if you want to do something different, whatever it is, we will support you. We can talk about it when I get back."

She squeezes his hand and stares down at her plate. Her chest feels heavy. She doesn't know what she wants. "Thank you."

"Did I...did I say the wrong thing?"

She meets his gaze. A gentle frown lines his forehead, making him look older than he is. Or rather, older than he was the last time she'd thought about it. So, in fact, his age. The years go by even if you aren't watching them.

"No." She shakes her head. "I don't know what's the matter with me. If I'd have asked my twenty-one-year-old self what I'd be doing in ten years, she'd have said headmistress or something crazy. Helping children to learn to read, a global charity for orphans, girl bossing it to the max. Maybe I just thought when you and I got together we'd be a team, taking on the world, owning it, a defiant king and queen sticking it to the man." She glances up at him. He's smiling at her. Her voice drops. "Or something..."

She looks around their kitchen with its matching decorative plates and potted plants. "I just don't know if this is what I expected or wanted. I never wanted to be the woman behind a great man. I wanted to be beside one."

He follows her gaze around the room. "We are a team, you and me," he says. "This family would be nothing without you. You're our foundation. There's no-one on this earth I'd prefer to be taking on the world with than you. When are you going to realise you are perfect as you are?"

She shrugs. Smiles, if only to put his mind at ease. "We'll talk about it when you get back." He tries so hard, and she doesn't want to sound ungrateful.

He kisses her on the hand.

There's a knock at the door.

Then it opens.

"Family Kilmore!" comes a booming voice from the hall. "Burt's in the hoooooooouse."

As if electrocuted, Dirk lets go of her hand and pushes himself to stand. "Burty the Mysterious!" he calls in his surfer voice. "Dude, we're in the kitchen."

"Ah, Dirk the Unstoppable." Burt invades firing finger guns. He wears wonky cut-off jean shorts and a T-shirt with a neon-coloured, sunglasses-wearing dinosaur on the front that says 'The Bodacious Period'. His curly brown hair is squashed down under a trucker's cap.

The pair jump and bump chests with a Neanderthal grunt.

Sadie tries not to slap a palm to her face. Fails. Boys are idiots.

"Never marry someone as silly as your father or his friends, Ellie," she says, patting her daughter on the hand.

"Ah," says Burt, spotting her. "How's my favourite best friend's wife?"

"We're fine, Burt. How's your mum doing?"

A little of the humour leaves his face. "OK, thanks. Doctors say she shouldn't be in much longer." He drops his cap on Ellie's head, covering her eyes, then pokes her in the tummy. She screams happily as he swooshes her out of her chair like a rocket.

That's family breakfast over then.

# GRANNY

"Have a good work, Daddy," says Ellie, wrapping her arms around Dirk's leg. "Sort out the meanies."

Dirk crouches and gives her a big hug. "Never fear, my dear, I will." He stands up and gives Sadie a kiss. "We'll talk about stuff when I'm back, OK?"

She nods.

They watch him trot down the garden path with his bag towards Burt's car. Heavy punk music pours out of the windows like a thick guitar-based soup. Burt head-bangs with zeal. Sadie's cheeks heat up. What must the neighbours think?

"See you soon, Gorgeousnesses," Dirk says with a wave, before jumping in.

Upon Ellie's insistence, they wait until the car is out of sight. She sighs as they turn the corner.

"Bye, Daddy."

Sadie looks down at her precious daughter standing with her on the doorstep. Of all the hardships that come from being a parent — the sleepless nights, the nappies, the sick, the tantrums — no one ever warns of the loneliness that somehow comes with the constant presence of a tiny human. A wonderful, little, awe-inspiring ball and chain.

The tangible things, the gross stuff, the tiredness, are often talked about openly. Almost jokes parents tell each other to keep themselves going. Perhaps because on the surface they appear hard, but in reality dealing with them is the easy part.

No one ever talked about the other stuff. The real stuff. The inside stuff.

She knows she's lucky. Knows how long it took them to get Ellie. The years of trying. Of watching friends and family pop 'em out like it was nothing. Of that awful, thoughtless question seemingly only ever repeated when she and Dirk were at their lowest, "when are you guys going to have kids?" Of having to bite her tongue and say "maybe soon", knowing they'd already been trying for what seemed like forever.

Asking a young couple about their plans for kids is thoughtless at best and heartless at worst. It's like calling someone out for being big, and then asking them when they're going to lose weight.

They either can't or don't want to, and in either case, it's nobody's fucking business.

Other people had it far worse. She knew that. Single mothers worked nine to five, making their own ends meet, whilst still finding time to wash, and cook, and clean, and keep their little human breathing. And in the grand scheme of things, two and a half years of trying for a child was nothing. At least they'd been blessed.

But that doesn't make her feel any better. If anything, it's worse. She isn't even that hard done by. Who does she think she is getting down about it?

So she tries not to feel anything.

*You should be happy, Sadie.*

*Or you could at least be tougher. Suck it up.*

Life isn't all roses. It's brambles and blackberries. And the blackberries are only good late summer.

She wishes she could talk to her own mum about how she feels.

Sure as hell can't talk to Jane. Perfect Jane with two kids and already thinking of going back to work. Jane, who's started running again. Jane, whose husband is out of the house every day from seven to six, working some corporate job in London, so she takes care of both kids, cooks, cleans, works, runs.

Perfect Jane, her only friend, who's actually lovely, and she's proud of her, and should tell her so. Not because girls have got to stick together, although they do, but because you should treat people how you wish others would treat you.

And for once, she'd love it if someone told her she was doing OK.

Mum's a no go. Can't talk to her.

Since that night, their relationship hasn't been the same. Sadie's not sure if it's her own fault. That, despite what Dirk says about the efficacy of his candles, she has some sort of stigma about her own mother being the dwelling place of a demon.

Not that she could be blamed. Having a demon-possessed mother isn't something they talked about the few times she'd met up with her NCT group.

Maybe it was time she bridged the gap she'd created between them.

She closes the door. "Do you want to go see if Granny's in?"

Ellie squeaks with glee, suggesting she does.

Granny's house is only ten minutes away, and with the day being sunny and bright, Sadie packs the pram so they can walk.

Still, it takes fifteen minutes, and at least one full-scale, foot-stamping, screaming tantrum to get out of the door.

The tantrums get worse weekly, so, liking to think she is a modern mother, Sadie has enlisted the powers of the internet and invested in an online parenting course.

She's only found time for the first lesson, but it had some expert advice on defusing meltdowns.

The advice goes: Acknowledge the feelings. Tell them it's OK. Remind them what you're doing next. Give them a choice. And repeat like a broken robot until the meltdown stops.

Something to do with baby brains not knowing how to deal with emotions yet. There's science behind it, but all Sadie cares about is if it works.

"Ellie, I know you're feeling sad," she says calmly, while Ellie screams into her face because they can't take her scooter. If nothing else, the girl has a bright future ahead of her as a vocalist in a death metal band. "And it's OK to feel sad. But we're going to Granny's in the pram. Do you want to wear welly boots or light-up trainers?"

Several repetitions later, with battered ears ringing, she promises Ellie a biscuit, which seems to fix the problem better than any sodding internet course.

After what had been such a pleasant morning, she pushes a shoeless Ellie out of the door feeling flustered and drained.

In her second year of uni Sadie took a job flipping burgers. With Dad gone and Mum's job at the allotment shop paying a pittance, she knew she wouldn't be able to rely on anyone for handouts.

Her first day on the job had coincided with the uni's volleyball tournament, and unfortunately for her, and more so her manager, what sporting young women want most of all after partaking in competitive ball slapping is burgers.

They had besieged the restaurant from the minute it opened.

Her superior had vibrated with frantic anxiety as he panicked his way through the most basic of training. His whole body shook like an old race car, desperately trying to go faster and further than it possibly could, as he churned out sub-standard meal after sub-standard meal with his utterly incompetent trainee trailing blindly behind him.

That is her life now.

Brain boiling with the need to be faster.

Be more efficient.

Get more done.

Be a better woman, mother, wife.

*Moremoremore movemovemove.*

It always makes her a little sad turning the corner on the garden path of the house she'd grown up in. Her parent's old detached cottage has fallen further and further into disrepair since her father passed, and seeing the cracking paint on the windowsills, the grass grown to knee height, reminds her he's gone. He'd never have let it get like this.

He always had a little list of jobs he was getting through, printed out in his spidery hand on a folded piece of paper tucked in his shirt pocket. Pruning the hedges, replacing the odd tile that had come away in a strong wind, clearing the garden of autumn leaves before spring.

He'd never been the hugging type. Was an old-fashioned man to some degree. But his love for Mum, and for her, came out in care for their shared home, by putting food on the table, helping her with maths and science. And on the odd occasion, after a beer or two had dropped his shield of masculinity, he'd hug them up in his powerful arms and dance them all around the kitchen. He'd been a clever man. A good man. And she missed him.

Mum had been the cuddly one. The bumped knee kisser. The one who tucked them in at night. The one who cooked and cleaned.

Perhaps that is the reason why she has allowed her life to go this way. Why she allowed Dirk to take on most of those more stereotypically masculine responsibilities. Allowed him to be the protector.

It had worked for her own parents. Why not for them?

The family home's deterioration is a reminder that Dad is gone. A reminder of everything that he had been, and everything he had done finally not mattering in the grand scheme of the universe. Like his life-force had somehow been connected to this inanimate thing.

No matter how hard one worked to keep everything together, it always broke in the end.

She knocks.

No answer.

Mum doesn't go out.

She tries again.

Nothing.

"Maybe she's in the garden?"

She pushes the pram around to the side gate. Black rusting wrought iron locked shut with a new chain and padlock. Ahead of her along the worn concrete path is Dad's old workshop. A dark wooden construct just big enough to fit a car. A place for his tools. A place he could go for a moment's peace or to repair anything that had broken. She swore sometimes he'd find fault in something just to get out of the house.

She calls. "Mum, are you in the garden? It's us."

Something clanks in the shed. Then the door opens. Mum's head peers around. "Who's it?" she says before looking. She sounds a little gruff.

Mum was up and down. Like she didn't know how the world worked anymore. Slowly losing touch. It would be an idea to take her to the doctor, but Sadie fears what they might find.

There was no online course for dealing with ageing demon-possessed mothers. Sadie knows. She's looked.

"It's me, Mum." Sadie waves.

She can't help but think every downturn is something to do with the demon. But then again, like everyone, Mums get no younger.

Mum's eyes light up when she spots Ellie in the pram. "Oh, look who it is."

She eases the door open and squeezes through the gap, then quickly shuts it behind her. Locks it with a key and another padlock. What was with all the new locks?

"I'll meet you round the front."

Sadie pushes the pram back to the front door.

Mum is already there. "Was I expecting you?" Her voice is croaky. Her throat sounds sore. She bends down and walks her fingertips up her granddaughter's tummy. Ellie laughs.

"Dirk's gone away for a few days, so we thought we'd stop in." Was this a bad idea? "What were you doing in the shed?"

"Oh, just fixing a broken something or other," she says, and beckons them in. "You all good? I'm aaaaall good. Should I put tea on?"

The way she asks is odd. Not as if she's checking if Sadie wants some, but more to check if tea is something one expects at a moment like this. She steps back and lets Sadie push the pram in over the front step. Closes the door behind them.

"Yes, please."

The floor of the hall is charcoal-black and page-white chequered tile. Some chips here and there filled in by her father. Some newer ones not. A great overflowing spider plant stands yellowing by the door.

"That looks like it needs a drink," says Sadie, nodding to the plant.

"Tea for four then," says Mum, with a serious nod.

Sadie laughs. Mum is one of those vastly intelligent women who people often mistake for being stupid because she refuses to hide her silly side.

The hallway is cool, white, open. The smell of cooking meat wafts from the kitchen.

"Making a roast?" says Sadie.

"Yeah. Something like that." Mum skips around to the front of the pram and unbuckles Ellie before picking her up for a squeeze. "Oh, I could just gobble her all up." She opens her mouth and moves nomming jaws towards Ellie's exposed stomach.

"Don't!" In a panic, Sadie dives forward, pulling her child from her mother's arms.

Mum frowns. "What's the matter?"

"Oh, she's...just being a bit funny at the moment." A weak excuse. If she's going to come and see Mum, she has to learn to stop overreacting. She needs to trust Dirk when he promises the candles keep the demon dormant; when he promises she has nothing to worry about.

Mum shrugs. "Seems fine to me." There's an awkward pause that Sadie doesn't know how to fill. "Tea then."

She disappears up the hall to the kitchen. Ellie moves to follow, but Sadie holds her firm and steers her towards the dim living room.

The television is on. Muted. The tennis.

The untrained eye might not consider the room a mess, but Sadie knows how Mum used to keep it.

First, she crosses the room and opens the curtains. She scoops them up into hooks screwed into the wall on either side of the windows while Ellie busies herself with a small box of teddies that Mum keeps in the corner. Then she fluffs the pillows on the sofa and neatens the books on the shelf.

"Need a hand, Mum?" she calls, once the living room is more to her liking.

"Don't think so. Do we have biscuits with tea?" She sounds unsure.

"Nah, I'm trying to cut down."

"Why?"

"Oh, ya know." But Mum has always been slim, so maybe she doesn't.

On the mantle above the fireplace stands one of Dirk's candles, burnt down to the stump. Melted blue wax hardened into a pool beneath the holder sticks it fast to the varnished wood. She picks at it with a thumbnail. Could never quite put her finger on its pungent scent. Like popcorn, but only in the way that burnt hair smells like popcorn.

She pulls the stump from the holder and replaces it with a fresh one from the drawer. Lights it.

Mum appears in the doorway with a short tray. On it sits four mugs, a plate holding half a digestive biscuit, and another with a hunk of what could be roasted rabbit or lamb. She looks at Sadie a moment, and a frown crosses her brow. Then she looks at the tray. "When did...?"

"A little snack before lunch?" Sadie nods towards the meat.

Mum smiles and gathers herself. "Sure."

She pops the tray on the coffee table in the centre of the room.

"Is that for me?" Sadie points to the half biscuit.

"Yes." Mum frowns. "Must get to the shops."

Sadie smiles, picks up the plate. Then the mug of tea. It's black. She takes a sip. It's coffee. "Mmm, just how I like it."

She and Dirk needed to have a proper talk about her, and soon.

"Oh, look who's here?" Mum's face brightens when she spots Ellie, who has set three teddies up on pillows, covered them in napkins, and is singing them to sleep with a nonsense lullaby. "And where's that husband of yours?"

"At work. He's gone away for a few days."

"Of course." She looks up. "Oh, getting a bit dusty up there."

Sadie follows her gaze. Dust-ridden spider webs cling to the corners of the room.

"Do you want me to get those?"

"Don't worry. I'll sort it." Mum sits, swallowed in her easy chair. She's so small. Her feet barely touch the floor when she sits against the back.

Is this who Sadie will become? Is this who she'll be if Dirk ever fails to come back from work? A tiny old woman sitting alone in her decaying house with only her daughter's irregular visits to look forward to?

"Everything OK then, Mum? Been up to much?" A snarl of crimson wool sits on the small table by her chair impaled by a crochet hook. "Making something?"

She picks it up. Stretches it out. It doesn't look like anything in particular. "I guess I am."

She glances over to Dad's old chair with its worn cushion flattened and faded. Still pointing towards the television as if at any moment he might wander in, kiss Mum on the head, and settle himself into it with a slice of Marmite on toast before sticking the news on.

She takes a breath as if to say something, then her body sinks a little. "I sometimes look at that old thing with a question on the tip of my tongue, thinking he's there. For a moment, I forget. Like he's just popped to the kitchen to get a slice of toast. I used to do the same when he was away with the army." Her lips purse as she chews the corner of her mouth. "But now I know he's not coming back."

Sadie's hand twitches on her lap. She wants to comfort her, but can't bring herself to reach out. Hates herself for this fear she has of her own mother. "He *did* love toast," she says, hoping it'll brighten Mum's mood.

Mum laughs the smallest of laughs. "I used to know how late he'd been up the night before by the amount of crumbs. I'd have to hoover that seat every morning when I got up before he came down. I miss his mess."

"Me too."

Mum lowers her eyes and reaches for her tea. "Oh, did I bring this in?" she says, spotting the hunk of meat on the plate. "I have Sunday roast cooking."

"On a Thursday?"

"Is it?" One eye closes a little. "You lose track of the days when they're all the same." She points to the meat. "Did you want some?"

Sadie checks her watch.

"I've got to get Ellie home for her nap, but maybe we could stop by later?" 'Maybe' gives her time to think of an excuse. Her stomach knots.

"I'd like that." Mum smiles. Sadie's gut twists further. "See if that husband of yours wants to come."

Her smile widens, sending a shiver down the length of Sadie's spine.

"I'd love to have you all for dinner."

# Night of The Wolf

They don't go back for dinner. Sadie finds an excuse. Ellie is tired. They won't be much fun.

She promises herself she won't see Mum again until Dirk is available to come and check on her.

She hopes she isn't making it up. Hopes she's not just seeing a problem where there isn't one. But it's hard not to see her mother for what's inside of her.

Maybe it would have been better if Dirk had just erased Sadie's memory like he'd done to the neighbour when Mum had eaten his dog. Keep the entirety, or at least the worst, of Mum's ailment a secret from her. But then again, would she know if he had? There could be things hidden from her that were much worse than eating a neighbour's dog.

Friday comes and goes. Saturday afternoon too.

Dirk often returns later than expected. His problem was that he gauged travel time as net zero.

If he had somewhere to be by 7 p.m., no matter how far away it was, he'd step out of the house at 6:55, start the car, return for his wallet and phone, and still expect to arrive at his destination early. Chuck Burt in the mix, and it's a wonder they ever get any demon hunting done at all. Especially if there's a Burger King en route.

She doesn't mind. They deserve a little treat now and then. Working hard in the shadows, keeping the world safe from the things that should not be. The only thanks they get for a job well done is to live another day. Another day to serve. She shudders.

His dinner goes cold, and she puts it in the fridge, wondering if she'll be eating it the next day for lunch. Once she's bathed and bedded Ellie, she catches up with her series. The one with the zombies, the one Dirk suggests isn't for him because of its lack of realism.

Zombies, according to Dirk, do not in fact eat human flesh raw. They are all vegan. Stripping the bark from trees, eating grass, devouring fruits and vegetables. A massive pain in the butt, but not as big a threat to society as the bigwigs in Hollywood would have people believe. Still, according to Dirk, the suburban zombie is a menace. If given a night, just one can lay waste to an entire allotment with its insatiable appetite.

They'd discussed it over drinks one night. He'd gone on to say it was all a conspiracy theory. Get people terrified of the meat-eating zombie apocalypse so that when it actually happens, and people find out it's their broccoli and not their brains that are in peril, they'll be less likely to panic, and more likely to get out there stoving in zombie heads with a spade.

She likes the show, though. Escapism at its finest. Normal people surviving abnormal situations. Lovely. Still, the more abrasive gorefests make her a little uneasy, knowing that Dirk might be out there living them.

Sometimes she tries reading, but can never get through a page or two before her mind switches off and her eyes close, causing her to either drop the book on her face while lying in bed or nod off on the sofa. She blames it on all the books she'd been forced to get through for her degree. Hasn't since felt the urge to read that she once had. Maybe one day, when she's sleeping a little better.

Dirk still hasn't returned when Sadie finally goes upstairs, despite watching a catch-up of Strictly to take the taste of zombie away. She often waits up, hoping he will come home before she falls asleep, which is always to her detriment when Ellie wakes at 5:30 a.m. the next day like the unstoppable, ever-waking juggernaut that she is.

She sends him a text and goes to sleep.

As regular as clockwork, the screams wake her on Sunday morning.

"Muuuuummmyyyy!"

Tired eyes crack open to check the bed next to her. Still no Dirk. His side remains untouched, as it was the night before. She checks her phone. No text.

But he does sometimes take longer on a job than he says he will.

Sometimes a hunt is more involved than the Bureau originally suggests. More bogeymen, for example. More werewolves. Sometimes there are complications. He'd often come home with bumps and bruises. Twice in the past he'd received such terrible injuries in the line of duty that she'd had to wait until he recovered before he could come home. And when he did, she'd fussed and fretted and nursed him back to health.

But he always called.

If he was likely to be away for longer than he said, he'd always call.

He'd ring tonight, she told herself. She'd wait until then before she got worried. Or at least, that's what she'd try to do. The worry usually starts creeping in the second he steps out the front door.

She pushes the feeling back. Buries it beneath busying herself. Spends the last few hours of the afternoon purposefully not looking at the clock, the way she does when she's doing a plank or the few times she'd tried a spin class at the gym. Not knowing how much time is passing often makes it go faster. Which is a shame because the time is rarely watched when it's being enjoyed.

At 6 p.m., she caves and tries his mobile while Ellie throws dinner around. Willing him to pick up, or if he's driving, Burt with a stupid, exaggeratedly deep voice pretending to be him.

But there's no answer. She tries Burt. The phone doesn't even ring.

What would she do if he never came back?

Stupid question. He always came back.

But what would she do?

She doesn't have a number for the Bureau. Doesn't even know where it's based. Only that it's nearby. She's always thought it a little strange that the headquarters of the country's primary defence against monsters and demons was in Hampshire, and not somewhere more important like London, but she's never asked why. Doesn't want to know. The reason could only be bad.

Did the Bureau have a plan when their hunters went MIA? Would she get that knock on the door from an official in a suit, hat in hand, there to tell her that her husband had made the ultimate sacrifice? Or would the news come in the form of a letter delivered by some sort of well-trained bird?

"Sorry your husband's dead," it would read. "Please give the pelican some tuna and send him on his way."

She doesn't know if she's supposed to know what Dirk does. He's never tried to hide it from her, but she keeps it a secret nonetheless. Not that anyone would believe her if she told them her husband was a demon hunter on the weekends.

If anyone bothers to ask, she says he's in a band. It seems a safe bet. Gigging weddings most weekends means he can never attend anything social on Friday or Saturday nights. She'd been careful to pick bass as his instrument of choice so that no one ever asked him to play them a song. Apparently, not even bass players like a bass solo.

The day drags. The meltdown at bedtime when Ellie wants to read another book escalates, leaving Sadie close to tears as she repeats the mantra from her course.

"You're sad because Mummy can't read you another book. It's OK to be sad, but it's time for bed. Would you like to cuddle Flopsy or Piggy?"

Miraculously, it works without sugary intervention, and once Ellie is calm and tucked in with Piggy, Sadie closes her door and sits on the landing shaking and taking deep breaths to expel the frustration and the negative energy.

She is a good mother.

Dirk will be back soon.

Ellie is just missing him.

They are both just tired.

Things are OK.

Things will get better.

A positive mental attitude is easy, but it's never enough. She could gloss over feelings for a few hours, or maybe a day, like papering over a hole in a wall, but unless the underlying problems were fixed, nothing would change. Staying positive won't save her husband if a giant spider tries to munch on him. And she couldn't meditate her way out of a manticore's sharp-toothed mouth.

*You're sad because your husband hasn't come home from work and you feel your daughter hates you. It's OK to be sad, but it's not OK to wallow on the landing while the house is a mess. Would you like a glass of wine or a whole sharing size packet of crisps?*

A glass of wine is possibly fewer calories, so she succumbs to two on the sofa in front of some more television. Nothing too strenuous. Something about couples getting married without ever having seen each other. Dickhead fodder, her dad would have called it. And though that makes her the dickhead, he'd have been right.

She only realises she's fallen asleep when she wakes. The remnants of that second glass are staining her favourite top blood red.

"Bugger." She sits up and places the glass on the coffee table, perching it on a coaster so as not to mark the wood.

She rubs the stain unconsciously with her thumb. Pouts and turns off the television, then checks the baby monitor. Ellie is still asleep. Her little white-noise box buzzes away in the background.

Sadie checks her phone. No calls. No messages. It's late. Nearly 2 a.m. A whole day late. Now is the time to worry.

Something creaks inside the house. The tenth step. She knows to avoid it because it wakes Ellie.

Dirk knows too.

On the monitor, Ellie's door stands wide. Had she left it open? Had it been open a second ago? The light from the hall throws the little camera's sensor off so most of the room is now obscured.

It hadn't been like that before. Had the door opened on its own? She peers closer. A strange silhouette in the corner by the wardrobe. A figure. A clawed hand moves. Inches forward out of the shadow. Reaches over into the cot.

She doesn't think, just moves. Instinctively grabs the wine glass from the table. She grips the base in her fist so its slender stem protrudes through her fingers. She smashes the top off on the door frame as she enters the hall, leaving a single fractured shard at the tip of the neck. In blind panic, she launches up the stairs two at a time, wrenching herself upwards with the bannister, not caring if she alerts whoever is in Ellie's room.

Her mind races out of control. She'll stab them.

No, that's murder.

She'll make them leave.

And what if they ran with Ellie?

She'd give chase. Throw herself on top of their car if she had to.

Ellie's room is at the top of the stairs. Whoever it is must know she's coming.

As she reaches the top, a sound from behind in the hall makes her glance back. Another figure, cloaked in black, follows. Her heart beats in her throat. She tastes the cold buzz of fear on her tongue. Fear for her child. Fear for herself.

She charges into Ellie's room. Slams the door behind her. Holds her back firm against it.

One at a time. Does she have a chance if she takes them one at a time?

She has no chance. Everyone likes to fantasise that if their child were in trouble, they'd somehow go into beast mode and trash anyone that might be a threat. But if there's a switch hidden somewhere inside of her, she can't find it.

The figure's hand is in the cot, resting gently on Ellie's chest. She lies still, quiet, eyes closed.

"I don't want to hurt you." His voice is a harsh snarl, almost a whisper. He wears black jeans, a black leather jacket. Boots. A get-up strangely reminiscent of Dirk's the first night they'd met. She can't see his face in the faint silhouette cast by Ellie's bunny nightlight. "But I will."

The door behind her shakes. The handle rattles noisily. Ellie's eyes spring open. She tries to roll over, but the figure holds her fast. She whimpers.

Sadie stutters, her mouth dry. She can't speak. She growls to clear her throat and the words break through strong and clear. "What do you want?"

"Just the child." He turns his head and looks down. The outline of his face is strange. A jaw, long and protruding like a hairless wolf, pink and grey. Eyes, shiny and black like a dead phone screen, stare hungrily at Ellie in the cot. A smile splits his fanged mouth. "We don't need you."

She squeezes the glass between the knuckles of her first and second finger. Presses it as close to her leg as she dares. The sharp tip digs into her thigh. Keeps her alert.

"Not happening," she hears herself say, as if she's not really here, as if she has a choice. "I won't let you take her."

He chuckles. A cold, dark sound. A laugh practised at the expense and pain of others. "I lied before, when I said I didn't want to hurt you. I'd enjoy it."

The door behind her rams open, shoving her further into the room. Another wolf-faced creature stalks in.

"What were you doing down there?"

"Parking's a nightmare. Why'd you not wait?"

"Hardly needs two of us."

Ellie shouts. She pushes against the long-nailed hand with her arms and legs, annoyed, not scared.

That's my girl. Brave and strong.

Sadie lets the tears come, and steps forward. "Please don't hurt her."

He doesn't bother to step back for the poor, defenceless, begging woman — she is no threat. His mistake. With a snarl, she jams her wine-glass-tipped fist as hard as she can up towards that long exposed chin. The shard glints in the yellow bunny nightlight, then disappears into his throat. She pushes him away with her other hand and tugs it free. The resistance sickens her as it tears from his neck.

He steps back but doesn't fall. Lifts a hand to hold his throat as blood gushes from the wound. He tries to speak, his voice coming out as a wet gargle.

The other stalks forward. Pulls some sort of hook from the folds of his jacket. Hesitates. "You OK, Kayder?"

Despite the blood that leaks from his chin and between his teeth, he nods to confirm he is. Gasps, "Kill her!"

Sadie grabs Ellie out of bed with one hand, positions her on her left hip, and retreats into the room.

"Where's my husband?" she shouts, jabbing the wine glass towards them. Blood drips from its tip.

"Oh, he's safe."

"Just leave us alone!"

The uninjured one shakes his head. "Can't do that." He raises the hook.

She clasps Ellie to her chest, wanting to envelop her, to keep her away from these horrors, and closes her eyes.

Something happens. A tiny sound that reminds her of the small birds that sometimes tap at their reflections in the window. Glass patters to the carpet as something whizzes through the air close to her left ear. Then a spatter of something warm hits her cheek.

She opens her eyes.

The previously uninjured dog man stands with his hook still raised above his head, face frozen in shock. His dark eyes widen, staring. He touches his other hand to his chest. Another tap and a hole appears in his forehead. His raised arm drops, and he flumps to the ground.

Kayder leaps for the door. Sadie ducks as several more shots pepper the wall with holes, following his movement. She looks up at the window. Dull orange streetlight streams through the shredded roller blind.

"Someone's here," gargles Kayder from the hallway outside.

Sadie stands. Pulls the blind up. Throws open the cracked window. Crawls out on to the roof of their kitchen with Ellie in her arms. Carefully eases herself to the edge, drops onto the garden bench, and then on to the patio. Goosebumps prickle across her skin. She holds Ellie to her chest, worried the girl's thin pyjamas won't be warm enough. Thankfully, she's not crying. Probably shock.

Sadie scans the rooftops of the houses opposite, looking for their saviour. Can't see anyone hiding amongst the chimney pots and television aerials. She jogs barefoot across the grass to the end of the garden and opens the gate onto the path that runs along the back of their street. Checks left and right, expecting to see both ends blocked off by packs of hungry wolves. But they are clear.

She picks her way across the broken concrete and shattered bottles, and runs for the only place she can think that might be safe. Mum's house.

# SHE SELLS SANCTUARY

By the time Sadie arrives at Mum's, Ellie is asleep, curled up against her neck, tucked inside her T-shirt to keep warm. Seeing that peaceful sleeping face turned up towards hers from beneath the collar of her wine-and-blood-stained top reminds her of the days when she'd kept Ellie in a sling swaddled at her chest. She'd loved having her so close. When had she stopped using it?

There was a last time for everything, and they seemed to come thicker and faster.

The lights are off when she turns on to the garden path. It is close to three in the morning.

She hesitates. She stands there without shoes as the damp and cold of the paving slabs leading up to the front door chills her feet. Is it fair to wake Mum at this hour? She will be so confused.

Mum had been the softness, the comfort. The one who remembered and knew everything as if she had some sort of psychic talent for it. She'd have done anything for Sadie. As Sadie would do anything for Ellie.

She presses the doorbell. Holds it firm. Pushes open the letterbox and shouts, "Mum, it's me. Please let us in!"

"Sadie?" The answer is immediate.

Along the hall, Sadie can see her. Standing in the dim light of the kitchen, half in the dark, wrapped in her light blue dressing gown. She looks around, seemingly disorientated.

"Sorry, Mum, I know it's late."

Mum hurries towards the door and opens it.

"What's wrong?" Her face is a picture of worry. "I was just...getting a glass of water."

Sadie looks her up and down. She is wearing one shoe.

"Oh, Mum." She shakes her head as Mum closes the door. Doesn't know what else to say. How did you explain what had just happened?

Before she can try, Mum wraps them in her arms. Still clutching Ellie beneath her shirt, Sadie leans into the hug.

"You're safe now," Mum says, patting her back. "You're safe now."

It's been so long since they've been this close. Sadie rests her head on her mother's shoulder and lets out a sob of relief, but it wavers with the fear she feels. The fear that Dirk is still out there somewhere. The terror that he might not be.

"Where's Dirk?" Mum holds her at arm's length.

Sadie wipes her eyes. Shakes her head. "I don't know. He didn't come back from work yesterday."

Mum ushers them through to the living room and Sadie sits on the sofa. The ache in her legs from running dwindles.

"Someone was in Ellie's room," she begins. How much of it should she share? "Dirk works for a government organisation." She risks sounding insane.

"Like James Bond?" Mum looks at her, a confused and worried frown on her face.

Sadie nods. Need she say more?

"Some...men came, and Dirk's gone, and..." She closes her eyes. Takes a deep breath. "Can we stay here?"

"I wouldn't have you anywhere else." Mum sits in her chair. On the edge this time, as if she might stand at any moment. Her face is puffy and tired. Sadie expects she hasn't been up at this time in many a year. "Do we call the police?"

"No!" Sadie blurts it out quick and loud. Ellie stirs on her chest but doesn't wake. She lowers her voice. "Dirk says that if anything ever happened, no police." She lays a hand on Ellie's back. "His organisation, it's a secret."

"The police must know, though, right?"

"They don't. They can't help."

"Don't worry. We'll think of something." Mum moves next to her on the sofa and wraps an arm around her.

It surprises Sadie how well she is coping with all of this new information. She had always been a rock. Someone she came to with those all-too-familiar teenage problems of cheating boyfriends and spiteful classmates.

"Has Dirk not left you anything? A back-up plan? Your father left me a nice file on the computer with everything in it, in case he had an accident."

She knows Mum's intention isn't to worry her, but her heart skips several beats at the thought of her losing Dirk like Mum had lost Dad.

"I don't think I can cope without him." It's suddenly hard to take a deep breath. Her head feels light. "We need him."

Mum's face falls when she realises what she's said. A mortified look that is enough to make Sadie want to comfort her rather than worry about herself.

"I don't mean to say he's hurt," Mum says. "But if his work is dangerous, they must have a contingency plan."

Sadie tries to calm herself, tries to think. Is there anything?

A light ignites in her brain as if turned on by an unseen finger. A card with an address. She had forgotten about it completely until now. It had been in his trouser pocket years ago when she'd been going through them before putting a wash on.

Its discovery had brought her to the edge of fury because she'd only told him the week before to "please empty your pockets before putting your trousers in the laundry basket." His used tissues, wrappers, and receipts were always creating seams of white throughout her nice clean wash.

She'd told him it was as if he'd left the card there on purpose. Which, thinking about it now, he may have done.

It had looked nothing special, but she had kept it. She remembers a strange tingle had seemed to radiate from the cheap cardboard when she held it between her fingers. The edges had been torn away precisely, leaving it in a little pillow shape. A shape that Dirk always seemed to doodle on any scrap pieces of paper as if he were practising something.

She'd put it in her box of special things. Didn't know why at the time. Something just told her it was significant. Like it had been there for a reason.

"I may have something."

But where did it lead? Could it be the address of the Bureau?

She looks up to the mantlepiece, where the fresh candle she'd lit earlier has already burnt down to about halfway. Chews her lip.

"Can I leave Ellie with you?" Her stomach bubbles. It'll be fine. Mum won't do anything. Dirk had assured her on multiple occasions that the candles worked. And there are at least three more in her drawer. "I'll be back soon."

Mum beams. "Oh, yes, please. Where are you going?"

"There's a card at home. It has an address. I'm going to get it."

"Is it safe? You could stay here with me. Go in the morning."

A sensible suggestion. Tempting, like the last few lines of chocolate on an almost finished bar made for sharing.

But, "I need to find him. We won't be safe until he's back."

Mum nods resolutely. "I could come with you."

Sadie hopes her feelings aren't evident in her expression. "I love you for asking, Mum, but I don't think you could help much if something happened."

Mum's eyes flick upwards. Then she smooths the crease of her dressing grown. "You're right. I've never been one for fisticuffs. But if you told me what you were looking for, I could go. You and Ellie could wait here."

Sadie's mouth tightens into a smile and she looks at her mother with nothing but love. What had she ever done to make herself worthy of this brave woman's care?

"I might need to get in and out fast," she says. She thinks she can do that. Maybe back through Ellie's bedroom window.

"Fast's not really me anymore."

Sadie stands and passes Ellie, still sleeping, to her mother. It hurts Sadie's heart to see she is almost reluctant to take her.

"Are you sure you're happy for me to...?" Mum's voice breaks as her lips crumple. She closes her eyes as her chin rests gently against Ellie's soft hair.

Heat tingles behind Sadie's eyes and she wipes them. She wants to say she's sorry for all the time apart. Instead, she crosses to the fireplace and lights the second half of Dirk's candle to be safe.

"If I'm gone longer than an hour, call the police."

Mum nods. "I will."

Sadie grabs Mum's parka from the stand as she moves to the door. Squeezes her feet into a pair of her flats. She doesn't want to go, doesn't want to leave her baby, but she must.

She needs Dirk. And, if her suspicions are correct, he needs her, too.

# BLIP

Sadie pulls the furry hood of Mum's coat over her head. Buries herself in it. The parka is thin and old and not much protection from the cold, but at least it will act as some sort of disguise as she creeps back along the alley behind their garden fence.

The backstreet is quiet, normal. A quiet Hampshire suburb surrounded by quiet Hampshire countryside where people work normal jobs and go to sleep at normal hours.

Here there is never any crime. No muggings. No burglary. No vandalism. The only piece of graffiti she has ever witnessed locally were the words 'Steve has a chode' written in marker pen on one of the supports for the swings at the park. And though it had made her snigger, she was happy to see that some Samaritan had washed it away by her following visit.

Any crime in the local area is often isolated to the Hanley Estate, situated a few miles west. A place no one normal goes. A place where robberies and muggings are common, say the local police. She's never been. Not even to drive through it on her way to somewhere else.

She passes the row of garages on the right, stops with her back to their own, and looks at the house. From here she can see Ellie's bedroom window is full of holes.

Who had helped them? And why hadn't they shown themselves? They would have seen her leave. Seen her run. Did they follow her to Mum's? Were they following her now?

She pulls the coat tighter to herself as the wind whistles through the alley. Something flies overhead. Quacks. Comes to land on their garage roof. The duck watches her. Its beak glints a golden silver in the orange streetlight. It's got something wrong with it. A weird grey growth on its back. It sort of squeaks. A strange sound for a duck. Poor thing. Ellie loved the ducks down by the pond.

With a deep breath, Sadie turns and marches across the alley, then through their garden gate, shutting it behind her so it doesn't click. She doesn't have a key so she's going to have to go in the way she came out. She tiptoes across the lawn to the back of the house, climbs on to the bench, and pulls herself up to the kitchen roof, careful to spread her weight.

She shimmies around the perimeter where it might better hold her, grips the sill of the still-open window and peers inside. The body is gone. Blood stains the light pink carpet burgundy. Seeing it fills her with a protective, maternal anger she's never felt before. A primal rage that makes her want to do terrible, terrible things to those who dare enter her home and threaten her innocent, sweet little girl.

With considerable effort, she pulls herself over the lip of the window sill, throwing her hands out to save herself from crashing face first into the carpet.

With held breath, she stands in Ellie's bedroom. Listens to the familiar silence of her empty house. Nothing in the room is out of place.

She steps over the spatters of spoiling blood. The thick carpet hushes her footsteps.

When she leaves the bedroom, she half-expects to see the house ransacked, but nothing is different. Except for the blood on the carpet and the holes in the wall and window, everything is as it is supposed to be.

As quickly as she dares, she skirts across the landing towards her craft room. A haven full of bits and bobs she'd collected for making and mending. A room dedicated to the recycled, reused, and redundant.

One day she will craft again, she promises herself. Knit a jumper, or finish that cross-stitch of a beautiful green woodpecker that has lain discarded in her embroidery hoop for almost three years. Something she envisioned going on Ellie's wall when she started it at two months into her pregnancy. Something she'll likely never finish.

Tucked away on the bookshelf sits her box of treasures. She removes it from the shelf. Kneels and opens the lid. Next to Ellie's first shoes, the battered paperback she'd hit Dirk with on the night they'd met, and a few other keepsakes, is the card. Heaven knew why she'd kept it. It hadn't been important when she'd found it. But putting it here had felt right.

She runs her finger across it. The torn edges seem to tingle once more at her touch. She holds it up to the moonlight coming through the window. A sparkling wave crosses it in the light. A mystical iridescence, like the surface of a soap bubble.

Judging by the postcode, the address isn't far.

She tucks the card into her pocket. Leaves the room. Listens once more to the house.

"Hello," she whispers into the silence. The sound of a motorbike passes outside. Its whining rise and fall startles her. Feeling a little braver, she speaks. "Dirk?"

No answer.

As if he would be here. She's talking to a memory. A ghost. The blue dark of an empty house at night.

She heads downstairs to the cupboard beneath and takes out the day bag she uses for Ellie's things. Stuffs it with a spare change of clothes for Ellie, some snacks, and Ellie's carrier, although she's a little big for it now. Swaps Mum's shoes for a pair that won't rub her heels. Grabs Dirk's thick, black hoody. The one she snuggles up in when she has a cold, and also the one that is perfect for night-based skulking.

She heads for the back patio doors. Glances back into the kitchen, at the table where they'd shared that too short but happy breakfast just a few mornings ago.

Will she be back? And if so, will they all be together?

She nods. Of course they will. This is just a blip. Dirk'll fix it.

She just has to find him first.

# PANDORA'S PASS THE PARCEL

Ellie sleeps, tucked up in a throw blanket on Mum's old, cracked leather sofa. Sadie can't help but smile. How she wishes she could be that oblivious to all the negative in the world. As oblivious as a two-year-old who knows nothing of war, or hunger, or the things that go bump in the night.

What did it feel like to be that innocent? You couldn't know because every time you learnt something terrible about the world, it tinted your vision like a scratch on an expensive pair of sunglasses you couldn't throw away.

Sadie often thought, while attending kids' parties, that life could be compared to a game of pass the parcel, but instead of filling the individual layers with the odd packet of Haribo or a tiny book, the mother (because it was always the mother), whilst wrapping up a stupid number of presents with a head full of a quadrillion other things (was the cake big enough? Would the weather be OK? Had she invited everyone? Would anyone come?), had mistakenly dipped her hand into Pandora's box for prizes.

The game was played alone over a lifetime, and every time you peeled back a layer, you would reveal a fresh horror that you couldn't stuff back inside and were expected to just accept and live with. And then beneath that last layer, the final super-duper whizz-bang prize wasn't a slightly bigger, more expensive book, or a cheap plastic one-button game where you had to get the hoops over pegs inside a container filled with water. Nope, the prize was growing old, if you were lucky, and dying, if you were human.

Sadie shudders. Why does her brain always go to such bleak places? Yes, dog men are after her baby girl, and yes, her husband is missing, but why be so down about it?

She grins like a maniac, a sure sign that things are going wrong behind the scenes, and tries to compose herself.

"Are you sure you're OK to have us stay here for a few days?" she asks, as she returns from her inner sad place to the warm comfort of Mum's living room.

Mum gazes just past her over the cup of coffee that props open her drooping eyelids. "Not at all," she says, dreamily.

"So, is that yes or no?"

"Absolutely."

Sadie takes it how she wants it. Sips her tea. Nibbles her chocolate digestive. A whole one this time, because damn society's expectations of what a woman should look like two years after squeezing out a massive fucking baby. Damn them to the frozen pits of Hell! Because, according to Dirk, Hell is actually pretty cold, and not, as the Christians would have you believe, hot.

It's an easy mistake to make. How is anyone supposed to know if they've never been? The god squad had a 50/50 shot. Really bloody hot or really bloody cold. It wasn't going to be a balmy 29 degrees, was it? Hell was not the Maldives.

Hm? Actually, now she's thinking about it, Dirk's knowledge of Hell's weather causes her to worry a little harder about where exactly he goes on his work trips...

But that's all beside the point. There is work to be done.

On the way back, she'd formulated a plan. Along with her father's rules for organisation, one of his mottos had been: "failure to plan was planning for failure". A saying that almost always characterised Dirk's spontaneous day trips with Ellie. The pair — both of them — would often come back from somewhere like the farm crying and starving. Sadie was the planner in this relationship, and, as long as she could put all her fears aside for a moment, she could damn well, blooming heck, organise her way out of this jam.

She doesn't know how well her plan will work, but she has to do something.

Step one: Follow the breadcrumbs. Go as far into Hampshire's seedy magical underbelly as the address on the card will take her.

Step two: Leave no stone unturned.

Step three: Um?

Really, there are only two steps. But all plans should have at least three steps. Step three probably goes something like — phone the police if the address on Dirk's card leads her to a dry cleaner's. With Dirk missing, and weird-looking hairless dog men hunting her and her child, what did she have to lose?

She reasons, because said dog men haven't arrived at Mum's yet, that they do not know where her mother lives. This, she hopes, means Ellie will remain safe at Mum's while Sadie is out there on the mean streets of Winchester, lifting metaphorical rocks off of what she hopes are metaphorical beasties.

She doesn't sleep well in her old bed. It's too small. Ellie lies curled up beside her on a small mattress Mum has made of pillows and duvets. Still, Sadie keeps waking with visions of those snarling dog faces, overcome with the worry that she'll roll over to see an empty space where Ellie had been.

Mum has kept her old room exactly as it has always been, with the posters of Duncan from Blue, and some boy band called Damage, who she can't even remember one song by.

From the position she rests in, she can see her old mirror still surrounded by faded and mostly blurry photos of the girls she used to hang out with at school.

They'd been a solid quartet. A gang. Four-fifths of the Spice Girls for most of junior school. All of All Saints once or twice. Regularly spitting girl power slogans at any stupid boys who might want to pull their hair or look up their skirts. Not that loads did. But there were some.

The other three moved away long ago. Got proper jobs. Married, had babies, disappeared out of town and out of Sadie's life. They'd all promised they'd be friends forever, but it's been years since she's seen, let alone spoken to, any of them.

Sometimes the dark of her mind takes her to a place where it was her they might have been escaping from.

As she lies there, she tries not to imagine where Dirk might be. Of what might be happening to him right now. But the thoughts sneak in on the backs of her worries and fears.

He can't be dead. If he died, she'd know. Like when her father had died, killed on patrol in Afghanistan, and she'd woken screaming, alone in the dark in her uni halls with the feeling that something terrible had happened. The next morning when the phone had rung and it was Mum, she'd known.

She holds on to that. Whatever is happening with Dirk, he is at least still here.

She rolls over and reaches down. Places her hand gently on Ellie's warm back. Knowing she will need all the strength she can muster over the next few days, she closes her eyes and concentrates solely on her breath, willing herself to sleep.

Eventually, with a tear in the corner of each eye, she goes.

# THE ADDRESS ON THE CARD

Ellie jumps up and down with a toothy grin upon learning she'll be spending extra time with Granny. Sadie suspects it's something to do with the copious amounts of mint choc chip on offer.

When she suggests, "Not too much. It's full of sugar."

Mum ripostes with, "I fed you ice cream every night when you were her age, and that never did you any harm."

"Maybe," says Sadie, on the backswing, "but you're always going on about how I didn't sleep until I was four."

To which Mum has a little think. Then nods. "Not too much ice cream, then."

Before she leaves for the address, Sadie lights another of Dirk's candles in the holder above the fireplace. Mum seems better now than she had a few days ago. More stable.

Sadie gives Ellie one last squeeze before she leaves. The longest they've ever been apart is a few hours.

"You need to be brave and strong for Mummy, OK?" she says.

Although, it seems, Sadie needs the pep talk a little more than Ellie, who turns and legs it off to the lounge to play with the teddies, screaming, "Byeeeee," over her shoulder.

With the address clear in her mind, and cursing her lack of organisation in not bringing a fresh top from home, Sadie leaves dressed in her dad's old David Bowie T-shirt. Her top from the night before is spattered with a fair amount of blood and wine. Though she may look like she means business caked in the brains of her fallen enemies, she feels walking around Winchester appearing as though she works in a boozy abattoir might attract some unwanted attention from the law.

She plugs the address from the card into her phone's satnav and hits the road in Mum's Peugeot 206.

After a fifteen-minute drive, she pulls into the car park of a large storage complex situated off a road quite close to Winchester's main high street. It's a short one-storey building comprising two parallel lines of roughly seventy squat, square garages and a glass-fronted reception. The sign on the front reads 'Rent-a-Space'.

It's not quite what she expected to find, but upon parking she realises the Bureau could be anywhere; hiding it in plain sight like this is probably the best way to keep it a secret.

Still, she feels a little let down. She had hoped for some huge, gothic, muse-um-style building covered in gargoyles, with the ectoplasm of the paranormal oozing from every crack in the stone.

She climbs out of the car and studies the building. Not a glob of slime any-where. She likes to think, having dealt with the outpourings of a small child for the last two years, that she'd be ready for anything gross, but worries that, if this investigation goes the way of her initial encounter with Dirk and her vomiting, backwards-headed, possessed mother, gross things like ectoplasm might become a problem.

Dirk had never broached the subject of ectoplasm. Not properly. He had once made a joke in the bedroom, which hadn't quite got the reaction he'd hoped for, and since said nothing. She'd just cross that bridge if she came to it, and make sure to use the hand sanitiser in her bag at regular intervals.

A few other vehicles sit in the car park. Nothing unusual about them. No orc wargs. No brooms.

It's a little underwhelming.

Sadie lifts her hands to either side of her face to shield the sun's glare reflecting on the blacked-out windows of the short blue reception building, and peers through, hoping to gauge what she is in for inside.

The interior shocks her.

Not in a good way. Not in a bad way. The shock is akin to that felt when, having taken a bite from last night's reheated kebab, one finds it tastes exactly as bad as it looks, and almost nothing like one remembers. So a very mild, somewhat disappointed shock. But a shock nonetheless.

A man stands at a small reception desk wearing a blue polo neck with the Rent-a-Space logo on his chest. Keys dangle on hooks behind him. He looks terribly bored.

He spots her and raises an awkward hand.

She steps inside. He stands as she crosses the reception. He fiddles with his hands and glances around as she approaches. The sound of a radio comes from a back room through an open doorway, along with the smell of something cheesy and microwaved for one.

"Can I help?" he says with a smile that looks genuine enough.

"Is this number 35, The Fairfax?" she asks, pointing to the ground as if being stood in the building isn't enough to illustrate where she's talking about.

"This isn't," he says, and the centre of his eyebrows dip down, unsure.

She sighs with relief. It's the wrong place. The satnav must be wrong.

He turns slightly and, with an impressive degree of professionalism, removes a specific key from the wall behind him without looking. Lets it dangle from his index finger, then moves to his computer and taps at his keyboard. "Here's the key, Mrs. Kilmore."

She frowns. He knows who she is?

He places it on the desk. The blue plastic tag reads 35.

"You're Dirk's wife, right?"

She nods. Looks around once more at the air-conditioned reception. Perhaps this *was* the Bureau. Maybe they know who she is, and judging by the high spirits of the man, aren't that bothered about Dirk's predicament. Could that be a good thing? Maybe Dirk is here, and OK.

"You're happy for me to just go in?" She points again in an uncertain direction.

"We're not really supposed to let just anyone in, client confidentiality and stuff, but Dirk said if I ever saw you here, I could give you the key." He tweaks his thumb and finger by his mouth as if locking it tight. Then his eyebrows lift. "How's Ellie? Still having a bit of trouble with the old tantrums? My boy's the same."

"She's fine," she says, sounding shorter than she means to. She doesn't like someone she doesn't know asking questions about her daughter.

A twitch in his lip shows he notices.

"Dirk has the authority to just let me in?" she asks. They won't just let her walk in, will they? She leans forward onto the counter and, despite there not being anyone else in the room, lowers her voice to a conspiratorial whisper. "This is the Bureau, right?"

He taps a finger on his lips. "Hm. Is that what he calls it?" He muses a moment longer, then leans forward and puts a hand to his mouth. They are two spies exchanging the toppest of secrets. "It's sort of against our Ts and Cs to work here, but I'm not gonna call him up on it." His eyes track up to something behind her. A slight widening of the lids suggests she should look too. Worried what she might witness, she inches around to see they are being watched by a little security camera.

"Like I say, I'm not supposed to let anyone into a client's unit without them being here," he continues, hand now scratching the side of his mouth to hide his lips, "but I'm just going to pop this here." He leaves the key on the counter, then moves over to his computer and starts tapping the keyboard like a cat controlled by their owner's hands.

She stares at him a moment with a lack of comprehension.

The corner of his mouth opens. "And whatever happens," he punctuates with a jump of the eyebrow, "happens."

She reaches across and picks up the key. It can't be this easy to get into the headquarters of the world's primary defence against the creatures of the night, can it? She stands there, fiddling with the key in her hand, unsure what to do with herself.

The corner of his mouth opens again. "You can drive your car right up if you're dropping something off. Just go around the side." He slowly spins his whole body to suggest the way.

"Thank you," she says, and before anything can happen to change his mind, she hurries out of the reception and back to Mum's car.

From there, she looks at the building again. If she could have just come here anytime, then why had Dirk never brought her to see where he worked? Is this even the right place? And if it isn't, what is it? Did he have something to hide? Something he wanted kept outside of the house and away from her and Ellie?

She starts the car. Pulls it casually around, passing under the barrier gate and up between the rows of units. Seventy in total. Dirk's is the furthest from the carpark. The furthest from prying eyes.

When out of the car, she hesitates in front of the large garage-style door, once more twiddling the key between her fingers. What was in there? There were possibilities. It strikes her that behind this door she might find some sort of magical staircase leading into the heart of the Bureau's subterranean headquarters.

Or she might not.

Whatever it is, is she ready to see what's on the other side? Is this another of those Pandora's pass the parcel moments? Does it matter if she's not ready? If Dirk is out there somewhere hurting, and if creepy dog men are out there hunting them, and if her daughter is being babysat by her demon-possessed mother who might turn at any moment and gobble her all up, did anything else matter?

She stabs the key into the lock and throws open the door.

# MONSTER BASHERS INC.

A strange smell. Ancient leather, dusty tomes, age, something like popcorn, but in the way burnt hair smells of popcorn. Where had she smelled that before? It's not unpleasant. No souring of mould or funk of damp.

Bookshelves line the walls either side of the garage, rammed to bursting with unmarked leather-bound spines of varying thickness and size.

In the centre of the room, two standing desks face each other a little way apart.

She steps in and pulls on a string that hangs in front of her face. A lamp on each desk activates, as do a series of other lights aimed up at a map of the UK comprised of many sheets of A4 paper pieced together with clear tape that covers the back wall.

Hundreds of tiny little coloured dots cover the map. As she steps closer, she can see they are stickers. Clustered around rural areas, mainly in and around Hampshire, the odd one or two in cities.

There are other stickers, taken from sets she'd bought for Ellie, stuck further afield. In one small town in Wales is a green dragon. To the southwest, near where Dirk grew up, a little way offshore, is a large red octopus sticker. There are others. A blue teddy bear not far from Winchester. A dog just north of London. Hadn't he talked about werewolves in Cambridge once?

She studies the map. Where had he said he was going this week? It was nearby, wasn't it?

Beneath the map is their old shoe rack; a knee-high wooden shelving unit from Ikea. She hasn't seen it in months. She'd wondered where it had gone. It holds a variety of strange artefacts. She looks at each in turn.

A gnarled blue horn. It is long and curved. Longer than any horn she's seen on any beast. She wonders what it came from and why Dirk might be keeping it. Next to the horn is an ornate wooden box with a picture of an octopus on it. And next to that are two stands. The finger-width depression in each suggests they might usually hold wands but both are empty. And lastly, something that looks like a fleshy head-sized blob of goo that gently pulses, occasionally giving off a cyan or pink light that brightens the shadow of the shelf that encloses it.

She leaves that well alone.

To the left of the map and shoe rack is a workbench, covered in tiny pots filled with different powders and liquids. The smooth, dark wood top is pockmarked with scars from corrosive and heated elements. A small digital scale, a pipette, and several pieces of string sit next to a measuring jug spattered with a hardened blue liquid that looks suspiciously like the wax used in Mum's candles.

It appears Dirk or Burt make them. What had she expected? That he bought them wholesale at some sort of Body Shop of the occult?

She scans the room once more. There's no way out except the main door. No mysterious portal. No staircase leading down.

Had she ever asked him to describe the place? Probably not. Hadn't wanted to probe into this part of his life. Didn't want to feel rejected if she pushed too far and he said no. Or, had she been worried about learning too much, of peeling away a layer of normality she could never put back? It was sometimes better to leave certain questions unasked.

Maybe she'd just filled in the gaps in what he'd told her. Tried to make believe that what Dirk was doing was official, and safe, and regulated.

She steps closer to the nearest desk. It's covered in books. Some open. Some shut. One is blasphemously wedged face down to record the reader's page. She fights the urge to close it and save the spine.

A little bronze plaque in front of the computer reads 'Burty the Mysterious' on top and 'CEO of Monster Bashers Inc' beneath.

Which meant...

She crosses the room.

The pieces of paper spread across Dirk's desk are covered in doodles. Mainly that pillow shape. The same shape as the card she'd used to find this place.

Two dried apple cores sit on the right side eaten down to the pips. Dirk's signature droppings. One book. A thick brown tome embossed with tentacles so detailed that they seem to writhe towards her off the page. Symbols that look like nothing she's ever seen cover the front.

Dirk's plaque reads: 'Dirk the Unstoppable –– Chief of Butt Kicking'.

She rubs her eyes with both hands, exhausted and frustrated. Boys were idiots.

Was this it? Was this what Dirk and Burt referred to as "the Bureau"? This poky little storage room? A familiar spark of annoyance ignites. Like catching him lying about hoovering or some other odd job he'd promised to do but hadn't.

She doesn't know whether to feel proud or terrified or furious.

On the one hand, the only thing standing against the dark oncoming night and all its mysterious dangers is her husband and his mate Burt. That could make a wife crazy with pride. What a man! What a guy!

But — and this was a big but — the only thing standing against the dark, terrifying night and all its horrifying dangers was Dirk and his mate Burt — the man-child who wore T-shirts covered in multi-coloured dinosaurs and referred to her as his "favourite best friend's wife".

Jesus Christ!

She leans her weight on the desk. Her head swims like she's stood up too fast.

The boys weren't part of a well-funded, professionally run government or-ganisation. They were all on their own. And no matter how mysterious Burt thought he was, nor how unstoppable Dirk could be, it meant there was no back-up, no help, no one to call if things went wrong.

And things had clearly gone very, very wrong.

And who was funding it? The state-of-the-art computers, the complex standing desks, the ancient library, her whole life since she'd met him? If there were no bigwigs telling them what to do, how was it that their bank account was topped up every month with a healthy enough sum to keep her out of work and everybody well fed?

Where was the money coming from?

She opens the drawer on Dirk's desk. Looking for something, anything, that'll prove her wrong. A secret button that might flip a bookcase or call up a magic elevator. A business card with a different address. But there's just an orange peel, an unwashed mug, and more indecipherable notes with that pillowy doodle in the margins.

She unhooks the mouse from a neat little charger screwed into the side of the desk. Neater than anything Dirk had ever done at home. She gives it a little wiggle. The computer screen lights up, and despite how she feels with him being gone, with him lying to her, she smiles. Tears prick her eyes. The background is them. A picture of their little trio holding ice creams sat on the beach on a precious weekend away to Brighton. They'd balanced the camera on Ellie's red plastic bucket. She'd kept trying to grab it. Her pudgy, ice-cream-sticky fingers reach for the screen, her face an adorable grimace of determination. Dirk has an arm around Sadie's shoulder as they grin in the background.

Unlike his physical desk, the computer desktop is ordered into three neat rows of folders. Only one document is left out. It sits in the centre of the screen labelled 'Hanley Estate Case'.

The Hanley Estate? Interesting.

She opens it. A spreadsheet with what appears to be a list of names. Each name has a date next to it. She scrolls down. To her, it's meaningless.

She closes the file and opens the first folder, 'Accounting'. Inside are more folders labelled with tax years.

She clicks the latest, revealing Excel documents labelled with each month. She opens the first and her mouth drops. The sums of money are huge. Far more than what comes into our account. Far, far more.

She scans the document. There's no indication of where it's coming from. Just a huge lump in every few weeks. On the right-hand side are three amounts. One titled DK, one BP, and the other TD. Dirk Kilmore, Burt Phoenix, and someone else. The DK one equates roughly to what Dirk is paid per month and is equal to Burt's, but the majority goes out to TD. What could that be?

The next folder is labelled 'Artefacts'. While that is very tempting, another folder calls to her. 'Gigs'. In Dirk-speak, that means jobs. He just calls them gigs because he thinks it sounds cooler, like he's some sort of rock star.

Once again, everything is divided up into years. She scrolls down to the bottom. The first folder is from sixteen years ago. The boys must have been fifteen.

She opens it. One scanned image file. Several blurry photographs taken on an old film camera. The image is faded and overexposed. The flash has turned their eyes red, but it is them. Dirk and Burt. Greasy teenage boys. And a girl who she assumes is Burt's sister, Betty. They'd met once before at a meal out for Burt's birthday. She's two or three years younger than Burt, and has the most amazing jet-black, curly hair.

They each wear big smiles and black, short-sleeved wetsuits. Hair plastered to their heads. Betty's is secured under a swimming cap.

The background of each picture is light brown, gleaming rock. A cave near the sea?

Dirk doesn't talk about his family much, but she knows he used to holiday down on the coast with Burt and the Phoenixes, somewhere near Lyme Regis in Dorset. She used to visit her great gran down that way and has put it to Dirk, more than once, that they may have passed each other on the beach or in one of the fossil shops. Looked at each other, smiled, not knowing how things would turn out. A romantic fantasy.

Dirk had known Burt since school. They'd grown up together.

In one picture, Betty holds an ornate box with an octopus on the front. Sadie looks up. It's the box from the shoe rack.

In another are two sets of hands. One holds the book now sitting on Dirk's desk, the one covered in squid-like appendages, and the other holds a wand. Wooden, curved, and carved like a reaching tentacle.

Did they find these as kids?

She reaches over to the book, unsure what she thinks she is doing. As her hand nears, a strange magnetic attraction draws her closer, as if her fingers are being pulled by an unseen force. With an uncanny amount of effort, she recoils. Rubs her hand down her trousers. It feels cold, slimy, as if gripped by some unfathomable thing from deep beneath the ocean that has impregnated her skin with its freezing touch.

Steeling herself, she flips the book open. The first few pages flutter past, pulled by the weight of the cover, landing on a diagram of the wand from the photograph. A hand demonstrates how one should hold it. The words are in English, inked by hand. Neat and easily readable.

She looks up at the mass of books filling the surrounding shelves. Had Dirk learnt everything he knew about magic from them? He'd never seemed that interested in learning anything new with her. When she'd suggested they take up gardening, he'd said, "sure, just let me know what you want me to do," and that had been as far as they'd got.

So many questions fill her head. She doesn't know where to begin. And none of them bring her any closer to finding him.

She scrolls back to the top of the folder on the computer, finds the current year and the latest document. A Word doc with Thursday's date. Mentally crossing her fingers, she opens it.

*Bogeymen. Old Sarum, Salisbury. Vick's whip?*

Hm. It's information. Not a lot. He had said he was going to the New Forest. Old Sarum must be the place.

Should she go? What might she find? She lets out a little growl of frustration. Why hadn't she asked more questions? Any normal wife would have asked for a number to ring so she could get him in an emergency.

But she wasn't a normal wife. She was married to a demon hunter.

She presses a loose strand of hair behind her ear. Her legs are suddenly jelly. She looks for somewhere to sit, to think, but there are no chairs in the room. Stupid Dirk and his stupid perfect posture. She makes her way to the shoe rack and plonks down on top of it. Something she'd done a hundred times before in their old house while putting on shoes.

With face resting on her palms, she gives her head a little squeeze, trying to force the brain juices into gear, to think up a solution, a means of finding him or at least finding out more.

A deep drone, like a whale song, sounds from somewhere beneath her, accompanied by the rhythmical wash of waves. The room seems to vibrate with it. A strange soporific motion seizes her, rocking her gently back and forth, as though the shoe rack where she sits has been suddenly transported to the deck of a ship at sea. The smell of seaweed and sand surrounds her. The salt spray of an icy mist strokes her cheek. Again, she hears the low and sombre song of some leviathan living deep down in the immeasurable inky darkness of the ocean.

It calls to her.

She stands, swaying slightly, and studies the artefacts. The sounds and scents wash away as her eyes fall on the octopus box, as if somehow it knows she's looking at it.

She kneels, feels that strange attraction once more. As if the air has thickened, as if she's enveloped in a frozen sea, being drawn on a wavering current. A slow, rolling tug draws her to the box.

With tentative fingers, she reaches out and touches it. Could swear it shifts so that its front is closer to her, like a cat nuzzling her palm. She lifts the box and places it on top of the shoe rack. As she does, the metal clasp, shaped like a gripping tentacle, falls silently open.

Her heart beats a little faster. Her fingers twitch towards the lid. Should she be messing with this stuff? She eases open the box and, as if sucked away, all sound around her ceases to be. Every ounce of her focus is on the contents. Lying on a soft velvet lining as dark a blue as the depths of the sea is the wand from the picture. A foot-long splinter of wood carved into the shape of a tentacle.

Feet scrape on the tarmac outside, bringing her back into the room like a deep-sea diver breaching the surface. Her defences drop and she picks up the wand, almost automatically, like it's hers and she needs it close. It's very smooth, almost to the point of being slimy in her grasp. Without thinking, she stuffs it into her bag.

She holds her breath and listens. The footsteps approach. She stands, thinking she should shut the door lest whoever it is might see what is in here. A tiny part of her suggests that whoever it is might not be an innocent passer-by. They could be here for her.

Why had she rushed in? She's down a dead end with no escape and no one nearby to help her. In Rent-a-Space, no one can hear you scream.

She looks for somewhere to hide, and ducks down behind a bookshelf as a woman steps around the corner.

Sadie recognises her, but it takes a moment to place her face. She looks different from the last time they'd met at Burt's birthday. The first thing Sadie notices about her is her hair. It's a huge tangled mess atop her head. Dressed in blue jeans, a black T-shirt, and a green bomber jacket, she looks to be in great shape, but her face is tired. Purple rings covered with fading concealer sit beneath her dark eyes.

Betty doesn't spot her as she steps further into the unit. Her hair catches on the underside of the opened door. She doesn't seem to mind, just bats it down. Her focus is on the centre of the room.

"Betty?"

"Oh," she says. Her lip curls in shock, and she puts a hand to her chest. "I didn't see you there?"

Betty tenses, wary, as Sadie drags herself from her terrible hiding place.

"It's me: Sadie." She brushes herself down. She must look awful. "Dirk's wife."

"Oh, of course. Sorry." Betty relaxes. "Have you seen them? Burt called me. Left a message on my phone. Told me something was wrong." She takes a card out of her pocket and holds it forward. "I have this. Thought I'd follow it."

Sadie looks. It's a copy of the one Dirk left her, but isn't ripped into a pillow shape. "Dirk left me one, too." She pats herself down thinking to retrieve it but stops. Betty doesn't need to see it. "That's how I got here." Some of the weight lifts from her shoulders. She's suddenly not alone anymore.

"What is this place?" asks Betty.

"I don't know. Their office, I suppose."

"So I guess Dirk is missing, too?"

Sadie nods. "Did Burt tell you the same lie about..." She bends two fingers either side of her head. "...the Bureau?" She watches Betty's face. "Looks like this is it."

Betty's hands go to her hips as she takes in the room. She shakes her head. Her hair flows from side to side like a bushel of seaweed in a strong current. "He hardly ever talks about it with me."

"Oh right! Do you not—" Sadie waggles an invisible wand around in front of her. "Abraca—!"

Becky gasps. "Woah, don't say that! You'll blow us all to Hell."

"What?" A bolt of nerves shoots up Sadie's spine.

Betty snorts. "Nah. Just kidding. I haven't got a clue about any of this stuff."

Of course. Sadie remembers Burt had said his sister did something in HR. A safe and normal corporate job.

Sadie nods towards the tentacle book, still open on Dirk's desk. "But you found that with them, right?"

"Oh, yeah."

"Where's it from?"

"Originally? No idea. One day I'll bore you with the story of how we found it." She lifts a hand to gesture to the room and the well-organised library around them. "I guess it's what got them into all of this."

"Do you have any idea where they might be?" she asks, as Betty passes her and walks to the map on the wall.

"I'm sorry. I don't." She puts her hands once more on her hips and studies the map.

"When did he call you?"

Dirk hadn't called. Why hadn't Dirk called?

"Friday night." She continues to face away. "What is this?"

"I don't know." Sadie moves parallel with her and looks up at the map. "Dirk says he hunts demons and monsters. I guess these mark where they've been."

Betty turns her head towards her. Rolls her big brown eyes. "Trust my brother to go around thinking he's some sort of hero. Mum always used to say he played far too many computer games."

"I heard she was in the hospital. Have you told her he's missing?"

"No. She's got enough on her plate." Betty returns her gaze to the map. "What about Ellie? Is she safe somewhere?"

"She's—"

"Mrs. Kilmore?"

The concrete beneath their feet hisses as they spin on the spot at the sound of another voice.

The man from reception stands in the doorway. His arms hang by his sides. He blinks slowly as he takes it all in. "Looks like you were right about them using this place as an office, then."

Had she said that?

He rolls his eyes and tuts in a way that suggests he isn't that bothered. "That Dirk, am I right?" He looks at Betty. "Do I know you?"

She shakes her head. "You know my brother, Burt."

He nods. "I do."

"How long have you known my husband?" asks Sadie, moving towards him.

As she passes Dirk's desk, something compels her to pick up the tentacle book. Without slowing, she stuffs it into her bag next to the wand.

The man looks at the sky and taps his chin. "Him and Burt have been coming down here just under eight years now."

Eight years? She and Dirk have been together for just over eight years.

"Does anyone else ever come here with them?" asks Betty, stepping forward.

"Not really." He looks at Sadie. "What's going on? Are you looking for Dirk, Mrs. Kilmore?"

This man, a total stranger, had seemed very knowledgeable about her, about Ellie, about everything when she'd arrived.

"How did you know who I was?" She steps forward, buoyed by Betty's presence.

He smiles, and with that innocent gesture, she can tell he's nothing more than the man who works at the storage place. "Dirk always goes on about you. We've become quite pally over the years. He comes in every week with a new picture or video of Ellie. Sometimes you're in the background. I got a son myself. They were born around the same time." He shrugs.

A smile touches her lips as a deep, bittersweet warmth grows inside. People only ever went on about their wives in movies and tacky romance novels. She never talked about Dirk to anyone. And she'd never just chat about him with total randoms from the storage company. She glances at Betty, who hasn't taken her eyes from the man, so doesn't see her blush a little. Dirk talked about her. Dirk showed her off to his friends. She stands a little straighter.

"We kind of compare notes," he continues. "I don't have many mates with kids — well, any, really. So it's just nice to talk about it with someone else." He looks down. Fumbles with his hands. "We went to the pub once. I thought that might continue, but we never got around to sorting another trip. He seems pretty busy. I expect he's got lots of real mates."

He didn't. Or as far as she knew, he didn't. Not in the life they shared. But perhaps he did in this secret Bureau-less life of storage units and messy little standing desks and hidden sums of money.

"He is busy." She takes a deep breath. She'd never considered that Dirk might need someone to talk to about the trials and tribulations of being a dad. And the tribulations were plentiful. Ellie often switched off to him, answering him with only screams or silence, wanting only Mummy.

"Do you know what they do here?" asks Betty.

He shakes his head. "I thought they were in a band. But they regularly come limping in with cuts and scrapes, so I had my suspicions." He purses his lips and glances at Sadie. Asks, "Is Dirk a spy?" Then covers his ears with a sudden look of panic. "No, don't answer that. I've got my boy to worry about."

Sadie looks at Betty. She's all out of ideas.

"Say they were missing," says Betty, "and you were us, how would you find them?"

Sadie shakes her head slightly in awe. What luck finding this woman who knew all the brilliant questions to ask.

"Missing. Hm?" The man thinks for a moment, then looks up. "I'd follow the money. Talk to their accountant, Jarrod Green. He pays the bills here. He's the only other link I have for them."

Accountant? Sadie looks back to Dirk's computer. Those Excel spreadsheets showed a lot of money coming in. Even if she can't get any more information on Dirk's whereabouts, she might at least find who is funding his operation.

"Do you have a number or an address?" asks Betty.

Lovely Betty with all the right questions.

He nods. "I have both. Follow me."

# I Spy Da Accountant

Betty's ride is a behemoth of a muscle car that would look more at home cruising the strip in Miami. Sadie stares at its wide black boot with only a small amount of jealousy from the driver's seat of Mum's Peugeot 206 as they sit in traffic heading to the accountant's. Satnav says it's a ten minute drive.

She calls Mum. By the white noise hiss of wind on the line, she guesses they're out.

"We've nipped to the park," Mum says, slightly out of breath.

Probably the same park she and Ellie visit. It sits between their two houses.

"She's having a right old time of it. She's made up a friend."

Sadie smiles. Ellie loves the idea of making friends, but hasn't started nursery yet, so doesn't know many other kids. She often comes home from the park with Dirk, having made a new best friend.

"Can you put her on so I can talk to her?" She just wants to hear Ellie's voice. Make sure she's OK.

"Sure." Mum calls Ellie's name a few times. The muffled sound of a phone passing over.

"She's here." Mum's voice comes from a slight distance. "You're on speaker."

"Hey, honey, are you having fun at the park?"

"Yes, Mummy." Her voice is so soft and small.

"And you're being good for Granny? She says you made a friend."

"Yes. Beebee. We're going on the slide." The phone goes quiet.

"Oh, she's run off," says Mum, with a gentle laugh in her voice. "I don't know when I'll be back."

"Don't worry. We're having a wonderful time."

She hardly feels herself as she drives to the next unknown location. Almost numb. Like she's switched the everyday part of herself off. Running on something more primal.

Dirk wouldn't give up if it were her who'd gone missing. So neither can she.

The sign outside the address reads JG Accounting. Again, not a building she recognises. And on the surface, nothing strange.

Betty parks up and jumps out.

Sadie pulls Mum's car into the space next to her.

"How we going to handle this?" says Betty, beeping her key fob. "Accountants can be slippery."

"I guess we'll just ask him if he knows where Dirk is."

Betty rubs her hands together. "Cool. I'll take your lead on this one."

Sadie looks over the names in the reserved spots. Jarrod Green. Sally Duncan. Olivia Price. Except for the one the guy from the storage place mentioned, she doesn't recognise any of them. But what would she know? She always tried not to eavesdrop on Dirk and Burt's work conversations.

Judging by the way it looks from the outside, the accountant's office was once an old house. Sadie twirls her wedding ring on her finger as she approaches the front door. Asks herself for the hundredth time if this is a fool's errand.

Betty hits the buzzer, then steps back, giving Sadie room.

"How can I help?" comes a nasal female voice through the intercom.

Sadie takes a nervous breath and bends close. "I'm looking to speak to Jarrod Green."

"Do you have an appointment?"

"No, but I really need to speak with him..." She glances up at Betty, who gives her a nod. "Now! Um...please."

"I'm afraid you can't come in without an appointment."

Betty leans forward. "I'm sure Mr. Green can take a five-minute break from wanking over the word 'boobs' on a calculator to talk to the wife of one of his biggest clients. Or does she need to take their business elsewhere?"

She stands back out of the way with arms folded.

There's a pause on the other end. "Please hold." The line clicks off.

Oh, Betty Phoenix, you're crude, but you get the job done.

Betty gives her a wink. "Got to be a bit forceful with some people."

Sadie laughs as if to say, of course. "Oh sure, yeah, I was about to get really forceful." She shakes a fist at the call box. "Watch out there, lady on the other side of the...bloody... uh—"

"Intercom."

"Intercom."

"You get 'em, tiger." Betty winks again.

You're not convincing anyone, Sadie Kilmore!

The day is sunny, but in the shade of a large oak standing out front of the building, Sadie's bare arms tingle with the cold. Goosebumps crawl across her skin as she gazes out towards the road. She counts the people walking by and wonders if there are more than there should be. She is suspicious that anyone looking out of place might be following her, watching Dirk's haunts, waiting for her to lead them back to Ellie.

A pair of old ladies sit at the bus stop. She squints at them, then shakes her head. It won't do to get paranoid. Yes, she had to be careful, but adding to her troubles whenever anyone slightly funny-looking walked by would only dampen her senses to the genuine threats.

"What's the name?" comes the woman on the other end of the intercom.

Sadie moves her mouth closer. "Er...Dirk Kilmore."

"No; *your* name."

The question stumps her for a moment, as if she needs to hide it.

"Sadie. Sadie Kilmore. I just need to talk to someone about my husband's account."

"Hm," comes the reply, and Sadie senses a hint of accusation in the tone. A hint of 'oh, another wife coming to check up on her husband's spending; let's all roll our eyes at her'.

The magnetic lock on the door clicks open. Betty immediately pushes her way inside and Sadie follows.

They haven't taken two steps when a sweaty, pale-faced man in a suit ploughs down the hallway towards them. He is skinny. Not the well-maintained slim of someone who worked out and ate right; more the rake-thin of someone who survived predominantly on late-night fast food taken at the office and multiple beers taken at lunchtime. His back is practically convex. He holds an arm out to shake. She's reluctant to take it, but does, gathering an unpleasant amount of moisture from his warm, limp hand.

He turns to Betty, who has her hands stuffed safely in her bomber pockets and doesn't look like she'll remove them for anything.

"Mrs. Kilmore, Jarrod Green," he says, somewhat forcibly, as if trying to impress his importance upon her, or perhaps upon himself. "I work with your husband."

"Good," says Sadie. "He's missing." She tries to keep her voice calm. Tries to appear collected.

The accountant coughs in alarm, and with it, his carefully waxed hair jumps out of place. He makes a nervous chittering sound. The rapid clicking of his tongue or tapping together of his teeth. It's unnerving, whatever it is.

"Missing?" Several beads of sweat drip from his forehead. He holds an arm out towards an open doorway and guides them into a private meeting room. "Step inside, would you?"

In the centre of the room stands a long table of metal and glass. It holds a set of tumblers and a pitcher of water. Scattered across its surface are a multitude of branded pens.

Sadie takes a seat. Betty leans against the wall to her side, arms folded.

With trembling fingers, Jarrod picks up the pitcher, pours himself some water, and pushing half the glass into his mouth as if he's about to eat it, drinks the lot in one. He then takes a deep breath as if someone has just tried to drown him, and repeats.

He catches Sadie's eye as he downs his second glass. His unblinking, drinking stare makes her uncomfortable.

He finishes and places the tumbler down with a heavy clink of glass on glass. "Sorry, do you want one?"

She shakes her head. Betty doesn't move.

He begins pacing. That clicking sound comes from his mouth. He moves to the window. Peels open the blind, peers out to the street. Chitters again.

He turns on them suddenly. "How did you find me?"

"The guy at the—"

"The guy at the storage unit." He clicks his fingers, then clenches his fists in annoyance. "Knew we'd get caught one day." His eyes travel to the ceiling, then he speaks as if talking to himself. "Well, I'd never done it before..." He trails off, then fixes his eyes on her once more. "How long's he been gone?"

"Since Saturday."

"But they sometimes come back a little late, don't they?" He sounds like he's guessing.

Sadie nods. "But never without a call."

He leans on the table. Not in a threatening way. Not leaning over her in a bid to intimidate. More to prop himself up, to steady his shaking hands, to stop himself from falling over. His eyes jitter about like flies, as if she and Betty aren't even there. He mumbles to himself in thought, calculating.

She is stumped as to what to ask next. It's clear he's going through something, and she doesn't know how much he knows. She looks at Betty, who watches him with clear and open disgust, lip curled up, a deep frown on her face. She doesn't look as if she's ready to take the lead.

"My husband, it seems, runs a business that makes a lot more money than I had originally come to believe, not all of which comes through our accounts. I don't know where the money comes from. I don't know where it goes. He's missing, and I have no idea where he is. And someone came to my home and tried to kidnap my daughter."

"Kidnap Ellie?" His tone rises in surprise. His eyes hold her gaze and his fidgeting, worried movements stop dead. "Is she safe?"

"She's fine. I don't think they know where I'm staying."

"And where are you staying?" He holds up a hand. "No, don't tell me. Don't tell anyone. I know Dirk has been, um..." He stops talking. His eyes dart between her and Betty. His neck bulges as he swallows. "Who was it? Who came to your house?"

She watches him for a moment. "I don't quite know how to tell you—"

He sighs, cutting her off. Lets his arms drop as if in defeat. Reaches up, removes his head, and places it on the table. Sadie nearly falls off her chair, nearly vomits, nearly dies, but manages, by some freakishly uncharacteristic means, to keep her cool.

After a minute's silence — just enough time for reality to set in — Betty shouts, "Holy shit on a stick!" and jumps to stand behind Sadie's chair. She presses herself against the wall.

Jarrod's body, though still standing, droops as if unconscious.

Eight brown, insectile legs, each roughly a foot in length, extend from the underside of his head and step up and out of the mock neck it had been resting upon. Sadie leaves her body. Retreats. Forget about it. Everything that is hers in that room, body included, is a complete write-off. They can have it. Might as well just forget it ever existed and become a ghost.

Unfortunately, she realises — while her spirit is off distracting itself with a little imaginary walk around Tesco's, up and down the aisles piling groceries in a trolley for a brief moment of calm, trying its best to keep hold of its sanity — that you can't stay out of your body for long, otherwise you die. And dead wives don't find missing husbands.

Something clicks, and she comes crashing back into that little meeting room furnished with a table, some nice comfy chairs, branded pens, and a fuck-off head with spider legs.

Her hands fly up to her mouth to hold in her scream and her eyes screw shut as the creature takes a slight step closer.

"I'd take my mask off too," says the head of Jarrod Green with a little unjustified laugh, "but that'd probably *really* freak you out." He smiles. "It looked like you were holding back, so I thought I'd show you that you can tell me anything."

"Wh-wh-wh—?"

"What the hell are you?" Betty picks up a pen from the desk and throws it at him. It bounces off his face as if his skin is made of rubber. She grabs another, clicks it open and points it at him like a blade. "I'll cut you. I'll cut you right up."

"In the simplest terms, I'm what you'd get if spiders had been allowed to evolve like humans had from apes." He looks up at them. "I'm not going to hurt you. I'm probably more scared of you than you are of me."

"Fuck off are you," says Betty, with venom.

"You can put the pen down," he says, lifting an appeasing limb.

Betty picks up another and duel-wields. "As if!"

Sadie nods towards his inert body. Forces her tongue to speak. "Is...robot?"

He laughs. "More like a plant. We have a symbiotic relationship. It's a little difficult to explain without getting into some real nitty gritty, which I could do, but I guess we don't have time."

She purses her lips. Squeezes the words out like toothpaste. "And you're Dirk's accountant?" Her head hurts.

He nods. Or at least she thinks he does. A nod is a curious movement for a head on spider legs.

"That's right. We're pretty good at numbers, us arachnids. It's all the web building — angles, load bearing, trigonometry. You're basically always doing maths when you build your own house with your butt."

She nods, if only to keep her eyes moving lest she stare too long. She doesn't want to appear rude, but she also doesn't want to go absolutely bonkers. "You're a...a spider-man?"

"An arachnid." Jarrod tuts with mock annoyance. "You lot are always putting 'man' on the end of things, as if talking and having some sort of cognitive function is strictly a human thing. It's a little bit rude."

"Sorry," she says, moving her hands to her lap. She does like to think she's inclusive. "I've not met a talking spider before."

"And you'll not likely meet another. I'm one of the last of my kind," he says, and though he wears a mask, the turn of his eye and slow of his breath are very human in their deep display of sadness.

"I'm sorry to hear that."

While the extinction of a whole species is a terrible, terrible thing, and she's an awful, awful woman for thinking it, she takes some comfort in knowing that she is unlikely to meet another giant talking spider anytime soon. Beings with more than four legs are very much not her thing. Looking forward into the murky but not too distant future, she decides this might not be the best phobia to have this week.

He brightens. "I'd probably be dead too if it wasn't for your husband and Burty. You won't meet two better humans. I'll do all I can to help." His voice becomes flat, business-like, for a talking spider with a man's face. "So tell me, who was it that came for Ellie?"

She shakes her head. "I don't know exactly. They weren't human. They were like weird hairless dog-faced me...guy...things?"

"Weird hairless dog-faced guys. Hmm?" One of his limbs bends up and strokes his chin. God, he has a lot of knees. Then he shakes his head. The mask slips ever so slightly, revealing something dark and chitinous behind his eyes. "Don't get many of those about. I know who you could try though: the Drake. He might know."

"The who?" Betty places her pens on the table and leans forward.

"He funds the guys. Finds buyers for all of their artefacts. He's the reason there's so much money flowing into their account. The reason they — oh dear!"

He skips around and propels himself up the front of his body with fast, precise movements that, if spotted a few metres away in the corner of a darkened room, would usually make her want to faint.

Jarrod settles himself squarely on top of his body's shoulders just as the conference room door flies open. A spotty teenage boy dressed in a billowing white shirt leans through the opening.

"Just wondering if you wanted a tea or anything, Mr. Green?" He glances right over Sadie, ignores her completely, and lands his wandering pubescent eyes happily on Betty. Buffs the lank, gel-soaked hair away from his forehead and says with a slight upward nod of the head, "Alright."

"No thanks, Carl." Jarrod's body raises a hand to cover his legs, which are tucked up under his chin. His actual neck still rests on the table like a thin slice of reconstituted ham. It looks as if he's choking himself. "I'll be back up in a minute."

"Cool." The boy gives Betty one last look, then disappears. His footsteps glomp back up the stairs.

"Work experience kid," says Jarrod, when he's sure they won't be disturbed again. "Lucky that boy wears such stupid, big shoes. He'd have caught me stretching my legs a few times now if I'd've not heard him stomping about. Doesn't know how to kno—"

He stops abruptly, catching Sadie's look.

Her cheeks tighten into an impatient smile, and she folds her arms. "You mentioned the Drake?"

# You Got This

As they step from the office, Betty lifts her phone to her ear.

"Yes?" she says. She holds her position in the centre of the car park and listens. Her face falls like something terrible has happened.

A breeze blows an empty crisp packet past Sadie's feet.

"I can't really talk right now. I'm with someone," she says. "OK. I'll just come." She hangs up and looks at Sadie. "Um." Her mouth hangs slightly open.

"What is it?" Sadie searches the eyes of this woman she barely knows. "What's wrong?"

"I can't go with you."

Her heart goes cold as Betty moves towards her car.

"Why...what do you mean?"

She stops and turns back. "I have to visit my mum." She lets out an unhappy sigh. "Something's happened."

No. She can't do this on her own. She's finally found someone who can help and now they're dumping her just when things are becoming a bit dicey.

She chews the corner of her mouth. "I could come with you...to see your mum," she tries. "We could go to see the Drake afterwards." She looks at the address on the slip of paper Jarrod had given them. She doesn't want to go there alone.

Betty takes a step closer. She places a hand on Sadie's shoulder. Dips her head to look her in the eye. "If it was anything else, I'd ditch it to come with you. But I've got to go, and time isn't on our side. I know we need to find Burt and Dirk, but..." She looks down. Fiddles with the zip of her coat. "Mum's taken a turn for the worse. She keeps asking why Burt hasn't been in to visit. I need to go and see her."

"But I can't..." Sadie begins. Betty's brow twitches in what looks like annoyance and she holds her tongue. Doesn't want to try to convince someone she hardly knows not to visit their sick mother. What kind of horrible person would do that? The sort of horrible person who might take comfort in the knowledge that an entire race of evolved arachnids had nearly been wiped out just so she didn't have to see another one. "I'm sorry about your mum."

"You got this." Betty takes her phone out of her pocket. "Give me your number. I'll call you when I'm done, then I'll come find you. Where are you staying?"

Sadie gives Betty her number. "I've been at my mum's," she says. A cold stone lies in the pit of her stomach.

"Where's that?"

"Not far."

Betty pauses. Opens her mouth, then closes it as she reconsiders what she's about to say. "I'll call you and come see you there later. We'll find them. Don't worry."

Sadie straightens her back, trying to look more confident than she feels. "OK."

"I'm sorry." Betty opens her car door. "I'll come find you at your mum's and we'll sort this."

"You've got nothing to be sorry about."

Betty holds up her phone, but doesn't smile. "I'll phone as soon as I'm free."

Sadie opens her mouth to apologise again about her mum, but Betty climbs in and closes the door before she can get the words out. She feels empty, like she has missed an opportunity to make a good impression, but the car is already reversing. She waves. Betty nods.

The poor woman. Imagine having that to deal with, too.

Betty pulls out of the accountants', and just like that, Sadie is alone once more.

# BREADCRUMBS

It's getting past lunchtime, and though her conversation with the accountant of her nightmares has pushed back her hunger, Sadie suspects it's difficult to run around looking for missing husbands on strength of will and hope alone, so she stops off on the high street and picks up a sushi meal deal.

While she sits inside her mother's car, putting off the next stage of her journey by precisely piling pickled ginger on to little circles of rice and cucumber, she goes over what Jarrod had told her and Betty.

The Drake is a conduit. Jarrod had said duct, but she knows what he means. Some sort of link between the seedy underworld of magical item collectors and Dirk and Burt's agency, which, it transpires, is a sort of private-investigator-cum-ghostbuster-style outfit. The Drake is a dealer through which otherworldly artefacts and money passes hands.

According to Jarrod, the story goes that Dirk and Burt, having disposed of a murderous monster, or thwarted the designs of some diabolical demigod, would steal and then sell whatever they found on site to raise funds so they could continue disposing and thwarting.

What were the ethics involved in such a practice? Was selling stolen goods or parts of exceedingly rare species OK if it meant you could continue saving the world one monster or demigod at a time? She wouldn't argue against it, but assumes someone with a swollen set of morals might in order to signal their virtue.

She isn't sure she understands what exactly this person can do to help her find Dirk, but Jarrod said that the Drake "knew the right people".

When he'd added finger quotes to the words "people", it led her to believe she wouldn't be dealing with people at all...

Preoccupied, she accidentally squirts soy sauce on to David Bowie's crooning face. A moment of panic passes as she searches for a tissue to remove it. Then she remembers it's her dad's shirt, and so likely to be more stain than print, anyway. Dad had an eating problem. Especially when it came to sauces, runny eggs, gravy. Caught on a desert island with one of Dad's frequently worn T-shirts and you could probably survive quite some time on the spillages alone. Dirk's the same. Is it weird she finds it endearing? She gives up and smears the brown sauce in with her thumb, giving David a little five o'clock shadow.

She pulls Dirk's black hoody out of her bag and puts it on. Doesn't want to show up with soy sauce stains all over her. Something solid sits in the front pocket amongst the used tissues. A little tub of VapoRub from her last cold. She holds it between finger and thumb and thinks about what Dirk had said over breakfast. Did Vick's know their cold medicine was used by demon hunters in the fight against evil?

As she finishes her sushi, Mum sends a picture of Ellie with a tea towel wrapped around her tummy like an apron, and a wooden spoon poised over a tray of unbaked cookies. '*Save one for me,*' she sends back.

When she'd been younger, and had day-dreamed about having her own children, Sadie had always presumed the three of them would do things like bake cookies or have little tea parties together.

But they never had.

It's not that she doesn't want to, and there had been plenty of time and opportunity. Sadie has spent many afternoons just her and Ellie, knowing Mum would be in. She's just been scared. And, thinking about it, as they'd spent more and more time apart, she's realised it's nothing to do with the possession either. She thinks maybe she's scared of asking too much of Mum. Scared of pushing her away, perhaps, just by asking her to be closer.

It's stupid. And she's stupid for thinking it.

She sighs and reaches over to stuff the wrappings of her meal deal into the glove box.

Things have to change. As soon as Dirk's back, everything has to be better.

The Drake's address isn't far. She recognises the location from the street name alone. The idea of going there tops up her dread levels almost to their limits.

The Hanley Estate.

It'll be her first time inside.

As if it could be anywhere other than the notorious council estate every child from her old school used to tell horror stories about. Kids who went in never came out. People got mugged, killed, disappeared. Yep, they "got disappeared," as if that was something that could be done to you in Winchester, of all places. It was all just playground conspiracy. Passed down from one judgemental parent to their gossipy child and spread like head lice. Spoilt kids creating as much division between themselves and the less well off as they could, just to make themselves feel better.

She enters the estate at a polite, but harried, 29 miles per hour.

Dirk had told her that he and Burt were highly trained operatives for a secret organisation. Had there been any truth in that? Or was Burt really just an old school friend with whom Dirk had found a magic wand and started battling the forces of evil? Had he just been massaging the truth, stretching it out like playdough? That secret organisation wasn't government-run, wasn't authentic or regulated. It was just him and his mate working out of some storage unit.

That would be typical of Dirk. Not to lie, but to stretch the truth to fit his narrative. Dirk, whose used plates only ever made it to the kitchen side and never into the dishwasher because he was in a hurry to do something else important. Dirk, whose discarded socks littered all areas of the house because they'd gotten a bit wet and were irritating his feet. Dirk, who always loved to play a grotesque game of garbage Jenga rather than empty the bin like a normal person because he was trying to save the environment and not use up too many bags. A likely excuse...

She huffs out a breath. It's not fair to slam him. Not while he's out there, possibly alone, possibly in mortal peril.

Possibly dea—

"No," she shouts to the inside of the car, and slaps a hand on the steering wheel hard enough to deaden her palm. The jolt shakes tears from her eyes. Tears she hadn't even known were there. She looks in the mirror. Wipes them away. Tells herself, "He's fine."

He is fine.

He had to be fine.

But denial is like fixing a bike puncture by nailing a piece of wood over the hole.

What would Betty do in this situation?

She screws up her face and pushes the car to an illegal 34. Smash the system! Screw the man! To the cold pits of Hell with the speed cameras! Mum doesn't have any points. Sadie can afford a ticket.

The Hanley Estate is like any other. Groups of kids play in the street. Jumpers for goalposts. Kicking a scuffed, semi-inflated ball between them. They stop their game for her to pass. The one holding the ball has red hair shaved short at the sides. He regards her with bright green eyes as if she were an infamous bandit with six guns at both hips entering his Wild West saloon, although, to turn an overused metaphor on its head, she feels strangely more like a Wild West saloon entering an infamous bandit.

Slender, silver-trunked birches skirt the street, stretching across with their serrated leaves, shading the children as they continue their play. She wonders why they aren't at school. It's a weekday after all.

A young mother with the thickest eyebrows Sadie has ever seen pushes a baby in a huge bassinet-style pram that could easily be a family heirloom. She stops, passes what looks to be a full-cooked chicken in, then smiles and replaces the child's blanket.

Sadie navigates the suburban warren of terraced houses, creeping between rows of filthy parked cars. Most look as if they haven't been driven in weeks — possibly months. They're covered in pollen and fallen detritus from the trees with moss growing from the seals and windows.

She is once again surprised to find the address isn't some sort of gothic mansion cloaked in cobwebs, circled by ancient decaying woods with permanent storm clouds grumbling and crackling lightning overhead. Once again, she is slightly disappointed.

The pebble-dash terrace she pulls up to stands at the head of a short concrete slab path surrounded by overgrown yellowing grass and a waist-high chain-link fence held up by concrete posts. Misty condensation covers the inside of the windows.

The only unusual thing is the two ducks stood on the apex of the roof and the third nestled in the pot of the chimney. They stand motionless and at first she presumes that they are a trio of strange roof ornaments. That is until one swivels its head to eye her cautiously. Its beak shines silver in the sun.

She removes the wand she'd taken from Dirk's lockup from her bag. It seems to writhe in her hand.

Could she defend herself with it? Were wands even used as weapons? She'd only ever seen Dirk use his twice. Once, the first time they'd met, to check her eyes for whatever he'd been checking her eyes for, and the second, to light Ellie's first birthday cake when they couldn't find any matches. But what would be the point in having a wand if you couldn't fight with it?

She stuffs it into her pocket. No one knows she can't use it. Might as well keep it on hand for intimidation purposes, at least. An unloaded gun is as much a deterrent as a loaded one if no one knows it's unloaded. Although if everyone else knows that the gun you think you're holding is just a gimmicky firelighter, then you're pretty stuffed. It would be just like her to bring a match to a gunfight.

She rubs her hands against her front to remove that creeping after-touch the wand leaves on her palms, then takes the VapoRub and dabs a smear beneath her nose to overpower what she judgementally expects, due to the condensation covering the interior of the house's windows, might be a bit of a smell inside. After Dirk's accountant, who knew what foul creatures of the night might await her? That said, Jarrod had been quite amicable for a giant talking spider.

Maybe she needed to check her prejudices. Didn't even know she had prejudices until a few hours ago. Then again, the thing about prejudices is that you don't know they are prejudices until you try to face them.

She takes a breath to steady her frayed nerves and catches herself in the mirror. Is she doing the right thing? Is she just chasing ghosts? Hoping that the next place she arrives will give her some answers and not just another brainful of questions.

She forces the worry back like a shot of tequila. An actual shot of tequila would go down very well right about now.

Betty would probably down a shot of tequila, then kick the door down, and shake the answers out of anyone unlucky enough to be on the other side with her crushing feminine power and her stunning, envy-provoking hair.

Though Burt's sister isn't here, it buoys Sadie to know she has an ally. It strengthens her. And with that strength comes a question — what would younger Sadie do? She wouldn't be sitting here quailing in her car. She'd be out there knocking on doors, busting chops!

Sadie slaps the steering wheel with both palms. Unbuckles. Throws the car door open. Steps out. Rolls her shoulders and straightens her back. Thinks positively. You are doing the right thing, Sadie. You are confident and brave and strong, Sadie.

She marches straight up to that garden gate and throws it open on shrieking rusted hinges. It bounces back instantly, catching her on the hip. One duck on the roof quacks. It sounds like a laugh.

Hm. Fuck you, duck!

She strides through the knee-high grass, raises her fist to bust the door down with the force of her knocking, but before her hand so much as scrapes the faded grey uPVC, it opens.

Her fist swings through, bopping a young man just out of his teens square on the nose.

"Aah!" he cries, falling backwards. "They're here. They're here."

He scrabbles up, retreating down the hallway, clutching his face, scurrying through into a back room that discharges the sound of video-game violence and some of the grimiest hip-hop she's ever heard. And back in uni, Sadie had listened to some proper grimy stuff…

The grit of the music helps her to bury that rising particle of guilt at punching some random dude and she strides after him through the front door.

The foot of the walls in the hall are black with mould. The grey carpet is almost soggy underfoot. Her lip curls.

A young woman, dressed all in black, with tattoos creeping up and around her throat and down her bare arms, peers past the man and frowns. She doesn't look particularly bothered.

"That's not them," she says, then rolls her eyes and disappears back around the open door.

"What do you mean?" the man says. He takes his hand away from his nose and inspects it, clearly expecting to see blood. He is thin and tall, with a big red nose that looks like it may have always been big and red, and not just because she's recently flattened it. A fluffy blue lumberjack's hat is pulled down around his ears. "Smacked me as soon as I opened the door."

Sadie holds an apologetic hand up, that particle of guilt growing and getting the better of her. "Sorry, I really am. I was knocking." She mimes a knock. He flinches. Her palms are sweaty. Her lunch jumps around her stomach like it's still alive. Why had she picked sushi and not something safe like ready salted crisps?

"That wasn't knocking. That was some Tyson Fury shit." He lifts his chin and looks to where the woman has disappeared. "Is it bleeding? Look, is it bleeding?"

"Don't be such a wuss," the woman says from around the corner. "Ask her what she wants. If she's selling something, tell her no thanks. I'm not buying a load of cleaning products from someone stuck in a pyramid scheme. Not again. I'm still trying to get through the last load. Cuts away grease like a hot knife through butter, my arse."

"He seemed legit," says the man. He glances back at Sadie, then gathers himself with a straightening of the back and a turnout of the elbows designed to make him look broader, but only really drawing attention to how lanky he is. "Who are ya, then? Go on!"

"I'm looking for someone called the Drake."

The sound of digitalised fighting ceases, followed by the music.

The woman's head eases horizontally around the door. She squints at Sadie as if to properly take her in. "You what?"

"The Drake."

"Ain't heard of him. You better leave." Her head pops away again. "Finch, show her out."

"Sorry," says Finch, making his cautious way back down the hall towards her, his hand out in front of him lest this crazy woman at the door come for him again. "Apparently, we don't know what you're talking about."

Sadie folds her arms and whacks him with a stare that has been known to stop a child drinking from the toilet from twenty feet. "Jarrod Green sent me."

He raises a finger and turns. "Er, Wren, she said Jar—"

"I heard what she said. What do you want?"

"I want her to leave so I can come back and play games…" says Finch, confused.

"She's talking to me, you dope." Sadie pushes her way past. The VapoRub does nothing to halt the stench cocktail of cigarette smoke and clothes that have taken too long to dry from creeping up her nose as she steps into the brown living room.

The curtains are closed. The orange bulb hanging naked in the centre of the ceiling gives her the impression that she is a mosquito caught in filthy amber. A TV covers one wall. Games magazines and an assortment of smoking paraphernalia are scattered across a two-legged coffee table propped up with bricks. Little bits of torn paper, ash-filled take-away coffee cups, sweet packets, and drinks cans litter the room. Like the hallway, the floor here is curiously moist underfoot.

"What do you want?" asks Wren. She sits cross-legged on the floor by the sofa with a gamepad on her lap and a crumpled rollie clamped in the corner of her lips. She brushes her hand over the carpet absentmindedly. It seems to move and shift with unusual eddies as she trails her fingers across its surface. She doesn't seem bothered by the wetness.

Sadie looks back at Finch, who remains in the hall. Surely this is the wrong place. These don't look the sort to deal in magical artefacts, to deal with the sort of money she saw coming and going in Dirk's account.

"You said Jarrod sent you?" Wren asks. She raises a plucked eyebrow as if to add, *and?*

Finch moves into the doorway, blocking it with folded arms.

"Um..." With her back to the wall, and no way out, Sadie suddenly feels very trapped. "I—" She clears her throat and balls her fists. "I'm looking for my husband. His name is Dirk Kilmore."

At the mention of Dirk's name, Wren's face lights up. "You're Sadie?" She stabs out her cigarette inside an ash-stained mug. "Sorry. We didn't know what you looked like. We have to be careful at the moment."

"Oh, wow," says Finch. He smiles, too. "You can see Ellie in her."

Wren nods to him. Her face is lean, the bones of her jaw sharp, when she smiles. "You can. How is the little one?" she asks. Her eyes travel around the room. A little redness touches her cheeks. Not enough, considering the state of the place. "Sorry about the mess." She claps her hands twice. "Stick the kettle on, bro. It's time for tea."

Finch wanders back down the hall.

"Sorry, you know who I am?"

Does everyone?

"Oh, yeah, Dirk's always going on about you. We've just never seen a pic."

Wren scurries across the room and scrapes an arm over the seat of an armchair, throwing clothes and assorted junk onto the floor.

"We didn't expect you to be dropping by," she adds, as she kicks the bits away with her bare feet. "Take a seat."

Sadie heaves a breath through her nose and sits gently on the armchair. Its battered cushion drops her several inches further than she'd planned for.

"Why are you here, of all places?" asks Wren.

Sadie explains.

"Ah," says Wren. "Yes, the card you found would have had some sort of influence spell on it that made you squirrel it away in case of emergency. Clever Dirk."

Finch returns from the kitchen, and points finger guns at each of them. "Kettle's going. What we having?"

Wren orders tea. Sadie declines, worried about the state of the cups. Her hosts insist, so she goes with a water. At least she'll be able to see if there's anything lurking in it...

"And did you want a TV with that?" Finch says, leaning his head to one side and shooting her dead once more with finger guns.

"I'm sorry?" She heard him. She just doesn't comprehend.

Wren scoffs. "Stop trying to sell everyone who drops by a bloody TV."

He turns a palm to the ceiling. "But Dad said to always be selling."

She gives him a withering look. "Not now, you hobnoblin. If Dirk wants a TV, he knows where to come."

"How about a vacuum?" He raises his eyebrows and gives a slight, questioning wobble of the head.

Wren flings an empty can at him. "Get back in the kitchen, wench."

Defeated, he leaves.

"I must apologise for my brother's idiocy," Wren says, turning her attention back to Sadie.

Wren props herself on the brick end of the coffee table, leans forward intently, fingers steepled in front of her chin. Her frame is all skin and bone. Doesn't look like she eats much, or well when she does. She's younger than Sadie had first assumed. Young and confident.

"When did you see him last?" Her concern is genuine. Sadie likes her for it. "Is Ellie OK?"

"Ellie's safe with..." She stops herself. Doesn't want to let anything slip. "She's safe."

Finch returns with her water, passes it over, then disappears again. She takes a tentative sip. Heavy chlorine taste, but nothing too strange. No bits.

Her mouth has gone quite dry. Lack of sleep catching up with her, as well as lack of coffee. Her temples are hot. Her eyes are blurry and sore. She rubs them. She's felt this way before…many, many times.

"He was supposed to come home Saturday night. Last time I saw him was Thursday. I don't know how much you know about him. I don't know where to start."

Wren takes her hand. Her warm smile suggests age beyond her years. "We know enough. Dirk's a slayer. A good one. They don't tend to get to his age unless they are."

"He's not old." She shakes her head, but freezes when she realises what Wren means. An icy finger strokes her heart. "Oh."

"Sorry," says Wren, leaning back. "I mean, if he's missing, then I wouldn't be too worried." She waves a hand as if to bat Sadie's worries away. "He's good at what he does. I expect he's right where he's meant to be."

To Sadie, that sounds like it means something she doesn't fully understand.

"Can you help me find him? Are you the Drake?"

Wren snorts a laugh. "Noooo. He's our dad. He'll be downstairs if he's not on the wing somewhere." She points to the floor.

Sadie frowns. It doesn't seem the sort of place to have a basement.

Finch enters with two teas.

"Finchy, I'll pop down. See if Dad's happy for guests. You wait here with Sadie K."

"Sure thing," he says, passing Wren her cup.

She takes a gulp and places it on the table. Winks at him. "Nice one. I'll be back for that."

She eases herself off the table to a seated position on the carpet. Seems to think to herself a moment before shifting a few inches to the left. Then, she pushes down on her knees as if to stand, but instead of her body moving up, her bare, black-nailed toes disappear into the floor. The fronds of the carpet swallow them like quicksand. Her calves follow. She manoeuvres herself as if to slide over the edge of a swimming pool, then sinks all the way under.

# It's Not Carpet

Sadie gasps and lifts her legs reflexively, wanting to be as far from this human-devouring quick-carpet as possible.

Finch puts a hand to his mouth. "Oh, gosh." Laughs through splayed fingers. "Sorry," he says, then jabs a thumb towards the empty space where Wren had been. "That must have looked a bit weird." He sips his tea and considers his next words carefully. He somehow decides the most appeasing thing he can offer is, "it's not carpet."

"I can see it's not bloody carpet," Sadie snaps, leaning forward to peer over the edge of her armchair, feeling as if she's looking over the side of a very tall building. "Where did she go?"

"She just went downstairs."

"Through the carpet?" Sadie feels like she's shouting. Is she shouting?

"It's not carpet," he repeats, to the same effect as before, then adds, "It's perfectly normal."

"It is *not* perfectly normal." She looks about the room to see if there's a chance of escape without touching the all-devouring floor covering. "Is she like a ghost or something?"

Finch snorts through his wrinkled nose as if that's the silliest thing anyone's ever said. "Noooo. The floor," he says, adopting the air of an expert academic, "he's a gelatinous guard cube." Then nods as if that is explanation enough.

She gives him nothing.

He taps his lips. Blows a little ponderous raspberry. "At the risk of sounding offensive, he's like a jelly that can hear what you're thinking. If you don't mean the person he's guarding harm, and you want to get through, he lets you through. If you *do* mean the person he's guarding harm, and want to get through, he lets you, but, um…" The young man scratches his ear in thought. "He sort of digests you on the way down." He smiles, surprised at having made it through that explanation alive and without sounding like a complete dunce. "He's called Topher. He's a good lad."

Sadie looks down at the floor. Prods it with her toe then recoils as it wobbles. Finch watches her.

Wren's head emerges from the space next to her armchair. Sadie lets out a little scream.

"Yeah, Dad's cool. Come on down." She disappears again.

Sadie glances at Finch as a feeling of horror builds. "Is there another way?"

He taps his lips with a finger, then closes one eye. "There is, but it's pretty gross."

"And sliding through a creature made of jelly isn't pretty gross?"

It is. It's the grossest thing she can think of.

And she'd once caught a surprise jet of warm prune and curry baby vomit…

…in her mouth.

Finch shakes his head. "Not really. You actually come out cleaner. I sometimes do it instead of having a shower. Saves on water. And Toph don't mind."

He raises his eyebrows as if his next-level money- and climate-saving ingenuity should impress her. Was it weird that it kind of did?

She puts her feet to the floor. Despite the wetness, it seems very firm. Sickeningly firm. Like a piece of thin, raw meat around hard bone.

"How do I—?" She heaves. "How—?"

"It's easy." Finch stands with her and holds out his free hand. "I'll show you."

Her heart quickens, and she chews the corner of her mouth. "Um." She takes a quick breath and readies herself. "OK. I'm ready…OK."

She's not, but she takes his hand.

"My first time, Dad taught me to think of it like a lift. You get in, push the button, and prepare for descent."

She nods. Then shakes her head. Nope. "How do I push the button?"

"Just ask him to see the Drake."

Finch wobbles slightly as he sinks up to his knees into the floor.

"Can I see the Drake?" she says out loud, although something tells her she could have somehow asked without words.

A tingling starts in the soles of her feet as if hundreds of tiny worms are trying to tickle her through her shoes. Then the floor seems to ease like wet sand on the beach. But it doesn't stop. She looks down as the ground absorbs her shoes, then her shins. A distressing notion enters her head, dancing nimbly out of the darkened depths uninvited.

"But, what happens if I mean the Drake harm?" she says.

Finch smiles. But a little dent appears on his brow. "But you don't, right?"

"I think I don't. But what if I do and I don't know?" The floor grips her legs tightly as she continues to sink. Did it always squeeze this hard?

"But you don't..." He leans his head forward ever so slightly to punctuate the next word. "Riiight?"

"No. But what if, like, somehow..." She's panicking. She's panicking. Uh oh! Abandon ship! "Like, somehow, um...the Drake does something that means I mean him harm, like in the future? Uh..." She can't breathe.

"Um."

How much do gelatinous guard cubes know? Her heart hammers in her chest. The floor pulls her down faster, gripping her stomach, then her chest. So tight around her chest. She's suffocating.

"What if...?" She presses her lips together as she drops to her neck. Squeezes her eyes shut. A little squeak of fear escapes her as the cube swallows her whole.

The exposed skin of her hands, face, and neck tingles as, for an unbearable second of absolute helplessness, she is fully submerged in cold wetness.

A green light shines beyond her eyelids. Her whole body is held firm. Is she really inside a living thing?

*You are*, says a pleasant voice, popping directly into her head. It rides on a wave of colour. The calming green of new leaves, of fresh grass. It's almost healing in its tranquillity.

*Oh. Hello*, she thinks back. *I don't mean the Drake harm. I promise.*

*Hi*, it says. *Don't worry, I'm not going to eat you. You'd be delicious, though.*

The green is shot through with swirls of royal purple and gold. The colours coordinate perfectly. The palette of Heaven's interior designer. She gets the feeling they are supposed to be a compliment.

*Thanks?*

*No problemo.* A strange vision of a happy piece of tofu waving goodbye filters into her thoughts. She doesn't know how she can tell it's happy because it has no face, or waving because it has no arms, but she just knows.

All is well.

Welcome dryness visits her ankles, then her midriff, hands, and neck. Her feet touch solid ground and she ducks down, allowing her head to slide out with a pop.

She opens her eyes and gasps in air. Air that smells sweet and clean and earthy. Wholly different from the room she has just left.

Above her, the ceiling crawls back, snail-like, up the wall. It looks identical to the carpet except for the faint translucent glow of the light bulb in the room above shining dully through it.

Finch stands next to her. He smiles, then lifts his mug to his lips. Frowns. Scoffs and looks up. "Oi, Toph, you drank my tea?"

Topher wobbles with what can only be described as amusement.

The room they are in is roughly the same size as the one above. The walls are compacted earth. Solid and strong, with white string-like roots running through them.

A blackboard stands in front of three rows of six mismatched tables and desks, much like a classroom. Ahead, a corridor leads down towards another larger room which must be situated beneath the house's back garden.

"Follow me," says Finch.

He holds up his hand. Tattoos of blue flame cover his forearm. He wiggles his fingers and they coalesce towards his palm, which begins to glow a brilliant blue. It lights the way ahead.

"Dad's very busy. We don't want to keep him waiting."

# THE DRAKE, I PRESUME

The archway leads to a short, low tunnel. Azure ripples of light beneath water twist and flow on the ceiling ahead.

Sadie gasps as she enters a great hall filled with treasure. Well, not quite treasure. Treasure maybe, if one of your hobbies is scouring charity shops for bargain toys and kids' clothes. Back in the day, when Dirk wasn't bringing much in, she'd hit the charity shops or car boot sales searching for bargains at least once a week. The joy of finding a diamond in all that rough sticks, even when you've got the money to afford new things.

Ahead, across a pool of water, sits a mountain of electrical goods amidst a decade's worth of jumble-sale junk. Several TVs, a couple of dodgy-looking vacuums, rusty lawnmowers and garden tools, hundreds of DVD cases, a stack of weird action figure bobblehead things in boxes, a sparkle of knock-off tablets, bin bags with clothes poking from the top, and piles and piles of kids' toys. A trove of car-boot-sale wonders.

She doesn't see anything that appears to be of any real value. None of the strange artefacts that Jarrod suggested were sold on for Dirk and Burt. Perhaps they are in another place, or sold on immediately.

The large pool that separates the small stone platform where they stand and the heap of junk shop riches is lit from beneath by some sort of bioluminescent glow. Swirling blue particles dance and ebb and flow in the stone-tiled depths. The water is so clear. Almost tropical. The bottom is a monochrome mosaic of white and midnight blue. The pool encircles the treasure island in the centre.

Grey stone blocks arch up and overhead, coming to a point in the domed ceiling like a cathedral. Through the shadows above, she can make out stunning paintings etched with vibrant colour and detail. Giant fire-breathing beasts battle men sheathed in armour.

"She's here, Dad," says Wren, who sits on the edge of the water. Her feet kick lazily in the pool, causing ripples of aqua reflections to dance around the stone walls and ceiling. She appears to be looking at something Sadie cannot see.

"Ah, Sadie, so wonderful to meet you finally." The voice is quiet, but low and firm. A bass sizzle. Cascades of teddies and nameless action figures tinkle down from the great mound ahead as something moves in the darkness.

"Er, hello?"

She squints, and suddenly, as if looking at a magic eye picture, all becomes clear. The round body with wings tucked in tight. The long, snaking neck. The bright orange webbed feet.

Jarrod Green hadn't said the Drake was a duct, as in conduit. He'd said duck, as in duck. A fifteen-foot-tall duck, to be exact.

He lifts his huge head and sniffs the air. He seems to shrink and stretch simultaneously as he waddles forward out of the shadow on the other side of the pool, slipping down the pile, transforming, until he gets to the island's edge and splashes into the water.

He surfaces as a man. Long brown hair floats around his shoulders as he doggy-paddles towards them with unusual grace for the stroke. He wears a black patch over his right eye. A scar runs down his clean-shaven cheek.

He climbs a series of steps out of the pool. The water runs off him and he's dry by the time he's next to her. His hair is perfectly coiffured, as if he's just been for a blow dry at a top salon. He stands about five inches taller than her and wears a brown jumpsuit done up at the centre with a purple silk sash. While getting out of the pool, an orange beret seems to have appeared on his head. He looks like he belongs on a Paris catwalk.

"Wren tells me you're here to find your wonderful husband," he says, catching her with his one good eye. He has a gentle way of speaking. Light and low. In this human form his voice is the auditory equivalent of a well-whipped chocolate mousse.

"You're the Drake?"

"I prefer Le Canard." He smoulders, puts a hand to his hip and delicately turns his palm to the ceiling. "But it's nice to go by many names. Makes one harder to pin down." His eye twinkles with good humour.

She looks at Finch, then Wren. Smaller ducks watch her from the wings. She feels so out of place.

"What is all of this?" She nods towards the contents of the island.

"Ah." He smiles, but she senses a sadness in it. "My hoard. Not as magnificent as it once was. But it does give the children something to work with. I like to train them in the art of the sale — for when they take over the family business — and what better way than at car boot sales and the odd jumble? They'll need the skill when they move onto artefacts of real value."

"She doesn't need a TV or a vacuum, Dad," says Finch. "I checked."

The Drake gives him a wink then puts an arm around Sadie's shoulder. "So tell me, what's happened to our man Dirk?"

"He's been missing since Thursday. He went to work and didn't come back."

"I take it you understand what he does for..." the Drake releases her and bends two fingers either side of his head, "work."

"I'm starting to."

He sucks air through his teeth. "I'm afraid it may be my case that has put him in his current predicament."

"I thought he just sold you things."

"Normally." He gives a worried smile. "He has been a great help to our cause. He and Burt donate books for the school and much-needed funds for the children of the estate, and in return I help find them buyers for the majority of the items they come across. I used to be somewhat of a mover and shaker."

Sadie glances back up the hall towards the rows of desks in the next room. Is that what they call a school?

The Drake smiles. "It's not much, but it's all the children have. The past few years have been tough on us all. But we can't afford to rest on our laurels. Sooner or later, Hell will make another demand, and we need to have someone ready."

She's curious to know what he means by that, but doesn't want to get off track. Dirk now. Hell's demands hopefully never.

"What did you have him working on?"

"Kids have been going missing from the estate," says Wren. She circles her legs in the water. "The magic users."

"There's more of you around here?" Sadie looks between the three.

"It's *only* us around here," says the Drake with a sad smile. He removes the beret from his head and holds it before him. "Don't tell us you haven't heard the rumours. We know there's a reason no one comes through here."

"This is where the Bureau stuck us all after..." Wren glances at the Drake, then clears her throat. "Everyone who lives here is either a magic user or a fae creature."

"They say it's safer for us all to be together," says Finch, folding his arms with a scowl, "but they just want us all cooped up in one place."

So there is a Bureau. She feels a twinkle of hope. There is someone official she can contact to help her.

"They don't like us out in front of the norms." Wren tuts.

"Dirk said he worked for them."

The Drake hums to himself in amusement. "Maybe once. I believe he may have been relieved of his duty after the war."

*War?* What war?

"Once upon a time, the Bureau had a modicum of integrity," he continues before she can ask. "Not now, though. Things have changed over there in recent months. The head of Hell Relations, she's different; compromised somehow. She has them under her spell."

"But aren't they like the police? Aren't they supposed to look after people like you?"

The Drake shakes his head.

"The Bureau can't help us," says Wren. "It's better to forget they exist now. We're on our own."

"It'd be easier to forget about them if they didn't come and arrest us every time we used magic outside of the estate," says Finch with a snarl.

Interesting. How would the Bureau know?

"Now, now, you two; some of the detectives still have their hearts in the right place. We know they are bound by bureaucracy. By the oaths they take." He looks at Sadie. "I believe that may be one reason your Dirk was discharged, but a lot of what happened around that time is fuzzy for me." He blinks and looks up to the ceiling. The drip drop of water fills the momentary silence.

"So," she says, loudly enough to snap him back. "Dirk was looking into your missing person's case, and you think wherever he's got to is something to do with that?"

The Drake nods. "Yes. He started a fortnight ago. Told us he might have something just last week. He'd compiled a list. Everyone who has gone. There's a connection. Each of the missing children can cast magic without a focus. Each has a natural gift for creating power from thought. Someone may be looking to harness that power."

"For what?"

"Unsure. All I know is it won't be good. In the past certain villains have used those that can manifest power as batteries for their own dark spells." He frowns, then closes his eyes. His hand whips out and hovers for a second over her stomach. "You have something in your pocket?"

Her fingers go to the wand.

He keeps his hand out. His frown deepens. "A focus."

Wren shifts on the floor. "Can I see it?" She pushes herself up.

Sadie removes the tentacle wand from her pocket. Each pair of eyes lights up.

"How did you come by such a piece?" asks the Drake, taking it in hand and looking between her and it. "Did you make it?" He shakes his head. "No. This is older than you are." He looks into her eyes searching for something, then cocks his head to one side. "Hm. It has history."

She clears her throat. "I found it in Dirk's unit."

There's a slight downturn in the corners of his mouth that she can't quite read.

Wren marvels over it. "Cool. Finchy, look at this."

Finch waves a hand and refolds his arms. "Not really into wands."

"Strange that Dirk never told me about this," comments the Drake, taking hold of the business end and passing it back handle first. "It likes you. You should keep a firm hold of it. This is a powerful tool when held in the right..." his eyebrows twitch, "or wrong hands."

She turns the wand over in her hands. "It likes me?"

The Drake nods. "Maybe because it's Dirks. Wands often form bonds with their owners. Some natural magic users create them as gifts for non-magical loved ones, but some people make them themselves. They are imbued with powerful magic. Each wand is connected to spells in a specific book, which allows the harnessing of the natural energy contained within the elements. Earth, air, fire, water, love..." He opens his mouth as if to add something else, then swallows. "The magic is in the book. The wand just harnesses it. You have the book?"

She nods and stuffs it back in her pocket.

"Good. Then you can learn the spells. People like you, Dirk, and Burt aren't gifted with magic. You can't do it without one of those." He points once more at the wand in her hoody pocket. "The children who have been taken can create the energy they need to cast spells within themselves. Books can guide them with what's possible, but with the proper training, they can manipulate those energies and create spells themselves. They become the focus. Someone just needs to teach them what they can achieve. They are naturals."

Her head spins. "I'm trying to keep up with all of this. You create magic from inside...um...your bodies?"

The Drake smiles with a slight wrinkle of his nose. "Sorry, I'm going a bit too fast. But it's important that you know, so you are aware what you're dealing with. Dirk and Burt learnt their skills, but they need a wand to do what we can do without. Spells use the energy caused by the reaction of specific movements, thoughts, sounds, even feelings to connect with the elements, either through a book or through the power of a natural magic user." He holds a hand out to Finch. "My boy, you put it so eloquently before."

"Think of it like tapping specials into a fighting game," says Finch. He waggles his thumbs as if holding a games controller. "Up C down C ABC start.

The wand and your mind are the controller. The book, the console. The spell, the game." He holds up a hand and allows the blue flame there to brighten. "It's hard, but if I work at it, I can play games without a controller or a console."

"Surely you must have *some* idea what whoever is taking the kids has in mind."

"There are a few spells." The Drake's face darkens. "A few terrible spells that require more energy than one person can summon. Whoever has taken our children has dark plans for them."

"And you don't know who that might be?"

"Before he went missing, Dirk told me it was risky for him to be investigating. For some reason, I got the feeling he meant him specifically. He didn't say why. But nearly twenty children have gone over the last four weeks. I couldn't stand by and do nothing."

The Drake rubs his head under his hat then adjusts it once more. Wren puts a comforting hand on his arm. "I tried to teach them, tried to protect them, but we just haven't had enough time. And none of the other elders take me seriously anymore. There were so many orphans left after the war. We're barely surviving here."

"What war?"

"I forget you don't know about it." The Drake stares over Sadie's shoulder, travelling time to re-witness horrors she couldn't understand.

"The battle between Hell and Earth," says Wren, putting an arm around his shoulders. "We won by closing the gate, didn't we, Dad?" Wren gives Sadie a meaningful look, which she doesn't understand, and pats her father's arm.

"But that shouldn't have been enough." The Drake's eyes scan the floor. Suddenly, all of his smooth charm has disappeared. He is hunched and small. "They shouldn't have given up just because we closed the gate. He's still out there somewhere. He's still here." He looks up to meet Sadie's eye. "We must be prepared. One day he will return. One day Earth will need a champion, and we must be ready." His voice shakes, descending to a whisper. "We must be ready."

Wren squeezes his hand. Her eyes connect with Sadie's. "The estate was originally a refugee camp for the orphans of those who fought. That's why it's mainly kids. Dad feels responsible for all of us."

She helps him down by the water. Cups some and washes his hair and his face.

Sadie looks to Finch. "When was this?"

Surely it would have been on the news?

"We're coming up eight years since the gate closed," says Finch. He gives her the same meaningful look as his sister. She still doesn't get it.

Eight years? She and Dirk had been together that long. And Dirk and Burt had started using the storage unit nearly eight years ago. Was there a connection between the war and their meeting and Dirk hiring the unit?

Wren glances up to Finch. "We should let him rest." Then to Sadie, "Can you come back later, maybe?"

"Sure," she says, but she is desperate to know more. "Goodbye, Drake."

He doesn't look up, just mumbles something to Wren. His decline is surprisingly swift.

Finch puts a hand on her shoulder to guide her back up the tunnel and away from his father.

"Some things came to my house," she says as he leads her back. "They wanted Ellie."

"Who?" he asks. His voice is low and comforting.

"Two guys with dog faces." It makes her cringe to picture them. "Like hairless werewolves."

"We're meeting tonight with the elders. We're going to pool what we know." He pauses at the end of the tunnel. "Do you have somewhere safe to stay?"

She nods. "I think so."

"You should come. I'm making snacks."

"What time?" Hopefully Betty will call. They'll both go.

She glances back down the tunnel to the Drake, who sits hunched by the side of the pool. Wren kisses him on the forehead. He says something like, "I'm sure it happened."

Finch takes a stepladder from by the wall and puts it into the middle of the room leading up to the underside of Toph.

"Midnight." He looks at her, then passes a sheepish glance back down the hall to Wren and the Drake. He smiles and rubs the back of his neck. "Sorry about Dad." He leans closer. "He thinks there was this war." He gives a humourless hum. "All the kids on the estate, including me and Wren, our real parents were killed by a disease. Something in their powers made them sick — all of them. The Bureau sent us here to quarantine us, but it didn't affect the kids. With nowhere else to go, we just sort of stayed here. A couple of adults made it, and now they take care of us. Other kids have grown up, started families. It's not great here, but it was getting better. Before..."

"So, he's not really your dad?"

Finch shakes his head. "No, but he always tried to look after us and the others. I hear he used to be a bit of a scoundrel. Like he never wanted this sort of life." He smiles and looks back up to the Drake with fondness. "He does his best. He doesn't look it, but he's really old. He gets jumbled. We just humour him, you know, otherwise it's worse. I guess worrying about everyone else takes its toll after a while."

# Pillow Talk (Smack Dat)

With Ellie bathed and bedded, Sadie sits downstairs with Mum and talks over her day. Mum looks exhausted, run ragged by a storm in the form of a little girl. Sadie tells her she plans to go out again tonight. While Mum is unsure of the idea, she heads up to bed early in case Ellie needs her during the night. They'll talk more in the morning.

Around fifteen minutes after Mum leaves, Sadie's phone rings. An unknown number. She hesitates as the interior of her bag glows. Cautiously, as if the phone itself is a dangerous creature, she answers.

"Sadie?" It's Betty.

Deep inside, something unknots, something that had been nagging at her since they parted, suggesting that Betty might never call, and she relaxes into Mum's sofa.

"How's your mum?"

She's relieved it's not someone with a ransom demand for Dirk. She's not sure how she might react to that.

"Holding in there. Where are you?"

"Still at my Mum's. Listen, I found the Drake. They are meeting tonight. Some sort of council at the Hanley Estate. Turns out lots of people have been going missing, and they're meeting up to do something about it."

She tries to explain what the Drake had told her about the missing kids being natural magic users and their ability to create power. Tells Betty the address and the time.

"I can make it. I can come get you first?"

Upstairs, she hears the familiar creak of Mum climbing into bed. The one that told Sadie and her father that it was OK to head to the kitchen for ice cream or toast and turn over to the horror channels to watch something Mum would hate.

"I'll meet you there." Mum's is a safe space. Everything and everyone has to be kept away from here.

Sadie hangs up feeling more confident than she has since that night with the dog men. She has leads, and she has friends.

Now all she needs is a way to fight back if it comes to it.

She removes the book and wand from her bag. Lies them flat on the table, not knowing what to do with either.

Had Dirk actually found these as a boy? Had a chance encounter really been the start of his journey into the occult?

She runs her fingers down the cover of the book. It has an unpleasant, greasy wetness to it, like rubber. It doesn't look like any leather she's seen before. Smoother, with less grain to it.

She picks up the wand. The Drake had said it liked her. How stupid was that? They'd only just met.

She flips the first couple of pages of dense writing with the wand tip until she finds something with pictures. The paper is old, a thick cream with faint touches of green-blue at the edges. Slightly crinkled as if it has been soaked, then dried again.

The instructions for holding the wand are clearly drawn in a reddish-brown ink. She readjusts her grip. It seems to wriggle in her grasp as if the wood were expanding to fill the lines in her palm. While somewhat revolted, she guesses this means she's at least holding it right.

She flips to the next page.

*"Move It"* reads the title.

Beneath that is another series of diagrams; numbered figures with arrows suggesting movement.

Below that is some text.

*"You may cause a force to affect a visible object targeted with the mind. A simple charm that will send the object moving in the intended direction with the imagined force. Combinations of concentrated forces can be quite useful in manipulating different objects."*

Hm? The movement's figures are arranged around the words, as well as a picture of a sigil, a sort of figure eight that she assumes she must draw with the wand. She flicks the page forward, then back. There are more details, but the instructions seem simple enough.

She chews the corner of her mouth. Could she learn magic with these pages? For some reason, she's always assumed Dirk and Burt had some ingrained talent, some gifted ability that had set them apart from others. She's never thought that perhaps they had just practised and become good at something.

Dirk had few other skills. He wasn't musical. Wasn't artistic. His cooking was often inedible. Back in the day, when they had friends, and they asked him to play pool at the pub, he'd whack the balls as hard as he could in the apparent hope that the more sides they hit the more likely they would be to find a pocket. So perhaps he'd misspent his youth with wizardry instead.

Could she do it too? Could she learn magic?

She picks a pillow from the sofa and throws it onto the rug in the centre of the room. It lands near Mum's gas fire, which still burns on a low heat.

"OK," she says, rolling her shoulders and tensing and untensing her grip on the wand.

She studies the diagram in the book. Traces the movements in her mind. Loops the wand over and under in the jagged figure-eight pattern. Then focuses on the pillow.

She flicks her wrist. Nothing happens. Not surprising.

She shakes her hands out and tries again.

Once again, nothing.

"Come on, Sadie," she mumbles to the empty room. "If a fifteen-year-old boy can learn magic from a book, then so can you."

She studies the writing once more. What did the bit about intended force mean? Did she have to imagine a force? Like in newtons?

She tries to clear her mind. What would happen if she thought too big, and the pillow smashed through the wall and killed Mum's neighbour?

So she starts small. Holds the pillow in her mind's eye. Imagines slapping it with her hand — pictures herself giving it a really good solid whack from right to left — and tries again.

She takes a deep breath and flicks her wrist.

A small dent appears in the pillow as if an invisible fat bee had just crash-landed there.

She stands silently, hands raised to the ceiling in the celebration of a hat-tricking footballer.

She. Just. Bloody. Did. Magic!

She was a wizard.

A witch?

A sorcerer. Sorcerer sounded good.

She tries again. This time imagining smacking it as hard as she can on top. Giving it a proper pounding. With a wave of the wand, the cushion flattens ever so slightly.

"Yessssss."

She looks for something else to try. Takes a used tissue from her bag and places it on the coffee table, then imagines kicking it with all the force she can muster.

It rolls, as if moved by a gentle breeze, right off the table, and on to the floor.

"Usssss." She clenches a fist.

The floorboard creaks above in Mum's room, and with the instinctual reaction of someone playing with something they shouldn't while their parents are asleep, Sadie stuffs the wand back into her bag.

Listens a moment. No other movement.

She smiles to herself, feeling most triumphant. Yes, perhaps the force isn't as strong as it could be. Yes, it would need refining before she went into battle. But she had. Just. Done. Bloooooody. Magic!

Not blood magic. According to every piece of fiction she's enjoyed on the subject, blood magic is not to be trifled with. So she'll make sure to steer clear of blood magic. For now at least.

She turns the wand over in her hand. Dare anyone mess with her now. Dare any sofa go with its pillows unplumped. Fucking dare it!

A warmth fills her. She's always considered magic to be something...well...magic. Locked away from people like her with the carburettors and the plumbing of toilets. Not something you could actually learn.

She checks the clock above the fire. It's getting to eleven. She needs to move if she's going to be at the Drake's meeting on time. She doesn't want to be late. Doesn't want to arrive last and walk into a room full of god knows what.

She's a little nervous. Who will be there? *What* will be there? But at least now perhaps she has some allies.

She pushes herself up to stand, tired, but itching for real answers. She grabs the bag with the wand inside. Walks into the silent, empty hall. Stands for a moment with her foot on the bottom stair gazing up towards her old bedroom where her daughter now sleeps. Listens for her. All is quiet.

Ellie will be fine with Mum. And she'd be back before either of them woke up.

Mum was OK. She was in charge. She'd been her old lovely self all evening. Sadie had checked Ellie over in the bath. No marks, nor anything to suggest any harm had come to her. And though her daughter was sometimes quite hard to decipher, she hadn't mentioned any strange behaviour coming from Granny. In fact, she'd been quite happy with their new arrangement. It was as different for her as it was for Sadie, and Ellie seemed to be taking it in her stride.

They'd be OK together. They had to be. What choice did she have?

# Off To See Le Canard

The estate is different at night.

The streets are empty. You might expect to see a dog walker out late with an incontinent pooch on an estate this big, but here it seems everyone is hidden away.

Windows are dark. No lights, no glow of a TV behind the curtains. No sound.

How many of these houses are home to orphans? Poor children all alone in the world. Apart from those who have grown to adulthood in the last eight years, is there anyone here to look after them? The thought hurts her heart. How scared must they be knowing that someone is snatching them one at a time? She has to help. Maybe she can.

Betty's car takes the space she had used earlier. More cars fill both sides of the road. Earlier that day, she'd thought they'd looked uncared for. It crosses her mind that they may have been here since the disease took their owners eight years ago. Had the Bureau just abandoned this place?

She eventually finds a space some distance away in a side street.

She's going to be late, but still she hesitates inside the car searching for courage. She pictures Ellie's face and finds it there.

The night is cool but pleasant. Up above, dark clouds obscure the stars. The full moon is a faint silver glow behind them.

She pulls her bag strap tight against her shoulder. Places a hand on the wand inside. Though she knows she can't do much with it, its almost imperceivable movement comforts her.

In the past, whenever she'd spoken to Dirk about his wand, she'd figured it was a weapon, like a gun or knife, but now she gets it. The shard of wood seems to have taken on a life in her mind, like that of a pet or, more closely, a guard dog.

As she turns the corner onto the main road where the Drake lives, she hears a voice.

"Wait."

It comes from nowhere.

She turns to see the boy she'd spotted playing football earlier; the one with the bright green eyes and red hair.

She'd just come through the spot where he now stands. He hadn't been there then.

He regards her with pale, freckled features.

"I can't. I'm running late." She frowns. She feels compelled to do as he says.

He holds up a hand. Gently. Weightless, as if performing a kata. There's something strange about him. Transparent almost, as though she can see the car behind him through him. He points down the road towards the Drake's terrace.

Sadie follows his gaze. Though she can't see the house from here, she can see where its garden pathway links to the pavement.

Betty emerges from the gate.

Sadie looks back at the boy. "That's my friend."

"Is it?" Those green eyes stare into her. She can't argue, so just watches.

Betty scans the road, but doesn't see Sadie tucked behind the hedge. She takes out her phone and puts it to her ear.

Sadie's phone rings.

"Don't trust her," says the boy, his voice a dream-like whisper.

He has some sort of hook in her.

"But—" She blinks sleepy eyes, then looks down at the ringing phone in her hand.

He catches and holds her gaze. She can't look away.

The phone rings off. She sees it's already 12:25. The time seems to have evaporated. What's happening?

Betty scowls, then climbs into her car.

The engine growls as the car pulls away.

"Be careful," the boy says from behind. His voice blends with the soft rustle of leaves in the breeze.

"What just happened?" Sadie turns back to him, but he's not there.

She searches, but he's gone.

She pulls the hood of her black hoody up and edges, head down, towards the terrace.

As it comes into view, she spots nothing out of the ordinary. The lights are off. The door is closed.

The waist-high, chain-link gate shrieks as she pushes it open. The sound grates against her teeth.

She knocks on the door. Waits. No answer.

A window stands next to it. She holds up her hands to block the glare of streetlights from the dirty glass. Beyond is a kitchen. A mountain of washing up sits soaking in the sink.

She prises at the edge of the window with her fingernails. It doesn't budge. She considers knocking again, but something tells her no one will answer.

She scans the road with its abandoned cars. Finch had said midnight. And he'd meant here, right?

Why had Betty not gone in? Surely she hadn't missed everything. Sadie hates the idea of wasting Burt's sister's time by bringing her here for nothing.

*Get away.* The thought creeps into her mind. Something brushes her shin, and she steps back.

At her feet, a tendril of jelly reaches out from the foundations of the house like a finger. Topher. She reaches down and touches it with her hand.

*Topher?*

The voice in her head is softer than before. Weaker. He's hurt. She can feel his pain. An all-encompassing ache coming to her on a wave of black and burgundy.

*Failed in my duty,* he says, and she can sense an overwhelming sadness. *Le Canard is gone, and Wren.*

*I'm coming in to help,* she thinks, hoping he can hear her.

She looks up at the window. Should she smash it? She scans the front garden for a rock big enough. The cracked corner of a paving slab might do. She eases it out. Feels the weight in her hand as something falls from the sky. There's a flutter of wings as a dark shape drops into the knee-high grass to her right. She presses herself against the wall under the kitchen window and freezes.

Hurried movement rustles towards her through the grass, parting it as it comes. Sadie's heart beats in her throat. What unthinkable horror is this? She grips the slab — ready to throw, ready to bludgeon — and a brown duck appears from within the grass. Its curious eyes watch her from atop its long, stupid neck. There's some sort of blob on its back. A grey-black thing with eight stumpy legs. A miniature rider.

The jockey jerks its head around. It looks right at her. A round, grey face with wide eyes and a funny little smile, atop the body of some sort of tardigrade-type thing. It wears a little hat like a cowboy. A black leathery duster. Now she's looking properly, she can see the duck wears a saddle and a few little stuffed brown satchels.

"Ah, are you late too?" He sounds gruff, but tiny, like a canary who's spent one too many days down the mines. He dismounts, taking the duck by the reins. "Hold on a second," he says, realisation dawning on his face as he gets a good look at her. "You're Sadie Kilmore." He clicks a set of fingers. The sound of a chia seed dropping. "Do you remember me?"

She shakes her head. Can't place an eight-inch-tall talking tardigrade that rides a duck. It's the sort of thing she'd usually remember—

"From the alleyway the other night. I did wave, but maybe you didn't see me. The name's Primrose Applewhistle."

Ah! The duck had been there in the alley when she'd gone back home on Sunday night. "Sorry, I thought you were a kind of duck tumour."

He pauses at that.

"Were you following me the other night?" she asks.

"The Drake wanted to know if Dirk was at home. He hadn't reported in for a while. He was worried."

"Do you work for the Drake or something?"

"Not really. He needed a fast friend, and Iron Bill is the fastest. And where she goes, I go."

"Did you see those dog things at our house?"

He shakes his little head.

She pushes herself up, brushes her hands together, and looks up at the house. "I think something bad has happened here. Toph's hurt."

The duck quacks. Its beak glints silver in the streetlight. Sadie leans forward. Squints. Its bill is made of razor-sharp metal. Pointed, like a knife.

"Sure thing, Iron Bill." Primrose turns to her. "My noble steed suggests we investigate."

It quacks again.

"Then, unless you have any objections," Sadie hefts the piece of paving slab, "I'm going to smash the kitchen window."

"Fantastic idea," says Primrose. "You sure know how to get the job done, don't you?"

Sadie hefts the slab and hoofs it through the glass. The sound is agonisingly loud in the dead night.

"Oof, good throw." Primrose gives her the littlest of claps. Though, with his six hands, it's a miniature applause.

She pulls her sleeve over her hand and removes the remaining shards of glinting glass, then reaches up and opens the window from the inside. She heaves herself up over the sill, but slips, dropping an arm up to her elbow in the full washing-up bowl. The water is cold and greasy.

The funk of mould has thickened since she was here earlier. Decayed.

She drops to the floor. It shifts beneath her like an under-inflated bouncy castle. Her feet sink up to the ankle, and she wobbles.

The duck flutters up to the window ledge and waddles inside. It springs up to her right shoulder.

"Oh, hello," she says. "Is that how we're rolling?"

"This is definitely how I'm rolling," says Primrose, who has somehow snuck up onto her left shoulder without her noticing. He grips a handful of her hoody for support, sword held in one of his other hands like a pirate riding the rigging, ready for boarding. "No point you talking to Iron Bill. She has no clue what you're saying. She's a duck."

Iron Bill quacks, and Sadie glances right into those dead, black duck eyes. They stare through her. Seeing into her very soul. Seeing each of her secrets spread out like the entrails of the dead picked clean by merciless mallard mercenaries. Eyes that have seen every horror that this world and the next can offer. The ruthless eyes of a killer.

Sadie clears her throat and tears her gaze away.

"Got a look on her, hasn't she?"

"Indeed she does," says Primrose.

"I don't mean to be offensive, but what are you?"

"How could asking what I am be offensive? Always good to question things. I'm a pixie."

Her face twitches.

"I know it's not what you expected one to look like. Disney has really ballsed up our image, but," he slaps his little grey belly, "this is me. Pixie through and through."

Now she's up close, she can see he has another sword sheathed at his hip, as well as some sort of miniature firearm.

"Pleased to meet you." She takes another step. Sinks further. She's conscious Betty could come back. "Toph," she says out loud. "What happened?"

The thought seems to travel up her legs. *I'll show you.*

With a rush of nausea, she drops up to her neck into the floor. Then eases the last of the way down until her head is submerged.

Wholly immersed, she can truly feel Toph's agony. It comes across as the burgundy of drying blood. The brown of rust, of poison and rot. Thoughts and images slip through her mind. A jumble.

They distil. The first thing she sees is a dog man. He has a bandage wrapped around his neck. The one from Ellie's room.

Kayder.

His colour is an invasive shadow of creeping charcoal.

Sadie sees him from floor level, from Toph's view, standing at the front door of the house. Finch holds the door open with a bowl of crisps in hand. He looks surprised. Kayder whips a hook from his pocket and strikes so fast Finch can do nothing to stop him. The hook sinks in below his sternum and the lad drops to the floor.

She knows his pain, his confusion, channelled through Topher. The sense of what makes Finch who he is drifts away as he closes his eyes.

She feels sick. A deep sadness fills her. A navy-blue wave of despair that is not her own, but Toph's. She is taken by it. Consumed.

Kayder removes a pouch from his jacket pocket. Takes a handful of powder and throws it before him as Finch bleeds out, dying on the welcome mat, his bowl overturned.

The powder lands on Toph's surface with searing flashes of yellow.

*Poison*, he says.

Kayder leans out of the way and Betty steps into view.

She holds a wand. Flicks it towards Topher.

Sadie senses a searing sensation across her skin as if she's suffering a burn. Then Betty drops through a hole in Topher's mass accompanied by Kayder. Another two dog men follow them through the growing chasm.

*Who is she?*

*I don't know, but her taste is familiar.*

*She told me she was Burt's sister.*

*They are similar, but something is off about her thoughts.*

She feels her brain spasm. An injection of nothing, of clear water, into all that black and red. She knows he's fading.

*Sorry*, he says. *I'm sorry...* His thoughts are barely there anymore. Like reflections on glass.

That poisoned rust colour runs clearer and clearer. Blacker and blacker. All-encompassing. Her own thoughts return and she sinks as the surrounding structure liquifies.

She kicks her legs, trying to stay up. *Who is Betty? What do I do next?* But it becomes increasingly like swimming through air.

She drops to the ground between the line of desks and chairs. A pounding wash of warm liquid splashes over her as Toph comes apart.

She ducks back as the living room furniture comes crashing down in the corner of the room. The sofa crushes a pair of desks in a splintering of wood. The brick-propped coffee table clatters down just to her left.

Finch's body lies next to her, curled in a foetal position. Primrose stands by it. He touches the young man's face, but he's gone.

"Damn it to hell. Where's the Drake?"

Iron Bill quacks. Sadie searches for her in the mess. The duck stands in the entranceway to the tunnel that leads to the Drake's treasure room. She quacks again. Then steps a few paces away.

Primrose jogs after her. From behind, he looks a bit like a tiny multi-armed Michelin man and has a waddle similar to his mount.

Sadie takes the wand from her bag and grips it firmly, then follows them both.

# BEAKY BLINDER

Four bodies lie on the central platform next to the Drake's pile of jumble. A duck, a man, a woman, and another pixie. The woman must be over two metres tall and slender. Two more bodies float in the pool. One is another man, as far as she can tell. He has wings like a butterfly, stretched out on the surface of the water. His still fresh blood radiates in a red cloud around him.

Sadie holds a hand over her mouth as Primrose and Iron Bill sweep across the pool. They land next to the body of the dead duck. Iron Bill prods it with one wing, then looks back at Sadie with grim determination in her eye and in the set of her beak. Primrose kneels next to the body of the other pixie. She can hear him mumble something from here.

Neither Wren nor the Drake are among the dead.

"It was Kayder and Betty. They killed them," she says.

Primrose replies, but his voice is too quiet to hear across the pool.

Betty. Who the hell was this woman? Why had she tricked her?

She'd been her only ally. Her only hope. Sadie claws her hands through her hair. This is too much. "Where's the Drake? Where's Wren? What am I supposed to do now?"

Something clicks behind her, and she wheels around as Iron Bill quacks a warning.

"You can start by telling us where you're keeping your daughter," says a figure standing back down the corridor in the classroom. Kayder. His voice is a strangled growl. He clears his throat, but it doesn't help. "Where's the girl?"

"Why do you want her?" Sadie backs away, but there's nowhere to go.

Kayder steps forward. The other two dog men from Toph's vision drop from the house above. All three hold those curved hooks.

She holds the wand at arm's length like Harry Potter in the films. "I'm warning you. I know how to use this. Dirk taught me everything he knows."

The other two hesitate, passing glances at each other, but Kayder smiles. "I somehow doubt you would have hit me with that shattered wine glass if you knew how to cast."

"Um…" She tightens her grip on the wand. Inches further back. Stumbles as her back foot comes up against the edge of the pool.

Kayder bares a mouthful of pointed teeth and the trio stalk towards her.

Sadie scans the hall for a way out. One other alcove stands on the far side of the room. A darkened archway that leads to god knows where.

With a whistle of wings and a pint-sized battle cry that could curdle blood, just not very much, the charging shape of Iron Bill and Primrose flash past. Lightning quick. Metal beak poised. The bird dives low, skimming the ground at high speed, then arcs upwards. The dog man on Kayder's right swipes with his hook, but he is too slow. Iron Bill is inside his reach before he can stop her. The jagged point of her beak stabs into his throat. She beats her wings at his gasping face as Primrose dismounts with two swords held aloft. The pixie dives deftly out of the way as the other dog man swings his hook, succeeding only in skewering the shoulder of his accomplice.

The killer duck rips herself from her victim's neck and lands on his head as the other dog man tries to tear the misplaced hook free. It's clear it's lodged in something hard, but he is too stupid, or too shocked, to let go. His eyes widen in alarm as Primrose, using the arm holding the hook as a bridge, charges. The pixie, once more yelling something too soft to hear, draws back his swords as he reaches the dog man's snout, then shoves both up to the hilt into his opponent's open black eyes. Jets of blood paint everything red.

The dog man screams, "my eyeeeeeessssss!" with the dramatic flair of an actor past his prime and drops to his knees. Primrose somersaults backwards and lands on the floor in front of his enemy, pulls his gun from his holster and blows a hole between his streaming, popped eyeballs. All the while, Iron Bill rakes the entrails from the other dog's stomach as he gasps through a destroyed larynx.

Sadie grimaces. Her stomach turns. She's heard ducks can be vicious, but this is an absolute bloodbath.

It has all happened so quickly that Kayder hasn't even had the chance to turn around. He spins on his heel, but is too late to help his eviscerated associates. While he is distracted, Sadie dives into the pool.

She drags herself desperately through the warm water, leaving the sound of screaming, of battle, of beating wings behind her. She drags herself up and out of the pool, and runs across the platform towards the archway at the far side.

She streaks into the tunnel and into the dark. Mud squelches underfoot. She takes out her phone and lights the torch. The walls glisten with green slime.

The tunnel leads around to the left. Something splashes into the pool back in the hall as she follows the path, so she quickens her pace.

Before long, she comes to a ladder. It leads up to a metal grate through which she can see the faint glow of distant street light. She drags herself up. Puts her shoulder against the heavy drain cover and shifts it to one side. Pulls herself up into some sort of drainage ditch beside a quiet dead-end street that ends in a small wood. She shifts the grate back across the hole and runs towards the cover of the trees. Squatting several feet inside the tree line, she fumbles with her phone to kill the torch.

She's freezing from the combination of her dripping clothes and the chill night air.

Holding her breath, and tensing to subdue the shivers, she watches for what seems an age until clawed fingers press up through the grate and throw it to the side. Kayder pulls himself up and out of the hole. He sniffs the air and looks around. Then, seemingly catching a scent, he runs off in the opposite direction.

Leaves crackle beneath Sadie's knees as she rests them on the forest floor. With a sigh, she closes her eyes, trying to still her galloping heart and the frantic thoughts of the possible end that she has just so narrowly missed.

Who are these dog men and why did they want her little girl?

With every second stretching out into an eternity, she forces herself to wait as long as she can before crawling from the forest. Hoping to find Mum's Peugeot without being spotted, she slinks through the unfamiliar streets.

Before long, she finds Iron Bill and Primrose already sat on the roof of the car. There's a gash across one of the duck's wings, bleeding, but it doesn't look deep. Primrose is covered in blood, but she can tell it's not his. He sits polishing his firearm with a cloth taken from one of the leather satchels on Iron Bill's saddle. The gun is reminiscent of a musket, comprised of brass and wood.

"How did you know this was my car?" she asks.

He stands, rubbing his ribs with a soft groan. "It's the only one that's not usually here."

"Sorry I left you...but you looked like you had it handled."

The duck quacks, nonplussed.

"Wounds heal. Scars are trophies," says Primrose, shoving his gun back into his holster. "And besides, I shouted for you to run."

She hadn't heard.

"I must apologise for what may have appeared to you to be an overzealous use of force," he says. "When you're my size, you make sure your enemies don't get back up, otherwise you're done for. My brother always said, hide if you can, go for the eyes if you can't."

"Your brother's a bright pixie. Those dogs sure weren't getting back up again."

"Was a bright pixie...got mashed going for the eyes of a combine harvester."

"Sorry."

"Don't be. He died doing what he loved." Primrose gazes at the stars. Sighs a tiny sigh. "Shagging his bird in the cornfield." He shrugs, then pats Iron Bill on the back.

"His girlfriend?"

"Yeah, his bird."

The duck hisses.

Primrose chuckles. "And you're not the best influence, are you, old girl? Charging in there like a duck out of Hell. You really stuck it to that dog, didn't you?"

"Do you want a tissue?" Sadie opens the passenger side door. She reaches into the glove compartment and finds the remains of her meal deal, along with a few napkins. She removes one and hands it to the pixie.

"Thank you. Most kind."

He wipes himself down. His little face tightens as he passes back the tissue. She takes it between finger and thumb, then encloses it inside her used sushi box.

"Who was it you said? Kayder and Betty?"

She nods. "They have something to do with my husband's disappearance. Kayder tried to kidnap my daughter. And Betty lied to me, told me she was looking for Burt."

"I don't know the names. But then, I don't usually get involved in these sorts of things."

"The other night, was it you who saved me and Ellie?" She nods towards his musket. "With that?"

He frowns. "How do you mean?"

She holds two fingers closed like a gun and fires off a shot. "You shot through the window."

He purses his lips and shakes his head. "Wasn't me."

Then who was it?

"Can't believe those blaggards got Daisy," he continues.

"Daisy? Was that the other pixie? Were they your friend?"

"Daisy Butterdew." Primrose's mouth tightens. "And yeah. What am I gonna tell his wife? He's got five larvae." He stands there shaking, looking a lot like the sort of cuddly but worn thing Ellie might pick up and instantly fall in love with in the toy section of a charity shop. "I said to him, let's not get involved. That it wasn't anything to do with us. It was you big ones' problem. But Daisy convinced me. He said, if it was gonna affect his kids, then we had to listen to whatever the Drake had to say." He grips the hilt of one of his sheathed swords.

"If only I'd been on time. I could have…" His voice rises from a self-directed mumble to a pint-sized roar, then drops again. He looks down.

"What was going to affect Daisy's kids?"

"The Drake said that whatever was happening here is big. Like Heaven and Hell big. Was planning to tell us his theory tonight."

"Do you know anything about the war the Drake remembers? The one from eight years ago?" The one that seemed to finish just before she met Dirk. Just before he'd hired his storage place.

"Not really. But I always feel a little weird when he brings it up. Not sure if it's old Drakey's gift of spinning a good tale, or maybe I've dreamt it, but I have visions. Demons pouring out of a gate. Battle. Terror. But they are just visions. Faded, like something left out in the sun. When I try to remember them, I can never keep hold of them, like trying to hold water in my hand."

She lifts a hand and rests it on the car roof near to where he stands. She feels sorry for him. Such a little thing fighting his way through this dangerous world.

"Don't give me that look."

"What look?"

"The, 'oh he's so tiny and cute and loveable, how will he ever survive' look. I'm eighty-five."

"Sorry."

He smiles. "Don't worry. It's good to be underestimated."

"Do you want to come with me?" she asks. He seems sad about his friend, and although he is tiny, after his and Iron Bill's display of gratuitous violence, she would feel much safer with him around.

The duck hops in and makes herself comfortable on the passenger seat.

Sadie turns her hand over as an invitation for him.

Primrose watches her from the roof of the car. She guesses he's considering whether he can trust her. With a nod to himself, he steps onto her palm. He weighs next to nothing. She places him down next to Iron Bill, then climbs in herself.

"I'm sorry about your friend."

He sighs. The sound of the gas escaping from an opened fizzy drink bottle. "Thank you."

She turns on the heaters and rubs her hands together. "What do we do now?"

The duck hisses.

Primrose tuts. "We can't just go around killing everyone, IB."

Quack?

"Because you can't."

Quack.

He puts his lower set of hands on his hips, then rolls his eyes towards Sadie. "Iron Bill says we should find them and kill them all."

"Well, you've made a pretty good start at that." Sadie pulls onto the main estate road, speeding, just wanting to get away. The street is still dead. "We have to help the children here, Primrose. They are all alone now the Drake's gone."

"I know. But don't that lot at the Bureau usually deal with this sort of thing?" says Primrose. Next to him, Iron Bill has her eyes half-closed.

Sadie taps her fingers on the wheel. "Do they? I only know what Dirk tells me, and that's not much. Maybe they don't know what's happening here. Do you know how to contact them?"

He raises a nostril. "Not really. It's generally best if us smaller beings keep ourselves to ourselves."

She grips the steering wheel in both hands. She knew next to nothing about the Bureau, but when they'd spoken earlier that day, Finch had said, "It'd be easier to forget about them if they didn't come and arrest us every time we used magic outside of the estate."

Maybe they had some sort of magical warning system? A fae-dar, as it were.

"I have an idea." She sits up in her chair and looks at Primrose. "You're magic, right? You can cast spells."

He laughs. "Bit of a weird thing to ask. Pixies don't do magic."

"But you're a magical creature, right? Otherwise, wouldn't everyone know about you?"

"When you're as small as us and living in a world built for giants, you learn to be sneaky." He gives his gun a little pat. "And when sneaky doesn't work, you start shooting."

She touches the wand in her pocket. Maybe *she* could make some magic? It'd probably take a little more than slapping a couple of pillows around, but there might be something at Dirk's storage unit that could create enough of a scene to bring the Bureau running. Then she could get some answers as to what the hell they thought they were doing about the Hanley Estate kids and her missing husband.

# RENT-A-SPACE, AGAIN

The car park is just as empty as it had been that afternoon. The light in reception remains on, but when Sadie holds her hands up to the glass, it doesn't look like anyone is in.

She tries the front door. Locked. She can see the key to Dirk's unit hanging on its peg.

"We need to get that to get into Dirk's unit," she says to Primrose. "But—"

"But you haven't got a paving slab." He wags a finger and winks. "No problem." He draws his weapon and with a small pop and puff of smoke blasts out the glass in the door's lower half with a silence-shattering smash.

"Bloody hell!" hisses Sadie, looking around to make sure no one is near. "I was going to check if there was a vent or something for you to go through."

He leans his head to one side. "I find the most direct route is often the best."

"Wait here." She pulls her sleeves over her hands and crawls through the newly made entrance in the bottom of the door. The cubes of safety glass prick her palms and knees.

She continues crawling all the way to the desk and behind. Waits a moment with her back against it. That's when she remembers the security camera aimed at the other side. It might not have seen her crawling across the floor, but as soon as she stands up and grabs the key, it will.

Maybe it's just recording and there's not someone sitting on the other side ready to call the real cops on her, but maybe there is.

"What are you doing?" asks Primrose, appearing right by her ear. He stands on a small shelf under the top surface of the desk. He points up. "The keys are up there. Can't you see them?"

"I can, but there's a security camera on the other side of the desk. I forgot about it."

"Ooh, a conundrum." He whips his musket out again.

"What are you doing?"

"Which key was it?" He waggles his gun. "I'll shoot it down."

A part of her wants to put a hand up to stop him, to say, *no, let's be sensible. No more shooting.*

But then it rethinks their position and comes back with, *you know what, fuck it. Shoot first. Ask questions later.*

"35."

A pop and a puff. And number 35's fob shatters, dropping the silver key to the ground with a tinkle. She picks it up.

"Good shot," she says.

"Thank you. Let's go." Primrose flips down to the floor next to her and runs off towards the door.

She scuttles after him on all fours.

She drives Mum's car through the barrier and down to the end. It's strange being here at night. The alley between storage units seems more cramped. More clinically claustrophobic thanks to the cool white LED lamps that hang over each door, obscuring the night sky above with their bright light.

Iron Bill and Primrose take to the sky, doing a little scout of the area, while Sadie pulls open the door and heads straight for the Ikea-branded magical artefact rack.

The gooey thing continues to throb with its neon glow. She wants nothing to do with it, so she picks up the blue horn and turns it over in her hands.

It looks like something you might find on an antelope, or, Ellie's favourite, a kudu. Roughly a foot and a half long, curved with a slight spiral. Hollow. The fatter end seems snapped, as if it were part of a larger antler. If this were just the tip, the creature it belonged to must be huge.

It must be magic, because it's blue. No normal creature had blue horns. She places it back and lets her hands fall to her sides, sighs and rubs her face. What was she doing here? She had no idea how any of this stuff worked.

She moves to the gooey blob once more. For a full minute, she stares at it, willing herself to at least pick it up. In the end, she decides she's just as bamboozled by it as the horn, and significantly more likely to pick up some sort of tropical disease.

"What is that?" says Primrose.

She starts. "Jesus Christ." He's on her shoulder. Iron Bill sits nestled on Dirk's desk.

He wiggles his eyebrows and pushes his top lip out like a rodent smelling some cheese. "Told you I was sneaky."

"I don't know. I was hoping you'd be able to help me here."

"Nope."

She moves to Dirk's desk. Wiggles the mouse. Heads for the folder labelled 'Artefacts.'

There's one file inside: 'Demon Leech'. A scan of a page from an old book shows a drawing of a blob in brown ink. It's the same as the one on the shoe rack. Another picture shows a person with the blob over their head.

Not something she's willing to do, especially as she doesn't know the outcome.

She closes the folder. The spreadsheet in the middle of the desktop catches her eye.

'Hanley Estate Case.'

She opens it. It's clearly a list of names of the children who have been taken. The dates correspond to when. She scrolls down. At the bottom, lower than she'd looked before, are some notes.

Primrose peers from his position on her shoulder. He taps his chin. "What's it say?"

"Sightings of tall men carrying large delivery boxes on the estate coincide with several disappearances," reads Sadie. "Black transit van." She sighs. "Nothing that can help unless I go wait for the next person to be abducted—"

"Well, we could follow them." He punches three fists into three palms. "I'm game if you are."

"It'd be dangerous, and we don't have any support. We don't know what we'd be walking in to."

She pulls the tentacle book out of her bag. Despite its sodden state due to the unplanned swim in the Drake's pool, the pages don't seem affected by the water.

She flicks through. If she couldn't use one of Dirk's artefacts, perhaps she could find a better spell. Something with a bit more whizz-pow. A bit more grandiose than pillow plumping. Something that might bring the Bureau running to arrest her.

Winchester high street is only a short walk. Maybe if she caused a scene there, they'd come. What did she have to lose?

She slows her pace remembering Finch and Toph, and those others in the Drake's chamber. Who would be mourning them tomorrow?

Of course, she had everything to lose. She had Ellie.

"Ooh, is that a spell book?" says Primrose.

Her lips tighten. "Yep."

Her eyes fall on a spell called *Water Whip*. The directions are similar to *Move It*. A move for the wand is illustrated by figures and arrows. A thought for the force and target.

She frowns. She must be missing something. The force she'd generated with *Move It* had been pathetic.

"Have you ever seen someone cast a spell with a wand before?" she asks, taking hers from her pocket.

"A few times."

She turns the book back to *Move It*. She screws up one of Dirk's many pieces of paper and drops it on the floor. Then she stands back from the table and holds up the wand.

"Can you tell me what I might be missing?"

She flicks her wrist, drawing the jagged figure-eight sigil she'd used before, and imagines kicking the paper as hard as she can. It rolls as if someone had breathed on it.

"Why didn't you say anything?"

"Say anything?"

He rips the stick from one of Dirk's apple cores and holds it aloft behind his head, like an Olympic fencing champion. "Human wizards are always screaming things at each other when battling with spells." He dances backwards with a spinning flourish, and shouts at the top of his voice, "Get on fire!" Then feints to one side, whipping his apple stick out once more, "And you, 'Explode!'" He drops the stick to the side. "That sort of thing. There are rules, I think. It's all a bit stifling."

"But what are they shouting? It has to be specific."

Primrose shrugs. Kicks a pip across the top of Dirk's desk. "I always thought it was just the spell name."

A light turns on in her head. There are markings on either side of the spell's title, ones she thought had been nothing but decoration. They look a lot like speech marks.

She aims her wand and her thoughts at the ball of paper again, but this time says, "Move It."

The paper ball jumps across the room as if she'd just kicked it.

"Yesss."

"Oh, magnificent."

She lifts the book back into her bag.

"Come on," she says, as Primrose mounts Iron Bill. "We're going up Winchester high street to see if we can drum up some back-up. Time to cause a scene."

# MAKING A SCENE

Tuesday night is student night, and Winchester high street is humming with well-dressed kids in their early twenties wandering between the Slug and Lettuce and Vodka Nightclub.

"Ah, Vodka," Sadie says to her pixie companion. "You know it's a classy place if it's named after a spirit."

From his vantage point in Sadie's handbag, Primrose says nothing, just watches as a gaggle of girls trot past on their way to join the queue.

Sadie had been like them once. She'd certainly raised the Vodka roof in her youth. Vaulted the Vodka bar. Vexed the Vodka DJ. Vomited on the Vodka curb. In fact, she'd been coming back from that very bar the night she and Dirk had met.

She could admit now that perhaps Student Sadie had been a bit of a disaster waiting to happen, but at least she'd had more fun. She'd been way more adventurous. Would Student Sadie cope better in this current situation than Mum Sadie? Who knew?

She sets herself up on the corner between the club and McDonald's. There's usually a high footfall here. She drops her bag on the floor in front of her like a busker, and removes the book.

"Are we doing this here?" says Primrose.

"As good a place as any."

Iron Bill settles herself on top of an electrical service box and watches with detached interest.

To their left, a group of lads stand outside McDonald's with chips and drinks. A couple of them watch her. The occasional car cruises by and she is in full view of the three taxis jamming up the rank on the far side. That's probably enough witnesses.

She draws the wand from her bag. Goes over the movement for Water Whip. A sort of wave shape.

She reads the instructions.

*"The handler may cause a jet of liquid, taken from the moisture in the air or a nearby body of water, to fire from the end of their focus towards something targeted with the mind. Works best on rainy nights or near a sink. If wielded right, one can remove even—"*

She stops reading and chews the corner of her mouth in thought. It hasn't rained recently. There are no puddles nearby. If she wants to do something noticeable, then she'll need water.

"Have you ever eaten at McDonald's?" she says.

Primrose shakes his head. "Pixies mainly eat fruits and seeds."

"Well, if you stay quiet, I'll see if I can get us some chips. You are in for a treat."

With the wand tucked inside her sleeve, she picks up her bag and heads towards McDonald's. Iron Bill flaps her wings and follows her inside.

A few tables are taken by drunken munchers. One or two of the men give her an interested look as she passes. Not as long a look as she used to get. These days she is only worth a short glance before the taste of a poor-to-average burger draws their focus back.

Someone mentions the duck waddling behind her. Someone else laughs, calls her a "duck lady".

"Hello," she says to the enthusiasm-draining black hole of a cashier. "Can I get five bottles of water, please?"

"Sorry," she says, appearing as unapologetic as is humanly possible. "Out of water. Delivery's coming tomorrow. You can get some then."

Sadie furrows her brow. "Do people usually wait?"

"No." The cashier stares gormlessly past, searching for the next customer. Her mouth works a piece of gum. When Sadie doesn't move away, she flops a pasty white arm in the air to indicate the menu behind her. "We've got coke. Would coke do?"

Hm. *Would* coke do?

She looks down into her bag. "Think coke would do?"

Primrose, lying flat on her purse, holds up his palms and says, "I don't know what that is, but fortune favours the bold. Give it a try. And don't forget my chips."

Sadie shrugs a shoulder at the confused cashier. "Yeah, worth a go, I suppose." She doesn't have time to be messing about. "Four large cokes please. And a small chips."

She pays.

While Sadie waits for her order, the restaurant fills with noisy, drunken students. Nerves tingle in the pit of her stomach. She removes the book and rests it on top of a bin. Iron Bill flaps up to rest beside it. She moves her head slowly, surveying the other restaurant patrons with a wary eye.

Sadie holds her bag close to the book and Primrose leans over the side on tiptoes to look. While they wait, she practises the motion of the spell's sigil with her finger.

Her drinks soon arrive at the counter, so she puts the book away and moves to pick them up. They are big. Since when did anyone need to drink this much coke?

First, she passes the chips into her bag. Primrose reaches out with six little hands and accepts them with a coo of excitement, and Sadie reaches her slender fingers around the cups as best she can under the apathetic gaze of the cashier.

Unfortunately, she lacks Dirk's skill for carrying many drinks. This, coupled with the cool condensation on the outside of each slippery cardboard cup, means she can't get ample purchase. The cups crumple together and drop, exploding across the restaurant floor in a fizzing brown puddle.

Several obvious tuts come from behind the counter, coupled with the brash guffaw of the group of boys seated towards the entrance. Others in the queue scootch back.

Even Iron Bill looks away, embarrassed.

No one offers to help her as she stands there alone, wading in the cola ocean.

Heat rises in her cheeks. One boy points and cackles. His friends join in, screeching like startled seagulls. She takes a deep breath. Closes her eyes. She'd come here to make a scene. So she would damn well, flipping heck, make a bloody scene.

She draws the wand from her sleeve, garnering a few noncommittal gasps from those nearest. She practises the movement once more with her finger, then decides on a target. Everyone in the restaurant is watching her now. This crazy, coke-dropping, stick-wielding duck lady who looks like she hasn't slept for days.

In the end, she thinks, kill two birds with one stone — make a scene and tidy up the mess — so she targets the flap of a bin on the other side of the room.

With a flick of her wrist, she shouts, "water whip!" Her words come out so loud and sudden that the nearest customers flinch back.

Other than that, nothing happens.

So she tries again. This time using her whole arm, waving the wand as if she were conducting an orchestra.

"Water whip!"

Once more, nothing.

She growls.

"Err, excuse me, lady?"

Sadie wheels on the cashier with the brazen fury of the terminally embarrassed. "What?"

The woman stands there with a palm turned to the ceiling in a 'what gives?' gesture. She points a nonchalant finger towards the puddle. "It's coke?"

"Oh, shut up," says Sadie, giving her the evil eye. Then, feeling somewhat petty, wanting to give this idiot girl an 'I told you so', she waves the wand again and shouts, "Coke whip!" just to—

A bomb goes off.

Or, for a fleeting second, that's what Sadie thinks has happened.

In a moment as infinitely small as a grain of sand, all the coke in the restaurant decides it wants to be near her. From the ground, from the cups of nearby customers, from the soft drinks machine screwed to the wall. Drawn to the tip of her wand and blasted in a liquid column across the restaurant and into the mouth of the bin with enough force to knock it over and explode the used trays from its top, sending them across the room and clattering against the far wall.

Except for Sadie, who remains surprisingly coke-free, there is not a dry eye in the house. Nor face. Nor body. Nor wall. Everyone in the room stares at her, dripping, mouths agape. The cashier wipes a hand over her face. The others are too shocked to move.

"Good show," says Primrose, through a mouthful of chip.

Iron Bill ruffles her feathers, seemingly unfazed, the moment passing her by like fizzy drink off a duck's back.

"Um…" Sadie holds the wand out in front of her. "I just did bloody magic," she says, finding her confidence. She gives an excited jump. "This was. Real. Bloody. Magic." She wangs the wand around to punctuate the words.

A man starts to clap, getting to three before realising no-one else is with him. He stops. Looks down.

Sadie glances at the kitchen area. The workers huddle at the back, terrified. They watch her with wide, frightened eyes as if she were a monster.

"Sorry," she says, meaning it, recalling her time as a fast food employee. "About the mess."

"Don't apologise to them," says Primrose, springing up from her bag to more startled gasps. He waves a chip at the bystanders. "All fear sorcerer Lady Kilmore, the Coke Dealer."

"Hold on, Primrose…"

"You know, like death, but you deal coke."

She shrugs. "You know what, yeah. Everybody fear me." She jabs a thumb at herself, then prods her wand around a bit more at her audience. If this is what it takes to get into the Bureau, then so be it.

She flicks her wrist again. "Move it." She blasts a straw dispenser off the countertop. This magic stuff wasn't so hard.

"Nice!" says Primrose, jiggling around in the coke puddle and periodically pointing back at Sadie like an overenthusiastic hip-hop hype man. "Fathers, lock up your straw-ters."

Then the screams begin. Those previously waiting in the queue scrabble across the slick floor, skidding and pushing each other back to get out of the door and away from the soft drinks spell weaver.

A red and blue light flashes outside. The woo of a police car. The opening and slamming of two doors. Frantic snippets of hysterical conversation bleed through the restaurant doors.

Sadie clears her throat and presses her hands down herself to smooth out her hoody. This is it. She holds her head up high as two police officers enter through the main door.

They stop at the far end of the restaurant, assessing the situation.

"Miss," says one, watching her from the far end with a hand on something at his belt. "I've been told you may have aannnn oooooofeeeeeenssiiiiive weeeeeaaap-pooo—"

Time seems to slow as they approach.

No. Time doesn't *seem* to do anything. Time actually slows as they approach, before grinding to a stop. The police officer's final syllable rings indefinitely in the air, like the sound of a humming air conditioner.

"Nnnnnn."

She turns to the right. Those who remain of the kitchen staff are still, their looks of horror frozen.

Iron Bill is also motionless, perched atop the bin. Primrose stands like a statue at Sadie's feet, looking in the direction of the police with one of his swords halfway drawn. Sadie waves a hand in front of his face. Nothing.

Everyone in the place is suspended in time. Some even have droplets of coke hang from their chins like icicles.

"Bit of a mess you've made here, young lady," says a voice to her right.

"Oh, yes," says another, but to her left. "I've seen it done with blood. Nasty business, blood whips. Difficult to get the stains out."

"Worst double murder suicide I've *ever* seen that, Thelma. Never seen coke, though."

"No, never seen coke."

She checks both sides but sees no one. Looks up. "Hello?"

"Could be a neat turn at a kid's party, maybe? Pretty sure it works with most liquids. Wonder if ice cream counts."

"Oh, get me on the end of an ice cream whip any day. Am I right?"

"Chunky choc chip with caramel sauce whip."

"Oh, stop it."

She finally looks down. A small, elderly woman surveys the mess. Her black-grey hair is pressed into a neat bun on top of her head, which comes to just a little higher than Sadie's waist. She wears a white shirt. Black trousers. She taps a finger on her folded arm and lets out a short whistle.

"That's an excellent whip you got there, young lady." Another woman stands on her right. Equally small. Similarly dressed. Kind eyes peer out from what appears to be a century's worth of wrinkles. She takes a notepad from her chest pocket and flips a few pages. "And forgive me if I'm wrong, but was it you slapping a pillow about earlier this evening with some sort of force spell? That we could have ignored, but not now. I'm going to have to write you up for both." She reaches up and takes the wand from Sadie's yielding hand. Studies it over the top of her glasses. "Hm." Then looks back at Sadie. "Where did you get this?"

"I found it." Sadie's throat feels constricted. Her words are clipped by guilt.

The first woman also brings out a notepad and, using the pointed end of her wand as a pen, starts to jot things down. She steps over the puddle and surveys the scene from a different angle.

"Um...are you from the Bureau?"

"We are indeed, young lady," says the one holding her wand. "And you're in a lot of trouble. Going to be tricky to explain this one to the odds and sods outside. Isn't that right, Devika?"

"Anyone would have thought she doesn't know the law, Thelma." Devika doesn't look up from her pad.

Thelma takes Sadie's hand and studies her palm. "Well, she's not naturally gifted, that's for sure." She regards Sadie with curious eyes, then sinks both hands into her pockets, and begins pacing, kicking her feet casually. She glances up, waggles the wand between thumb and forefinger. "So, let me get this straight. You found this and thought you'd just pop down McDonald's and blast the place with coke. Seems unlikely."

"I was trying to contact someone from the Bureau. I don't have a number. I just hoped you'd, um...hear the magic, and someone would come."

Thelma chuckles. A soft, warm sound. "Get that down, Dev? Wasting Bureau time on top of the charges for magic use in a public place and possession of an unlicensed wand." She turns her attention back to Sadie. "Why would you be trying to contact someone from the Bureau?"

"My husband hasn't come home from work."

"And that's Bureau business because...?"

"His name is Dirk Kilmore." She feels stupid saying it, but still adds, "maybe you've heard of him?"

The corners of Thelma's mouth turn down. "You know any Dirk Kilmores, Dev?"

"Does he run the potion shop next to the pie shop?" Devika stops writing and chews the end of her wand.

"No, that's Derek the Kraken. He's a kraken." Thelma eyes Sadie. "Ain't married to a kraken, are ya?"

"No." Least, she didn't think so...

"Of course not." Thelma raises a sordid eyebrow. "Krakens can be a lot of fun, but boy, are they handsy." She sticks out her tongue and wiggles her fingers like a creepy lech. "Derek's alright, though. Keeps himself to himself. Bit old for you."

"Either way, missing husband or no," Devika says, looking greatly disappointed, "you can't go around slapping pillows and drowning the denizens of burger restaurants in coca cola. It's against the law."

"Those things specifically?"

"What?"

"Nothing. Sorry." Sadie scratches the back of her neck and looks around at the mess she's made. She catches sight once more of the motionless police officers, frozen mid-step at the end of the restaurant. "Have you stopped time for me?"

Thelma glances at her watch. A coggy little thing with a few extra hands and strange symbols. "Gosh, no. We've just magnified the moment using the unpleasantness-to-perceived-time conundrum."

"The what?"

"This is first-year eldritch physics."

Sadie shakes her head.

Thelma lets out an annoyed breath. "You know that when you're having a rubbish time the hours seem to stretch?"

"Yes. That I do know."

"Well, we've just magnified the effect. You probably feel guilty now for making such a mess. Or perhaps for getting caught. Who knows? So we've used that feeling to elongate this moment for you. Makes catching criminals much easier. Crime doesn't feel good."

"And it doesn't pay," says Devika, plain-faced.

"OK." Sadie lets out a tired breath. Is anything going to make sense ever again?

Devika squints past her and nods. "You recognise that duck, Thelma?"

Both Sadie and Thelma turn to look at the frozen duck sitting atop the bin. In the stark restaurant lighting, Sadie can see flecks of dried blood on her beak.

"And there's a sword-wielding pixie at the woman's feet," adds Devika, pointing downwards with the end of her wand.

"A pixie and a duck, hey?" Thelma squats down to inspect Primrose, who still stares straight past her towards the police at the far end of the room. She hums in amusement. "What would a member of the Beaky Blinders be doing in town?"

Devika shakes her head. "Don't know. Legendary wands. Metal-mouthed ducks. Maybe we need to have a word with our friend the Drake." She squints at Sadie over her pad.

Sadie opens her mouth to speak but Devika continues without stopping.

"Puts a bit of an unlikely spin on the old 'I found a wand and decided to trash McDonald's just so I could talk to someone at the Bureau' story, though, doesn't it? I think we should take them all in for questioning."

She flips her notepad shut and puts it away, before drawing a loop of twine from a pouch on her belt and slapping it over Sadie's wrist. Her hands are suddenly bound with a force so strong it feels as if the flesh of her wrists is fused.

"I'm arresting you for using magic in a public place, use of an unlicensed wand in front of non-magic users, and slapping a pillow about."

Thelma picks up Iron Bill, tucking her under one arm, then does the same with Primrose. Then she moves closer to Sadie's right side. "Not to mention making a bloody nuisance of yourself," she adds. She seems to consider Primrose a second, then says, "Should really wrap him up, too."

Devika takes out some more of that twine and pins each of Primrose's six arms to his chest with it. Then she turns to Sadie.

"You do not have to say anything, so please don't. Blah blah blah. Off we go." She clicks her fingers.

With the laborious ascension in pitch of a record player grinding into gear, time starts once more.

Something flashes.

Suddenly, she has a feeling they're not in McDonald's anymore.

# THE BUREAU

"Come on, you."

Before Sadie has the chance to take it all in, Devika grabs her by the elbow and leads her across the immense reception area where they now stand.

Iron Bill wrestles in Thelma's grasp, flapping her wings to get free, but Thelma draws some of the twine Devika had used to bind Sadie's wrists and wraps it around the duck's body, holding her fast.

"Be still, Iron Bill," says Primrose. He looks down at his bonds but doesn't struggle. "They used the unpleasantness-to-perceived-time conundrum, didn't they?"

"First-year eldritch physics, apparently," says Sadie.

"Did we get to where we're supposed to be?"

"I hope so."

Devika drags her towards a reception desk manned by what looks like a bad stone carving of a bulky man.

The click-clacking of hundreds of feet reverberates around the room. Sadie watches as a giant, knee-high centipede passes them. It raises a leg and tips a bowler hat towards Thelma and Devika. "Ladies." Then disappears around the corner segment by segment.

Sadie shivers. Centipedes were worse than spiders.

Waiting at the reception desk is a sort of tall human with butterfly wings. She looks a similar species to the body in the pool back at the Drake's. A green, tusked fellow, with his arms bound behind his back, waits with her. She grips his arm as if he might run away.

Other creatures come and go. Three other little old people like Thelma and Devika sit in a corner of the room heatedly discussing something over tiny polystyrene cups of steaming black coffee.

A graceful, slender man with pointy ears spots them and approaches. His hair, braided and plaited with coloured beads and small bronze flowers, lies in a tail along his back. He looks like her first celebrity crush, Orlando Bloom.

"Evenin', girls," he says with a thick Liverpudlian accent. He stops and folds his arms, like he's digging in ready for a good chin-wag. "Who you got?" He nods towards Sadie.

"Says she's just a norm who found a wand," says Devika. "Pretty cut and dry. Gonna confiscate, then delete her memory."

"You're gonna what?"

They ignore her.

"Wait a minute—"

"I reckon there's a little more to this one." Thelma bobs her head from side to side. "Found her with this pixie and this duck." She leans her head, and a small frown dents her brow. "You heard of a Dirk Kilmore, Ther'Per'Fliff'Floff?"

Ther'Per'Fliff'Floff shakes his head. His gently jingling braid swings in stunning slow motion. "Doesn't he run the potion shop by the pie shop?"

"Aaah," says Devika, pointing a goading finger at Thelma.

Thelma rolls her eyes. "No, that's Derek the Kraken."

"Gork might know." The elf nods towards the statue behind the reception desk, which now appears to be filling out a form with grinding, precise movements.

The butterfly woman and the green guy stand before the desk, checking in with him as if this were a hotel.

"But I ain't done nuffin'," complains the green man around a mouthful of sharp teeth. "That kebab shop was like that when I got there."

"Good shout," says Thelma. "We'll ask."

There's an awkward pause while they wait for Gork to process the green guy, before Ther'Per'Fliff'Floff comes to realise the conversation is over.

"Anyway, gotta get on," he says. "Gonna go see Kay. He got attacked again tonight. Banged up pretty bad. The boss has got him working on something serious." He eyes the duck under Thelma's arm, then catches himself. "See ya, girls."

"Later, Ther'Per'Fliff Floff," says Thelma.

"Dodged a bullet there," hisses Devika when he's out of earshot. "Can talk the hind legs off a dire donkey, that one."

"Oh, he's alright," says Thelma.

"Sorry, but where am I?" says Sadie, gazing around the room.

"You wanted into the Bureau, you're here, love," says Devika, giving her a gentle shove forward as the muscle-bound green man is dragged off by the butterfly woman, who, despite her delicate appearance, has no trouble wrestling her resistant charge away.

"I was only coming here because my husband has disappeared. He's a magic user."

"Magicians do disappearing acts all the time, love," says Devika. "It's what they're known for."

"Husbands more so," adds Thelma.

"But—"

"Gork," Devika says, greeting the statue. She drags Sadie forward by the binding on her wrists. She and Thelma both climb up a short series of steps, bringing them level with the desk.

"How's the sunburn?" says Thelma.

Gork tips his head from side to side.

"Still stiff, hey?"

He nods.

Devika jabs a thumb at Sadie. "This is the one who blasted Winchester McDonald's with soft drink."

Thelma places Iron Bill and Primrose on the desk. "We found her with this duck and this pixie."

Primrose straightens his back and lifts his chin. "Good day, troll," he says to Gork. He looks slightly embarrassed.

Gork nods, then grabs a pre-printed form and starts ticking boxes.

"You haven't heard of a Dirk Kilmore, have you, G-Man?" asks Thelma, leaning an elbow on the desk.

Gork stops, which isn't much different from Gork going. He studies Sadie for a moment. Something changes in his eyes. They soften. Then he shakes his head with a grating rumble of stone. He looks back down at the form. Seems to reconsider one of his answers, makes an adjustment, then punches it with a stamp and passes it down to Devika.

"Room 1?" she says, looking at the form. She glances up at Gork. Raises an eyebrow. "You sure?"

He shrugs, then makes a gesture with his hands.

"Fair enough," says Devika.

Thelma removes the tentacle wand from somewhere on her person, as if pulling it out of thin air. Passes it across the desk. "This is what she did it with. Says she found it. Came with this book too. You know whose these were, right?"

The lines of stone that make up Gork's brow knit together and he nods slowly before taking the wand and book. His eyes swivel to Sadie once more. There's an urgency in his gaze. Something she can't quite determine.

"Come on, you." Thelma grabs the binding on Sadie's wrists and leads her away from the desk. "Time to find out what you think you were doing with that wand, and where you got it from."

# Smoking Mirrors

The room where they leave Sadie appears to be the sort of standard interrogation room you might see in any detective show. She sits at a table in the centre of the room, her twine cuffs stuck to its surface as if by a powerful magnet. A mirror hangs from the wall in front of her.

The only alteration to the stereotypical cop show decor is that the mirror is oval and decorated with a frame of gunmetal-grey swirls. In its centre is a black and green face. It watches her with the grim gaze of a grizzled detective, occasionally curling its lip in disgust. It's a look that tells her she is going down. Down for life. That she's got a one-way ticket...straight to jail. All that mirror needs is a confession.

And by God, it's the mirror to get it.

It catches her staring. Squints back. Takes a drag from its cigarette.

The Bureau detectives had left for coffee and to take Iron Bill and Primrose to a different room. The duck had looked exceedingly nonplussed as they carried her away. Primrose had told Sadie not to worry, that there wasn't a cage that could hold a pixie for long.

Sadie tugs at the loop that secures her hands to the table. The thin strand of twine bites into her wrists, stronger than any metal.

She's starting to think this wasn't such a good idea.

Why isn't anyone listening to her?

She'd got it into her head that, because the guy at the storage unit and Wren and Finch had known Dirk, the people at the Bureau would know him too. Like all magic people just knew each other. Like when you meet someone from Albuquerque when you already have a friend from Albuquerque, so you tell them you have a friend who lives in Albuquerque as if everyone from Albuquerque knows everyone else from Albuquerque.

How wrong could she be? Not only did they not know who he was, they didn't seem to care one bit about finding out.

Maybe they had bigger fish to fry right now. Krakens probably... Or maybe they thought she was just wasting their time.

She rests her forehead on the table. The cool metal feels nice on her skin. She's shattered. It isn't an unfamiliar feeling. That juddering, bone-deep weariness that makes every thought fuzzy as if you're drunk and every moment slow and hard. It has been long over three years since she's intentionally stayed up so late. But she's been running on a sleep deficit ever since Ellie was born.

She closes her eyes. It's amazing what the human body can do. But it isn't half torturous.

She shakes herself back to the moment. Talking of torture, what is she in for? What laws bind the magic police? Did they have human rights here? Devika had mentioned memory erasure. How far back would they erase? Would she forget about Dirk being missing? Forget everything she'd learnt?

The door handle creaks as it eases down. The door glides open towards her so she can't see who's entering.

This is it.

The statue from behind the reception desk, Gork, inches in. Following him, with the cock-sure waddle her species is known for, stalks Iron Bill.

Gork closes the door behind her. Waits a moment. Listening. Looks down as if willing himself on. Gathering confidence.

He glances at the mirror. Holds up a grey hand. Fingers splayed. Take five.

The man in the mirror nods, then turns and disappears in a wisp of green smoke.

Gork studies her.

Is this bad?

This must be bad.

Must it?

Detectives in those shows only ever pull the plug on the CCTV, and ask everyone else to step out, when they are about to beat a perp to a pulp. Is she about to become perp pulp?

"I can explain..." she starts, her voice rising.

Gork places a finger over his lips.

He approaches like a bad plasticine stop-motion puppet. Her book is under his arm and he holds a wriggling manila envelope in one hand. He places both on the table.

Primrose rolls from the envelope, then stretches out with some side bends and neck rolls. "Bit of a squeeze in there."

Gork glances towards the clock. Holds his fingers up again. Five minutes. He touches a finger to her restraints. They come loose.

She flexes her wrists and rubs the life back into them as Gork pulls three pieces of paper from inside the envelope. Judging by the way he holds it, there is something else inside.

Iron Bill flaps up to the table to stand by Primrose as Gork spreads the papers in front of them.

Primrose folds most of his arms, then taps one finger on his chin. "What have we here?"

One document looks like a kind of report. Spoken word, transcribed. And two photos.

One photo takes her focus. Dirk and Betty. Her bottom lip shakes. They don't stand close. Not as if they are "together" together. Just talking. Though it's evident they are friends.

What did it mean? Why would he be talking to that murderer?

She sniffs. Gork's stone face turns down, and he pats her on the shoulder with the comforting tenderness of a car crusher.

He points to the picture, taps a heavy finger on Dirk's image, then holds up a hand in an OK gesture.

"Dirk's OK?"

Gork's mouth spreads though his lips remain firmly closed. Maybe. He taps his wrist where a watch might be, and with splayed fingers, waggles his hand.

"But he doesn't have much time?"

He nods. Then points at Betty. Gives a thumbs down gesture.

Iron Bill makes a hocking noise, and spits on Betty's face.

"Who is she? She told me she was Burt's sister."

Gork looks pained. Glances up at the clock. Not much time. Shakes his head. Taps Betty again, then points upwards.

She doesn't understand. "I'm sorry."

He points upwards again, this time with more insistency.

"I think the troll is saying she's upstairs," says Primrose.

Gork nods. He holds his hand out with splayed fingers and tips it from side to side.

"Sort of..."

Primrose moves to stand on the other photo. In it, two of the tallest, skinniest men she's ever seen stand either end of a long wooden box. The box is roughly the length of a person. They are loading it into the back of a black van.

"Are these the tall men Dirk spoke about in his note?" he asks.

"These must be the ones kidnapping the kids from the Hanley Estate," says Sadie.

Gork's face brightens, slowly like a sunrise, in surprise. He nods. Gives her two thumbs up, then, somewhat patronisingly, ruffles her hair.

"Where are they taking them? Do they have Dirk and Burt too?"

He shrugs and points at the document.

She moves it towards herself. It's some sort of report.

"What is this?"

He glances towards the mirror. A green mist coalesces into the face of the man. Gork's eyes widen, and he hurries to scrape the pieces of paper together into the envelope. His movements are too slow and cumbersome, so she helps. She picks up the book and slots it under her arm.

"Are they going to help me here?" she whispers.

He shakes his head.

"What can I do? I don't know magic. How can I escape?"

Gork upends the envelope and shakes the final things from it. The wand and Primrose's little swords and gun. Primrose hurries to collect his armaments as Gork holds the wand up to his neck as if at gunpoint. A look of worry crosses his stone face. Then he places it in to Sadie's hand.

"I don't know what to do with this."

Gork motions for her to stand as the man in the mirror returns.

"What's going on here?" he says. "Gork?"

"I'll tell you what's going on here," shouts Primrose, catching on fast. He flips up on to Iron Bill's back, takes the reins with one hand and brandishes his gun with the other. "We're walking out of here and there's nothing you can do to stop us, glass face."

Gork shrugs, hands raised.

Sadie takes the initiative, jumps up, and places an arm around his neck. "Get me out of here, stone man, or else I'll 'Move It' your bloody head off!"

Gork frowns, but goes with it. He lumbers forward, dragging her with him. With subtle care, he places the envelope with the pictures and document into her hand. Iron Bill and Primrose swoop around the room, quacking and shouting.

"You've got nowhere to go," says the man in the mirror. "This place is crawling with cops."

Sadie does her best to pretend she's pushing Gork on as he pulls her towards the door.

"Jeez Louise, she has the strength of an ox," says the man in the mirror, aghast. "Goddamnit, Gork, resist. Resist!"

Gork turns his hands over apologetically, then tows her towards the door. He blocks the view of the handle from the mirror with his body and performs a complex series of turns with the knob, like unlocking a combination safe.

A cool breeze blows in when the door opens. Goosebumps stand on Sadie's arms. It's dark inside. The dark interior of a building at night. A different building. Iron Bill swoops past her shoulder and through.

"Get moving," she says, for the mirror's benefit.

The static of a radio sounds from the mirror. "This is Man in the Mirror to all available officers. We've got a code thirty in progress. Back-up to room—" His voice cuts off as the stone man drags them both through and shuts the door behind them.

Broken glass crunches beneath her feet.

She glances up. The stars are visible through the smashed and fallen corrugated tiles of the ceiling above. Long vines of ivy grow up the walls, stretching across girders of corroded steel, their leaves silhouetted in the orange-purple glow of light pollution from nearby streetlights.

She turns. A crumpled wooden door stands in a frame with no wall. It says 'Private' on it. She suspects that if she were to open it, it would not lead back into the Bureau.

She lets go of Gork's neck and steps away from him. With a heavy sweep of his arm, he smashes the door from its frame. He taps his wrist again and shakes his head.

She holds up the envelope.

"Is whoever wrote this report a detective at the Bureau?"

He nods.

"Is someone at the Bureau trying to cover something up?"

He nods again.

"But," she shakes the wand, "I don't know how to use this. I can't fight."

He pushes the hand holding the wand to her chest, points at it, then points at her face. Some hidden meaning she doesn't understand.

Iron Bill quacks. Gork holds up a wrist and she lands there.

"You are not alone," says the pixie. "Primrose Applewhistle is with you."

She smiles at him, but nausea builds in her stomach. "What would have happened to me if you hadn't come?"

Gork's lips tighten and he shakes his head.

That told her everything.

"Thank you," she says. She moves forward to hug him. It's like embracing a brick house.

He smiles, then flicks his fingers. Go.

She nods. "But how will I find him?"

Gork taps the envelope in her hand. The answers would be in the document. She hopes she'll be able to decipher them.

# Got The Horn

It doesn't take long to recognise where she is. Sadie deduces Gork picked this particular spot to drop her off because he knew where Dirk's unit was.

There was a lot more to this than she'd first considered. Dirk had uncovered something in his investigation, either intentionally or by accident — something that someone high up in the Bureau didn't want people to know. Something that meant the kids disappearing from the estate could go unnoticed and unchecked.

But then there was Betty. Who was she? Dirk had met with her recently. To him, she was more than just Burt's sister. She knew magic. She knew about his investigation. Everything she'd said had been a lie.

Were she and Dirk working together? If so, what did *that* mean? The dogs were with her, so she was clearly a bad guy. Sadie's heart flutters in her chest, causing her to cough. Dirk couldn't be a bad guy, could he?

She hurries along the road to the storage unit. The street is quiet. No other cars. No other people. Mum's car is still in the car park. She'd almost expected it to be gone.

She glances up the alley that leads towards Dirk's unit. Her heart races. Someone is there. She dives behind Mum's car and glances out between the wheels. It's Kayder. Waiting, leaning against Betty's black muscle car, arms folded, facing towards Dirk's unit. Out in the open, not caring if he's seen.

After a moment, he climbs into the passenger side of the car as Betty emerges from the unit carrying a black holdall. That unmistakable mop of hair falls like Niagara around her shoulders.

Iron Bill leaps from Sadie's shoulder.

"Woah there, IB," says Primrose, pulling on the reins.

Sadie catches the duck by the foot, and with great difficulty the two of them manage to wrangle her back.

Iron Bill growls at Sadie. Most people never get to hear a duck growl. Lucky them. The sound would haunt her nightmares for longer than the sight of a giant spider with a man's face.

"Wait," Sadie hisses.

The duck calms. Floats to the ground. Primrose dismounts and jogs under the car for a better look.

Betty puts the bag into the boot of her car. Takes one look back to Dirk's unit, then climbs in.

Sadie lies on the tarmac as the car purrs past and out on to the main road.

"I will follow them," says Primrose, as he reappears from beneath the car and jumps atop his mount. "And if they have your husband, I will find him."

"What if I don't hear from you?"

"If I cannot rescue him, I will come to you." He looks up at the sky. "By the stars I see it is four of the morning. I will be to you by nine, with or without information." He slaps the reins and Iron Bill flaps her wings, ready to fly.

"And what if you don't?"

"Then it is up to you to think of something else. Where will you be?"

"I'm staying at my mum's. 42 Abbey's Hill."

"I'll find it. Until we meet again, Lady Kilmore." He kicks his feet and they take to the sky.

She watches them go, then climbs into Mum's car. She grips the wheel and stares at the open doorway to Dirk's unit.

Betty had taken something, but what? What could Dirk have that this woman wanted?

She places Gork's envelope, along with the spell book and her bag, on the passenger's seat. Then, with a firm grip on her wand, she climbs out of the car and creeps along the alley.

The place is still as neat as when she'd left it. She pulls on the light.

Nerves bubble in her stomach. Could whatever Betty had taken be the reason Dirk had gone missing? Had it been the reason Betty had come earlier? Maybe she'd only stopped then because Sadie had been there. Maybe she'd been hoping Sadie would lead her to Ellie. If so, why had she disappeared? Why not just follow Sadie around for the rest of the day?

She spots the two gaps in the shoe rack.

The blue horn and the demon leech are gone.

She hurries back to the car and heads for Mum's.

As she pulls up, the faintest line of lightening sky far off to the east tells her it will be morning soon, and so only a few hours before Ellie is up and absolutely at 'em.

Sadie drags her weary body out of the car and into the lounge, where she falls onto the sofa.

She'd been nodding off on the drive. Unable to keep those micro-sleeps at bay even for a minute, but as soon as she lies down in her mother's living room, her mind races.

She empties the envelope onto Mum's coffee table. Studies the picture of Dirk. A slight frown crosses his brow as he speaks seriously with Betty. His eyes are aimed at someone else out of shot. The curve of a nose protrudes in from the side. Burt?

The focus of the shot, though, is her, as if the photographer were trying to capture Betty, and Dirk just happened to be there.

She places her hand over Betty to cut her out and looks at her lost husband. Studies the contours of his face. His clothes. She lets out a breath. It leaves her as a soft moan. Oh god, she prays he's OK.

He's wearing what he'd left in on Thursday. Maybe the picture had been taken that day.

Who was Betty really? And what did she have to do with the missing kids on the estate?

Sadie picks up Gork's document. Scans it first. It is indeed a detective's report. Something spoken and then transcribed. It looks like a photocopy of a printout.

*G-man, I don't know if this'll reach you, but I have to try. I've found out who's responsible for taking the missing kids from the estate. You were right, it's got something to do with our own head of HR. Or at least she's the one covering it up, the one making it so that we don't investigate. But I can't understand why.*

*They are using delivery men to capture and move the kids. They take them around mid-afternoon. It's the tall men. So you know what that means. The witch is involved, but I can't figure out the connection.*

*They take someone new every other day. I think they're choosing the younger ones because they're naturals, or maybe because they're easier to take without anyone knowing they're missing.*

*Why would the witch be after naturals? And what is she using them for? Surely these kids have been through enough.*

*The guy in the photo with her is Dirk Kilmore. He's a PI. I looked him up. Not much else in the records. Although one mentioned he used to work for us. Only found it because I put a typo in the search. But no one else remembers him, and it was just his name spelt slightly wrong in a crime report transcript. It's like someone deleted everything on him, but missed that record because of the typo.*

*I'll keep an eye on him. I can't tell if he's in on it, too. Or on to it, maybe? The other guy — the nose on the right — I haven't got anything on him. Not even a name. He works with the PI. But I think I can see a slight family resemblance, maybe? That curly hair.*

So Dirk had worked for the Bureau. But then, why hadn't they heard of him? Had someone deleted his records? Had someone performed some sort of memory-erasing spell on everyone there?

She keeps reading.

*They were talking about something called Bergerberg. Think it's a name. I've asked the Librarian, but she can't find anything about it, which seems suspicious in itself.*

*I took the photo Friday. Think they were talking about the disappearances, which is why I think Kilmore is investigating it too. He was questioning her. What was the Bureau doing about it? That sort of thing.*

*Maybe worth talking to him if you can find him.*

*It's weird the kids are going missing, and we're not doing anything about it. We put them there to protect them. I'm going to see the duck Monday night. He contacted me to talk about the disappearances, along with a few others. He's off on one of his conspiracy jobs again. Thinks something big is going down, but we all know that guy is as nutty as a fruitcake, so it could be nothing. Still, I'm leaving no stone unturned.*

That meant the person who wrote this was dead. There had been a man in the water, with wings, like the woman at the front desk inside the Bureau. Could it be him who wrote this? He'd been on to whatever conspiracy Sadie had stumbled upon. She continues reading.

*I'll try to contact you Tuesday, but if I don't, you know who's to blame. Don't know how you're going to pin it on her. She's never done anything like this before, so it'll be hard to convince everyone. We both know Betty Phoenix didn't get promoted to the top of Hell Relations based purely on her looks.*

Betty Phoenix.

Everything crashes together.

She's the one behind the disappearances.

And she works at the Bureau.

# HELL TO PAY

Sadie doesn't know she's fallen asleep until she wakes up to the gentle rip of a small hand stroking through the tangles of her hair.

"Wake up, Mummy."

She opens an eye. Ellie hugs her hands to her chest inches from Sadie's face. Mum stands in the living room doorway, a dreamy smile on her face.

"I'll get the teas," she says, then disappears. Her voice carries down the hallway. "And then you can tell me what you've learnt."

Sadie rubs her hands firmly over her eyes. Coloured spots dance in her vision. She glances at the clock. Seven. She's had less than three hours' sleep. Her sore eyes water. Her lashes stick.

"Hey, baby," she says, pressing herself up to sit. "Where's my hug?"

"Mummy." Ellie smiles wide and throws her arms around Sadie's torso. She always manages to land her full weight, elbows first, on a boob. Left this time. Dirk had said the same was true of his soft parts. They were a magnet and Ellie's hinge joints were the purest, toughest iron.

Sadie groans, but hugs her child tightly. "How did you sleep?"

"Good."

"No bad dreams?"

"No. Beebee was there. He watched out for any meanies."

Mum returns holding two mugs. "I haven't the foggiest idea who this Beebee is," she says. "Keeps banging on about him."

"She's not mentioned him before." Sadie wraps her arms around Ellie, who has curled up in her lap.

Ellie often makes up names for things. Her cuddly toys went through a whole range of monikers daily. And she often carried imaginary dogs, and kangaroos, and babies around the house as if they were really present.

Mum crosses the room and passes a cup over.

"Thanks."

"We were just about to have breakfast and then go out for another walk to the park. I was going to let you sleep. But then she spotted you. You were back late. Did you want more?"

What had she been worried about? Mum was taking this all in her stride. She is clearly unaffected by the demon inside her. Dirk had been right. She feels like crying. They'd missed so much time they could have spent together. Instead, she smiles.

"You didn't wait up, did you?"

Mum presses her lips together. "Oh, I don't sleep much these days," she says. "You can use my bed. It's much comfier than the sofa."

"Thank you, Mum." Her traitorous voice cracks, so she clears her throat.

"What for?"

"For looking after Ellie. For letting us stay."

Mum frowns. "I won't hear it." She looks at Ellie and smiles. "I know you know what I mean when I say the day that you were born was the day that I stopped worrying about my own comfort. You were as dear a little thing as she is. And in my eyes you've not changed. You and her are all that matters to me. Being with her is a joy. And having you here is a pleasure." She swallows. "I've missed you." She blinks. Catches herself. Places one wrist on her hip and wags a finger. "Now get upstairs, young lady, and go to sleep. I'll wake you when we're back and you can tell me what you've learnt about your errant husband."

"But—"

"You're worried about him. I know how that feels. But you have to give yourself permission to take care of yourself. You're no good to anyone in this state. Bed."

She stands with her tea and heads for the door. "Someone is going to pop by soon, so can you stay here? He's a little unusual. Comes with a duck. Wake me as soon as he gets here."

"A duck? Sure." Mum nods. "I have some Sominex in the bathroom cabinet. Take two if you think you'll struggle."

Despite everything flying through her head, the sleeping tablets work, and Sadie manages to drop off.

When Mum next enters with Ellie, Sadie is dragged back to consciousness as if she were being brought back to life.

She opens an eye as Mum closes the bedroom door behind her. Dad's dressing gown still hangs on the back. It swings out like a ghost.

Sadie is immediately alert. "Did he come?"

"Who?"

"The pixie. Primrose?"

Mum squints one questioning eye and leans her head. "A pixie? No one's come."

"What time is it?" Sadie pushes herself up.

"Just after half-nine. I tried to let you sleep longer, but she can be quite insistent."

Ellie rushes forward and throws herself at the side of the bed, arms over the side, legs kicking the air, trying to haul herself up. Sadie lifts her on to her lap.

"Beebee says it's time to get up." She nibbles an obliterated piece of toast scrunched up in her fist.

A glance to Mum. A shrug from her.

"And who is this Beebee?" Sadie leans her forehead against her daughter's. Rests her fingers on her small back.

Ellie turns and points towards Mum, who's sat herself on the end of the bed, towards the door where Dad's dressing gown still rocks from side to side.

"I've made you something to eat," says Mum. "We can get it down you while we wait for your friend. Are you ready for it?"

It worries her that Primrose hasn't arrived yet, but she's famished. Breakfast can only be a good idea. She lifts Ellie up and slides herself out of bed. "Sure am. Coffee?"

She pulls on her hoody from the night before. The wand is still tucked in the front pocket next to her cold supplies.

Mum smiles. "I put an extra spoon of grounds in. Don't worry. I know how to wake someone up. Your father always needed it after one of his late-night toast marathons."

Sadie laughs.

The trio head downstairs to the kitchen. The smell of toast fills the air. Mum's old filter coffee machine bubbles and hisses, filling the room with a dark and rich aroma that reminds her of mornings spent with Dad. Of waking so early that Saturday morning kid's TV hadn't even started yet. Of sitting with him through Trans World Sport, munching on toast and waiting for the cartoons to begin. Mum takes a single mug from the line of hooks under the plate rack that hangs on the wall.

"Sugar and milk?"

"I've been taking it black."

The toaster pops. Sadie grabs butter and blackcurrant jam from the fridge.

"There's peanut butter too," says Mum, pouring the coffee while Ellie busies herself with rolling the apples from the fruit basket along the floor.

Sadie smiles as her mum brings her the jar. A mother never forgets. Peanut butter and blackcurrant jam, just how Dad had taught her.

"A meal in itself," she says.

"That's what he used to say."

How long has it been since she's made herself one of these?

She takes a bite and closes her eyes. Transported to another time. Heaven.

Two eggs sing next to a sausage in the pan. The familiar crack and pop, the salty smell of sizzling fat, warms her. She is a girl again. Safe at home.

Mum ushers her to the table and places the mug of coffee in front of her on the same chequered tablecloth that's been there so long it has moulded itself around the wood.

Sadie takes another bite of her toast. Closes her eyes. Wiggles her sock-covered toes on the black and white tile floor.

She glances at Mum's clock. Coming up to ten and still no Primrose. She'll have to come up with something if he doesn't return. But for the moment, she wants to enjoy these five minutes of peace.

She closes her eyes. She'd read once that the best way to get some normality after a tragic event was to pretend. So for a moment, she pretends. Looks to the future where she, and Ellie, and Dirk, would share a breakfast like this, here with Mum. Maybe they could do that. A monthly, no, weekly thing to make up for the time they'd missed.

Mum plates up her breakfast and brings it over. Ellie is happy on the floor, so Mum sits opposite while Sadie eats. It's a unique quality of a mum to be able to sit and watch someone eat without having food themselves. As if they derived as much pleasure from feeding as being fed. She'd found the opposite was often true of a dad, who might lurk at the edges of your plate like a wild dog.

Sadie reaches across the table and gives Mum's hand a squeeze.

"I'm sorry I haven't been more..." she searches for the word. "More present."

"I remember how it was." Mum squeezes back. "It's hard to know what to do. You're just about surviving, trying to keep hold of them and treasure them while they're still small. Trying to memorise everything that happens. Trying to make the most of that time as it races by you when you've had no sleep and you're barely functioning, knowing you'll only ever get the one chance. Hoping and praying you don't waste it. Wanting to be near them. Wanting to be yourself. Trying to figure out exactly who you are now that you're a mother. It's hard." Her eyes sparkle. "I wanted you all to myself, too."

Sadie sniffs. Blinks. Pushes through.

Mum pats her hand. "Now's not the time to get maudlin about the un-changeable past. Tell me, what did you learn?"

"I don't know how to tell you what's happening. It's too crazy."

"You can tell me anything."

"Dirk..." she starts, not really knowing how she will finish. "Dirk can use magic." She takes the wand from her pocket and places it on the table between them. "I think he found this when he was younger. Since then, he's learnt how to cast spells with it. He fights..." this sounds so stupid, "he fights the forces of evil."

Mum lets go of her hand. Reaches out gingerly to pick up the wand. "It's funny how the past can catch up with you, isn't it?

Sadie squints. "How do you mean?"

"I've seen something like this before. My grandmother was a...well, my mother called her a witch." She turns the wand over in her hands. "She had something like this. Could do all sorts of things with it." Mum laughs to herself. "My mum says when she was little, Granny had a spell that would send them straight to bed if they were being naughty. With a wave of the wand, she'd say 'Straight To Bed' and off they'd go. And I believe it. Granny Joan took no lip."

Sadie shakes her head, not believing that someone in her own family had the ability to wield magic like Dirk. The world was a small place. Could it be a coincidence? Or perhaps magic, like technology, had a way of making the world smaller. Of drawing pieces together to make an unbelievable whole.

Everything was connected by physics; why couldn't it be connected by magic too? Maybe there wasn't much of a difference.

"Granny Joan was a magic user?" she asks.

"Is that what they call them?"

"That's what I call them." She studies Mum's eyes. "Do you know any magic?"

"Oh, just a few bits and pieces that she taught me when I was a girl. Granny stopped doing it later on in her life and after that I just sort of forgot. Put it away with tooth fairies and Easter bunnies. Don't know why she stopped. Wouldn't talk of it again, despite my pleading with her. She'd get cross about it sometimes." Mum's lips tighten into a thin white line. "I had almost forgotten completely until one night, consumed with grief about your father, I went looking through the attic and found one of Granny Joan's old books. I found a spell that said I might be able to talk to him." She frowns, and rubs her temple, and for a moment Sadie glimpses the confused look she's associated with her mother recently. "I don't really remember what happened." She looks Sadie in the eye. "I feel we grew apart after that."

Should she tell her? Tell Mum what had really happened that night? No. Not yet. It would only scare her. So she continues with her story.

"Young magic users on a local estate have been going missing. The um...magic police aren't doing anything about it because someone's trying to cover it up. Dirk stumbled upon it, and I think they got him."

"Who?"

"I think his partner's sister is involved. Someone else is doing the actual kidnapping, though. Wait a second."

Sadie stands and jogs to the living room to grab Gork's envelope from the coffee table then returns to the kitchen.

"Here." She places the photo of the men carrying the box on the table.

Mum's eyes flash wider as if she recognises them. Then she clears her throat and frowns. Rubs her forehead. "I don't like the look of them."

"These are the people who have been kidnapping the kids from the estate. I guess they pretend to be delivery men, then pack them in boxes and take them somewhere."

"Where?"

Sadie shakes her head. "I don't know." She chews the corner of her mouth. "I need to find him, Mum. He's in trouble. No one else is there for him. No one else even knows he exists."

"What about your friend? The pixie?"

"Primrose said he'd come find me, but he's already an hour late."

Mum takes a long inhale and sighs. "I sometimes think I never told your father I loved him enough. If I'd have known he'd be gone from us so soon, I'd hug him and never let him go." She looks down. "We all know from the start that everyone we ever love is going to leave us at some point, and though we take that for granted, it's the deal we make when we fall in love. The sad thing is you never know the real price until it's paid." Mum places the wand down and takes Sadie's hand again. "I'd give anything just to see him again, so I know if there's anything you can do, you'll do it. And..." She wipes her eyes with the sleeve of her jumper. "And I'll do all I can to help."

Sadie looks at Ellie, still content with bruising apples.

"You know what you have to do, don't you?" says Mum, knocking a knuckle on the table snapping Sadie back.

"I have no idea."

Mum lifts the picture of the two men and shakes it. "You need to wait for this pair of galoots to strike again. And then you follow them. And then you call the police, the army, whoever you can, make up some story about terrorists if you have to, and you come down on them hard as a hammer. You squash them flat."

Her heart rate quickens. "But what about Ellie?"

"She'll be safe with me."

"But—"

Mum cuts her off by leaving the room. Ellie looks up to watch her go, then takes a bite from the apple clenched in her fist. Mum returns and slaps Dad's rifle on the table. She then takes her phone from her trouser pocket and passes it over. "That watch on your wrist, you got the Find My Watch app?"

Sadie touches it. Nods. What is Mum thinking?

"You take my phone. Give me yours. If you're not back here with Dirk by tomorrow morning, I'm coming to get you." Mum's lip hardens, and for a moment, she looks truly terrifying. She lifts the rifle. Her voice lowers to an almost inhuman growl. "And whoever we find there will have hell to pay."

# TALL MEN DELIVERY SERVICE

Sadie drives Mum's car once more into the Hanley Estate. A place that, until yesterday, she had avoided at all costs. And now here she is, back in the same place her school friends warned her never to go to for the third time in two days.

A single road bisects the entire estate with warren-like crescents and closes running from it. On the far side, the road leads out towards the New Forest.

The kids are playing street football once again. With them, she spots the green-eyed boy who had warned her the previous night.

She smiles at the kids as they stand out of the way and watch her pass. Parks once more outside the Drake's home. The house sits near the centre of the main road, one of many identical homes that line the street. She wonders if anyone has been in. If poor Finch's body is still there, untouched.

She climbs from the car and scans the road left and right.

How is she going to find a black van in this maze of parked cars, let alone the right one? It could disappear down any side street, then escape back out of the estate and she'd be none the wiser.

She checks her watch. It's getting to eleven. Might she already be too late? The report said the van came around midday, which could mean any time from now until 1pm.

She glances back up towards the kids and their game. Perhaps she could enlist some help.

She starts towards them, reaching for her wallet. The kid with the green eyes stops playing and regards her as she approaches. The ball rolls to him and he picks it up, holds up a hand, and the others mobilise into a V formation behind him.

"Hey, you," she says tentatively, trying not to sound or look like a paedo. Women could get away with talking to kids they didn't know, right? Could get away with paying them cash to run a little errand without seeming too weird, right? "It was you I saw the other night."

The boy neither confirms nor denies. Just watches her with those eyes. Emerald eyes. Eyes that seem to sparkle. That draw her in. Threaten to drown her like mysterious pools of molten bottle glass.

She shakes her head, feeling a little dizzy. "I wonder if I might proposition you."

The boy screws up his face. "You what?"

*Proposition?* Kids, Sadie. Kids. Simplify.

"Do you dudes," she tries, "wanna make some sweet, sweet cash?"

The children behind him break into whispers.

"You a Bureau narc?" the boy demands, folding his arms.

"Um...no. You know I'm not."

A girl with a plait of red hair down to her waist — maybe his sister? — hisses in his ear. "That's what a Bureau narc would say."

"That's what a Bureau narc would say," he repeats.

This doesn't seem like the kid from last night at all.

She takes a tenner from her purse. "You didn't think I was a Bureau narc last night. You helped me then."

His lips pinch together. "You must be thinking of someone else."

She shrugs. "Sure, whatever. All I want is for you to maybe play your game up near the main road." She points towards the end she means. "And then one of you calls me if you see a black transit van coming in. Ideally one with a couple of tall-looking men in the front seat."

More whispers. Nothing she can catch.

"We know the one. Twenty now and we'll do it."

Sadie digs into her wallet. She only has the tenner. There's some change, though. Damn the ever-increasing cashlessness of society.

"I don't have that much on me." She tips the coins from her purse into her hand. "I've got about eleven quid in change here. You can have this now, and I'll give you the ten after?"

The boy raises unbelieving eyebrows. "You'll run off without paying."

"I won't."

"Where you gonna be?"

She points back up to the other end of the main road. "I'll be watching for the van, too."

He takes out a battered phone; an obvious hand-me-down with a cracked screen. "Give us your number. We'll call you if we see it. A couple of us'll follow and the others'll lead you to it."

"Aren't you the shrewd little businessman?" She takes his phone and taps in her mum's number.

His eyebrows press together once as he takes it back. Then he holds out his hand.

She deposits the eleven pounds in coins. He clicks his fingers and they disappear.

She can't help but smile. "Neat trick."

"That's nothing."

"Call me as soon as you see them. Don't approach. Just let me know where they are."

The boy nods, then throws the ball back into the street where the game erupts once more.

He shouts after her as she walks away.

"Don't look at them. Not in the eye, anyway."

She nods. Butterflies dance in her stomach.

She heads past her car towards the far end of the estate. She hasn't stepped ten paces past the Drake's house when her mum's phone vibrates in her pocket.

"They're here," says the boy. "Down Amber Close. Back up here on the right. Meet you at the entrance."

That was quick. She thought she'd have time. Time to come up with a plan of action, at least. She pushes her arms above her head, stretching out the anxious nerves that have suddenly made her lethargic.

What is she going to do? She jumps into Mum's car and races back towards where the kids had been playing.

Just the green-eyed boy stands at the corner of the street, now next to a sign that reads Amber Close. She pulls up to the curb. Winds down her window.

"Down there," he says, then leans into the car. "You got my money?"

"Hold on," she says, wary for a moment. "I don't see a van."

He points. "There."

She swallows. He's right. Parked up a little way along. The black transit. Like a rotten tooth. A dark omen. The passenger side door opens and an impossibly tall man unfolds. He stands like a sapling with a long and slender frame. The top of his head easily meets the height of the van.

She takes the tenner from her pocket and holds it out to the boy. He grabs it then jumps back to the curb.

"Remember what I said," he says, pointing to his own eyes with two fingers. "Don't look them in the eye."

She nods, then turns the steering wheel and pulls off the curb with eyes focused on the van yet trying not to look at its occupant. She doesn't dare blink in case she might lose them. She crawls the car up the road as another man steps out.

Looking around, pretending to be lost, she parks a few houses down.

Using sideways glances, she can see the pair wear loose navy boiler suits, their frames lost inside the baggy wealth of material designed for much broader men. They skirt around the back of the van and remove a long wooden box like the one she'd seen in the photograph.

She ducks as they scan the area, and when she pokes her head back up, she just catches sight of them disappearing down a garden path.

This is it. Someone is about to be kidnapped. And here she is just watching, knowing it's about to happen, using them as bait. A guilty sickness builds in her throat. She puts a hand to the wand in her pocket. Should she try to help?

She'll never find Dirk if she dives into the rescue. And she might only make matters worse, for herself, and for the person she'd be trying to save.

Moments later, they return carrying the box between them. They shove it into the back of the van next to another just like it, and climb back in.

The van does a U-turn, then starts back down towards the main street. Now she can see there are three of them squeezed into the front seats. She ducks again as they pass, forces herself to wait a few breaths, then turns the car around and follows.

When they reach the end, she expects them to head right back out of the estate. Instead, they go left and further in.

The children have gone. The roads are empty.

The tall men pass the Drake's house and head into another street. She continues to shadow them. Ahead she can see the boy with the green eyes walking alone. He disappears down a garden path.

The van pulls over. Are they going for him next?

She parks up. Sits immobile in her chair with indecision weighing her down. She can't let this happen. Despite what he said in front of his friends, he saved her last night. Is there anything she can do?

She undoes her belt and climbs out of the car as the tall men move around the back of their van and withdraw the second box. She squats down behind Mum's car and fiddles with her shoelace. That's what an undercover agent might do, as if the men could even see her.

The scuff of their shoes on the pavement tells her they are heading away. After the boy. She skirts past the car, holding the wand up against her chest like a spy with a gun from a movie. In her mind she traces the sigil for 'Move It'.

As she nears the back of the van, she listens. There's a knock on the door of the house that the boy had been heading to. A whizz and a pop and a sigh, and then the clunk of a wooden box closing. She glances inside the vehicle. The interior is clean. The other box rests on the bare metal. In the driver's seat, the third tall man sits motionless, oblivious to her presence.

This is a bad idea. She should get back in the car.

She shakes herself. Takes a deep breath. She's not helping anyone if she gets caught. Clamping the edge of her teeth on the corner of her lips, she turns away and walks as normally as she can back towards Mum's car.

Her legs are jelly. Is this normal walking? Does she usually lift her knees this high?

She doesn't look back.

Suddenly, the hairs on the back of her neck stand. A chill runs the length of her spine. The gaze of something truly predatory is upon her. She feels it. She knows it. An ingrained primal sense screams at her to flee, telling her that something has eyes on her. Something horrible.

Somehow she just knows her fate is being considered. Her fingers tighten on the wand. It squirms in her grip. It takes everything she has not to run.

The van doors clang shut, and, like an excruciating pressure headache suddenly growing dull, that feeling of dread evaporates, leaving her rotten and trembling, knowing she has been a whisper away from terrible harm.

She eases herself into Mum's car. The van passes. With eyes in her lap, she grips the wheel to steady her shaking hands. After counting to three in her head to put some distance between them, Sadie wrestles the car into gear and follows.

# FOLLOWERS

She follows for at least twenty minutes. Could have sworn on more than one occasion she'd been made, but there had been no indication from the van's occupants that they'd spotted her, and that all-encompassing sense of dread she'd felt back on the estate hadn't returned.

On two occasions she'd run a red light, but the van didn't stop, so neither did she.

At last they turn down a country lane with a sign that reads 'Airfield Only'.

She doesn't take this last turn, feeling it might be a little obvious if she does. Instead, she passes by and pulls up on the verge just beyond.

She presses her fingers against sore eyes. Blinks. The vision in her right eye is starting to blur. She closes the left to test it. It just won't focus. God, she needs sleep.

But this is it. This is the moment everything has built up to. Make or break time.

She calls Mum, who picks up on the first ring.

"Sadie?" By the waver in her voice, Sadie can tell Mum is trying to hold it together.

"I'm fine, Mum. I think I've found it. Some airfield out Salisbury way."

"Is Dirk there?"

"I don't know. I'm going to go in and have a snoop. I just wanted to call you before I did, so you knew where I was. Did Primrose come?" She expects Mum would have called if he had, but asks anyway, hoping she won't need to go into the airfield alone.

"Nobody came."

She hopes he's OK. "I'll call you again when I know."

Mum's voice shakes. "I know I said I understood what you needed to do, but I'm still scared. Just be careful. Don't take any chances."

"I won't. I love you, Mum."

"I love you too."

She squeezes the steering wheel in her fists. She can do this.

She reverses back past the turning and heads in.

Hulking oak trees line the road, shading it with their long, gnarled branches. Usually, it would be a pleasant drive, but now she just wants to throw up. Will she find Dirk down here? If she does, will he still be alive? Or is she just heading into a danger that she can't possibly fathom for nothing?

What had it said in the report Gork had given her? Something about a witch and a Bergerberg? What was a Bergerberg? A person, a place, a thing?

She grits her teeth. And who was Betty Phoenix and how had she come so far from her brother?

Oh.

In that moment, it strikes her that if Betty Phoenix was an enemy, Burt might not be on their side either. Had he ever given her reason to doubt him?

He'd been Dirk's friend from the very beginning. Despite his child-like dress sense and bachelor lifestyle, he'd brought Ellie thoughtful presents for each of her birthdays. Been there for every one of the parties they'd had. Got drunk and danced in their living room to Bon Jovi dressed as the head of a pantomime horse while Dirk, the legs, made his own cocktails with the dregs from their cupboards.

Burt was a good part of their lives. He was on their side.

The airfield comes into view through the trees. Little white pleasure planes are parked in lines of three on the grass. Three hangar buildings jut up from the ground. Huge semi-circles of white, like a baby's first teeth. The runway, a long strip of cropped grass.

A small plane takes off as she approaches, floating off over the picturesque Wiltshire countryside.

She parks in a bay outside a small cafe. No one seems to pay her any attention as she waits.

It's not busy, but not empty. Other cars are parked with hers, but it's quiet. Inside the cafe, a few older gents sit drinking teas and dunking biscuits, looking out over the grassy strip. A man and a woman stand by one plane preparing it for flight.

It seems a strange place to bring kidnap victims. Though it sort of makes sense. Out of sight. Out of the way. Somewhere with a lot of storage and an easy escape route.

None of the planes seem big enough to carry one of those wooden boxes, so she assumes they aren't flying them off site. That's a relief. It would have opened up the whole world for places Dirk might be.

She spots the black van parked outside one hangar. Two of the tall men leave the hangar through a side door and proceed to the van, where they retrieve one of the boxes.

The driver remains in his seat while a fine mist of exhaust gathers around the van. Maybe they would leave after their drop-off and she'd have time to investigate.

After a moment, the two tall men return from the warehouse, closing the door behind them. They climb back into the van and leave.

This time she doesn't follow.

She rubs her hands on her knees, steels herself, then climbs out of the car.

Casting sideways glances to make sure no one is watching, she strides across the car park towards the hangar. Tries the handle of the door the tall men had used. Locked.

She holds her hands up to the frosted glass, but can't see anything inside.

"Can I help you, miss?" comes a voice from behind. She jumps back from the door.

A young man watches her with a wary eye from beneath a black sports cap. He wears white overalls and holds a bucket of foaming, soapy water in one hand. A string of keys dangles from his belt.

"Oh, I wonder if you can," she says, thinking quickly, putting the back of her hand to her forehead, damsel-in-distress style. "I left my car keys inside and the guys have locked the doors. They've gone and won't be back until tonight. You wouldn't happen to have a spare, would you?"

The man smiled. "I might."

He wrestles with the chain of keys at his waist. Filters through them one at a time. "Ah." He steps forward and places it in the lock. "What are you guys using this place for, anyway?" he asks, opening the door and stepping inside.

She follows him. She has to fight down her horror and surprise when she sees what's inside.

"Oh, just storage," she says as, in her head, she tries to count the rows of boxes in the middle of the room. There must be at least forty. Ten rows of four.

Why did they need so many boxes? Why couldn't they just use the same ones unless...the kids are still inside.

Dirk might be among them.

"Hm." The man chuckles. "Well, you must have something big planned to move all these. Isn't the lease up tomorrow?"

"Oh, yeah." She nods and waves a finger at the boxes. "Gonna get all these gone by tomorrow, don't you worry."

He stands next to her a moment, as if on pause, watching her, waiting for something.

"Thanks?" She looks back at him, hoping he will leave.

"Aren't you getting your keys?"

"Oh. Quite right." She moves towards the boxes in the centre of the room while he stands at the door. How is she going to look in all of them with him standing there?

"I've just remembered I've got to do something here," she says. "I might be a while. I'll come find you to lock up once I'm done."

He holds up his sponge. "Sure. I'll just be about scrubbing planes."

She smiles. He leaves.

She steps to the nearest box. It's clean. No markings. Smooth like a coffin. A shiver travels down her spine. She touches the lid. Eases fingers around the edge and lifts. It opens on a hinge.

Inside, eyes closed, is the green-eyed boy boy. He looks so peaceful. For a moment, her heart stops. He's dead. But then she sees the gentle rise and fall of his chest. She reaches in and touches his wrist. Cool, but there's a pulse.

"Hey," she hisses. She grips and shakes his shoulders. "Wake up."

He doesn't.

She scans the rows of boxes. She should check them all. Dirk could be here. But what if the tall men come back?

She closes the boy's lid and hurries to the next. Lifts it. Inside is a girl. Maybe fifteen. She sleeps too. Acres of auburn hair billow around her shoulders and pale face. Her sharp elf-like features remind Sadie of the man she'd seen in the reception at the Bureau.

In the next box is another teenage boy, a little older than the girl.

She loses hope halfway down the second row. If the report from Gork is correct, and the tall men are taking kids every other day, and if these boxes are lined up in the order they are taken, then she's already gone back to before Dirk went missing.

Something clicks inside the room, followed by a hum. The huge hangar doors judder, then begin to roll upwards.

Panic grips her. Her knees weaken. They're back. She lifts the lid of the nearest box and rolls in next to the young girl inside. She pulls the lid closed, sealing out all light.

Something digs into her hip. She fishes the VapoRub from her pocket and stuffs it in to her hoody next to the wand.

The girl in the box breathes quietly, peacefully. She seems unaffected by Sadie's presence.

A rumble from outside. The roaring engine of a lorry reverberates inside the hangar. The floor vibrates beneath her.

She closes her eyes and tries to listen.

"You have one hour." A woman's voice. Sadie's lip curls. Betty. "I want each of the children awake, prepared, and ready at the church to begin the song of opening. We must have everything in place for when we find the first-born of the vanquisher. There must be no delays. Time is running out." There's an edge to her voice. A waver that could be worry.

Sadie holds her breath for fear of making a sound. Nothing else is audible over the noise of the truck as it draws nearer.

It's not long before she feels the box being lifted. There's a tingle of motion in her stomach as she is carried swiftly along, then passed up and into what she presumes is the truck.

She grips the wand in her hand as other boxes are lumped on top of hers. Tells herself that she'll be OK as the back doors of the truck are closed. Prays that she'll see Ellie and Dirk again as it cranks into gear and rumbles away to an unknown destination.

Believes that she won't.

# BOXED IN

Sadie takes a deep breath and reassesses her situation while she lies in darkness and listens to the slow peaceful respiration of the girl by her side in the box.

Hm.

Assessment complete. Situation terrible.

At least she has her wand. But she'll need water for a good solid whip. Unless she can cast 'Move It' with enough power, the short tentacle-shaped piece of wood is useless. The most violent thing she'll be able to do is jam it in someone's eye.

She goes over the jagged figure eight in her head. Traces it with her finger while she grips the wand in her other hand.

She clears her mind and dances the wand around and around. Going over the shape. Perfecting it. Wiring it into her brain, into her muscle memory so she can perform it without looking, without thinking.

She'll need quick reactions if she's going to defend herself.

She prays it'll work. Prays something will happen. Something big. Something that might save her so she can save Dirk.

She just had to conjure enough force in her mind.

Once, back when her father had been alive, he'd been driving them home from the cinema when a drunk driver had swerved across the road and front-ended their car.

Airbags had exploded inside the tight space. Sitting behind her mother, Sadie had seen her father flung forward against his seat belt, powerless despite his strength, into the white balloon that had bloomed like a puffball fungus from the steering wheel.

Sadie had been thrown forward, even before the cars had collided, thanks to her father breaking when he saw what was about to happen. The smells of exhaust and washer fluid and petrol had flooded the car. Mum hadn't been able to open her door, the chassis so badly mangled that it had been shunted backwards into its frame. Sadie could still clearly envision the way that the fumes from the engine had oozed out of the bonnet through the glare of the smashed headlights once they had been set free by police.

The thing that stuck with her most, like a splinter of recollection that the other memories grew out from, was the sudden screeching grunt as the two cars ploughed into one another. What sort of force would be needed to create that much damage, that much chaos? They'd been on a main road, so both cars had only been going thirty. And she guessed her father's quick thinking had slowed them considerably before the actual collision.

What if the cars had been going seventy or faster like those vehicles thundering past on the motorway that time when she and Dirk had run out of petrol on the M3?

She tries to solidify that force in her mind. That speed.

Almost hypnotised by the movement of her hands and the coalescing of that powerful force behind her eyes, she zones out. Doesn't even notice the truck stop. Only breaks free from her trance when she hears the back doors clunk open.

Footsteps outside the box. The grunt of men lifting heavy things. Working without talking.

The trip hadn't been long. Although there was no way to tell how fast they'd been going, she had only felt three or four turns. They couldn't be far from the airfield.

She tenses as she listens. Flinches when the lid of her box scrapes with the sound of the one above being removed. Hers is next.

While they carry her box, she is so focused on the lid, watching for that split second when it might be removed and she might have someone to aim at, that she doesn't feel the passage of time correctly. Everything seems to slow.

What had that little old Bureau woman called it? The unpleasantness-to-per-ceived-time conundrum.

They set her box down with a thud.

The lid is removed with the click of a latch, and her eyes are stung by glaring fluorescent bars shining from the ceiling above. Two round heads peer down at her. One on each side. The delivery men.

She raises the wand, focusing on both heads. Flicks her wrist. Distils that image of two cars colliding and screams "Move It!".

The faces staring down at her have no time to register what is happening as they are catapulted upwards. Their bodies are launched as if some giant hand has gripped their heads and thrown them at the ceiling like rag dolls.

One smashes against a light, shattering it. The other strikes the bare stonework of the arched ceiling with a crunch of bone.

They drop, lifeless limbs flop like overcooked spaghetti, and land on either side of the box. Broken glass tinkles around her. She rolls over, shielding herself and the girl in the box.

Then silence.

She opens one eye. Rolls back. Wand pointing to the sky. No sound comes from outside. No sign that anyone else is there nor seen what has just happened.

She raises her head over the wooden parapet.

The room is roughly the size of a school dinner hall. The floor is flagstones. The ceiling, ancient stone arches. No windows. The only natural light comes through an open archway that leads out into the back of the truck.

The day is still bright outside.

Her box sits next to several others. Each open. Each empty.

The two crumpled, gaunt bodies lie either side, their thin limbs splayed inelegantly. One has come crashing down on the box nearest hers. His body is bent at an awkward angle over the top. He looks a little like a baby bird she had once discovered fallen from its nest and sprawled on the pavement.

She'd done that. She'd killed these men. She's not surprised to find she doesn't care. In fact, she's glad she could do what it took when the time came. She feels no remorse. Perhaps something she's learnt from Iron Bill.

But there had been three in the vehicle. And she had heard Betty's voice back at the hangar.

Sadie glances out towards the truck. Aiming the wand all around her, she climbs from the box. The poor girl in the box hasn't stirred.

She slides the wand up her sleeve and lifts the girl's torso. She pulls her from the box and lies her next to it. The girl doesn't wake. Sadie considers carrying her. But they'd not get far, and if they were attacked, she'd have no hope of defending herself.

The best thing to do would be to follow Mum's plan. Now she knew where they were bringing everyone, she should leave and come back with help.

"Sorry," she whispers. Her eyes tingle with tears.

She creeps towards the exit arch. She should get somewhere safe and call the police.

The truck door slams outside. The third delivery man approaches. Her heart jumps. She's trapped. She retreats behind the empty box.

Footsteps near. She freezes. Back against the wood.

"Brothers?" The word hisses, seems to echo inside her head, bigger than sound.

From her limited vantage point, she looks for another way out. One other doorway leads further into the building down a darkened, descending stair. She shouldn't go in, should she?

She only has one option.

"Freeze!" she shouts, jumping to her feet and drawing a sort of cube shape with the wand hoping she might stumble upon a new spell and turn him into a block of ice.

Alas, he remains warm and mobile, though he does raise his gangly arms overhead and halts his progress towards her.

Result.

She watches him through her peripheries, trying not to look directly at him. But she feels her eyes drawn, like the way your brain sometimes wants you to peer over the edge of a very high cliff or at a nasty car crash on the other side of the motorway.

She catches herself as her gaze wanders towards him. Jerks her head away.

"Don't move. I am a powerful sorcerer and I will blast you across this room with the force of..." She hesitates. Pick anything. Any number. "Ten..." Weather? Maybe try weather? "Um...hurricanes, you...you lanky prick." She nods to herself. That sounded pretty damn threatening. "Yeah."

He says nothing. Just puts his hands down.

The silence stretches out. And she can't help it. She steals a look at him and is caught — a rabbit in headlights. Something is off about his face. Something hypnotising. His features are so plain as to be almost invisible. Like, he has a mouth — does he? And eyes — does he? — and —

"My god." Sound doesn't leave her lips as she mouths the words. The skin of her arms breaks out in goosebumps. Her voice cracks. "Where is your face?"

He grins. But he doesn't. She just has the feeling of sharp gnashing teeth behind a sinister slit in his flesh. He stalks towards her. Fingers working in strange shapes, drawing runes in the air before him. Black shadowy tendrils snake out of nowhere, reaching towards her.

She focuses her mind. Focuses that force of the car crash once more. Flicks the wand.

"Move It."

The tendrils flicker and something crackles, the sound of electricity discharging, but he doesn't slow his steady march across the room. She tries again. This time, nothing.

"Your force spell can't hurt me, now," he says.

What should she do? A different tack, maybe. Instead, she focuses on the wooden box that stands open between them.

"Move It."

The box awakens like a stampeding bull and shoots across the room, crashing as it goes through the man's lower body, and flipping him up into the air. His legs flail behind him as his chin careers into the smooth resin floor. Something cracks like an egg, and he lays still.

She's going to be sick. Her ears ring with the sound of his head smacking the floor.

But there's another sound. She listens carefully. It's not her ears. There's a wail that had started as soon as the tall man's head hit the ground. She steps closer to his body, but he is silent and still. Dead, she hopes. The sound isn't coming from him.

It's coming from behind her. Down that flight of steps. Further into the building. She listens. It's a man, crying, screaming in pain. Gasping for breath.

She looks back to the arch leading outside, leading to freedom. But something about that voice... She's never heard him like this before. Never. But she's sure it's him. Time stretches out as she listens. She works up her courage.

He needs her. She can't leave him.

She's spent all this time searching; she can't turn her back on him now. It's time for her to do something about it. To go in wands blazing. Time for her to be tough. Tough like Dirk. Tough like Ellie. Tough like her father and her mother.

"I am brave and strong," she says. The wand shifts in her grip as she climbs down the steps deeper into the building with the screams of her husband ringing in her ears. "I am brave and strong."

And terrified.

# Portrait Landscape

The stairs lead down to join the centre of a darkened corridor, wide enough for four people to walk side by side without touching. To both the left and right, roughly ten metres away, the corridor rounds a corner. It sounds like Dirk's voice is coming from the right, but Sadie can't be sure.

She holds her position. Takes everything in. Rushing in won't be good for anyone.

The floor is wooden, varnished dark, with a purple, almost black, swirling carpet that runs along the centre. It looks like the sort of hallway you might find in an old National Trust property.

No other doors lead from the corridor.

Portraits hang from the black-papered walls at five-metre intervals. She moves closer to the nearest. A woman stares back with cruel black eyes. She wears a flowing black dress that one who has dabbled in the odd sexy period drama on Netflix might pin as from the Georgian era. Something about her face makes it impossible to tell how old she is. Her skin is smooth and free of wrinkles, but a darkness lives in her eyes. The curve of her mouth, a snarl of some illicit contempt, suggests a confidence and a hatred that can only come with the experience of decades.

A creeping fear prickles at Sadie's neck, similar to the feeling she'd had when the tall man had been looking at her back on the street. Dread. As if she stands not before the painting of a woman, but face to face with some carnivorous dinosaur capable of devouring her whole with no pity or remorse. Something so primal, so malicious, so radioactive with evil that just to be in its presence could cause harm.

She takes a deep, shuddering breath. Strange how just a mixture of paint on canvas can breed such horror.

Who is this woman? Perhaps the witch referred to in the detective's report.

Sadie steps back and scans the other paintings. They are almost exact copies, although there is a slight difference to the angle of the face and of the eye in each. She lets out a low moan. Every single one faces towards her. She backs away and rounds the corner towards Dirk's voice.

The next corridor is identical. His voice sounds no closer.

Keeping her eyes ahead, she creeps further, not wanting to look at the paintings. She can sense those malicious eyes tracking her. That and the sounds of pain from ahead are enough to take anyone over the edge.

This corridor is devoid of doors. She reaches the end and turns right again.

Another corridor. Identical. No doors. Only paintings.

Dirk sounds no closer, but no further away. His moans of pain have become less frantic.

She looks back, confused. The paintings along this hall are fractionally different. A slight lift at the corners of the mouth. A hint of glee in the eye.

She hurries along and to the right once more. It makes no sense. Why have a stairway leading up to a square of identical corridors? Who would build this?

The paintings here are different again. That uplift at the corners of the mouth, moving further into a twisted smile.

She sprints along the corridor as fast as she can. Her footsteps clomp on the thick purple carpet. She turns right, back into what she presumes is the first corridor. She will leave and come back through a different entrance to find Dirk.

But it isn't the first corridor.

The door back down to the storage room isn't there.

The paintings grin at her. She fights herself not to go mad, to control her breathing and her heart as they race.

She turns and runs back again. Somehow, she's become confused. This is just a clever architectural trick. She must have missed a doorway somewhere.

In turning back to the third corridor, she realises she isn't confused at all. She has gone insane. The woman in the paintings now has her head thrown back in a laugh. And Dirk isn't screaming in pain anymore. He's laughing too. Shrieking with maddening glee. It's all in her head. Her vision blurs.

She runs, turning left and turning left, headless, heedless. The paintings reel past like a zoetrope, laughing and laughing until finally she has to stop, out of breath and unable to run anymore. Her thighs burn with the strain.

She rests her hands on her knees and tries to catch her breath.

"Tired of running?"

She looks up through lank, sweaty hair. Betty stands in the centre of the corridor flanked by two tall men.

"I'm impressed." Betty folds her arms. "You've come a long way."

"Where's Dirk?"

"Oh, he's somewhere." She waves a hand. "Maybe you heard him...but I don't think you did."

Sadie pushes against her thighs to stand. "Betty, why?"

She grins. "I'll be honest with you: I'm not Betty Phoenix."

"Then who?"

"My real name is Azalea Williams."

"But you were in the photos with Dirk and Burt. The report said..."

She laughs as if Sadie is stupid. "Oh, this is Betty's body. My last one was getting on a bit, so a couple of months back I lured her here and we swapped. It's not the first time I've done it, and it won't be the last, but I think this one'll do me for a couple of decades yet. And it comes with a lot of perks." She holds up her fingers and starts ticking them off. "I can subvert any Bureau investigations. I have close contact with some of Hell's biggest players — more close with some than others." She raises an eyebrow suggestively. "And — this one's the kicker, so pay attention — I'm now the one who's informed when Hell makes a demand for souls, and I get to put forward Earth's champion."

The Drake had mentioned something about that. "What do you mean?"

"Hm. The Bureau do such a good job of hiding it, you people have no clue what's really happening behind the scenes." She points to the ceiling as if having a great idea. "I won't waste my time explaining it to you. I have a busy night planned. Maybe you should ask your husband. He's downstairs right now. Not doing so well, I'm afraid." The corners of her mouth turn down in mock sadness. "I've been looking for him for nearly eight years now. I found it strange that no one was willing to spill their guts about him, even after I'd spilled their guts." She smiles wistfully at the ceiling as if remembering better times. "Strange, considering what he achieved all that time ago. People should know your Dirk, should love him, but nobody does. Nobody even remembers that there was anything to stop. It crossed my mind for a time that I'd gone raving mad." Her eyes light and Sadie can see the psychopath hiding beneath Betty's pretty face. The same malicious confidence she'd seen in the eyes of the woman in the painting. "But I wasn't the one who'd lost their mind. It was everyone else. Imagine my surprise when, just two months after I begin my masquerade as the head of Hell Relations at the Bureau, your husband crawls out of the woodwork to come and ask me for help with a missing person's case that I am in fact responsible for. Changed my plans quite considerably."

Sadie glares. "What are you planning?"

Azalea looks disappointed. "Let's just say it's time for a change of management."

"Why do you want Ellie? I don't understand why you didn't just follow me earlier. Why pretend you were going to see your mother?"

"You weren't going to lead me to your daughter after what that accountant told you. And I've had a lot to do over the last few days. Lots to arrange with those downstairs." She points to the ground. "A whole show to put together. There are many pieces to my plan. But now it looks like we have everything we need."

"You'll never get Ellie."

Sadie wants to appear furious — furious, brave and strong — but she knows she has nothing left. Her ears buzz like a cloud of flies. The centre of her vision has gone grey. She doesn't think she can hold herself up much longer.

Azalea's lips tighten as if she's happy to disagree, but won't say it.

"You should ask your husband why this has happened to you. You'll be with him soon enough, and you'll have time while you both rot. He has a lot of explaining to do. It's all his fault, you know?" Azalea clicks her fingers. "Take her."

The tall men stride forward.

Sadie raises the wand. Steps back.

With a nonchalant flick of the witch's wrist, the wand is ripped from Sadie's grasp. When Azalea catches it, her eyes widen. She hisses in pain and drops the wand to the carpet. She holds up her hand: an angry red line like a jellyfish sting runs across her palm.

"Hm." She shakes her hand out and the line fades. "A neat trick. But I assume that was more the wand than you." She lifts her eyebrows and leans her head to one side.

Sadie's body tenses as the two men lurch forward. Black tendrils appear around them like spider's legs. She can't breathe. She can't move as they surround her and drag her across the hall to a door opposite the storage room. A door that hadn't been there before.

Azalea laughs, a piercing, mocking hoot. "Say hello to Betty for me, too," she says, as they force Sadie down into cold darkness.

# WATCH OUT, SHE'S MENTHOL

Water drips somewhere nearby. The smell of mould clings to the air.

Sadie's cell is barred all the way around. A cage almost her length if she lies down. And half as wide. No furniture. Not even a mattress. Just cold, wet floor. Darkness hides almost everything beyond.

She sits pressed up against one corner. Hugging her knees to fend off the cold, to isolate herself from everything else, to squeeze away the horrific images that keep trying to invade her mind.

Hers is central in a row of three cells. Another three are setup across the slim hall. One light from further down the corridor reflects off the rusted steel bars and wet flagstones.

As far as she can tell, as her eyes adjust, the cells closest are empty, but the corners hide in shadow, and when she listens, beneath the constant dripping, beneath the strange vibrating rumble that seems to shake the floor below, rattling every lock on every cage, she can hear the rise and fall of laboured breath.

"Is that you, Sadie?" The voice from the darkness to her right startles her. It is frail and wavering, as if every word takes a great effort. A shadow shifts in the corner of the cell next to hers.

Sadie moves so she can pierce the gloom. Can just make out the shape of a small woman wrapped in a long black cloak.

"Betty?"

"Ah, you know, I was trying to figure out how I was going to explain."

"How long have you been here?"

"Two months, five days." She holds up an arm to reveal a series of tally marks on the wall.

"Alone?"

A faint noise. Not quite a sob. An affirming crackle of an old, parched throat. "Until last week." Betty takes a breath. "Two of our officers had gone missing. I came with my number two. You may have met him, Kayder. He betrayed me. They took my focus. They took my body. Locked me up down here." Her voice finally cracks. "She said she wanted to keep me around for the sentimentality, like an old dress you were never going to wear again, but didn't want to throw out. And all this time she's been out there pretending to be me. Taking my life."

Sadie can't imagine it. Being here all that time alone, knowing no one was looking for you, that no one, not even your closest friends, were missing you. Waiting here to die.

"Has Dirk been here?"

"Yes. And Burt." She blinks slowly and looks down with a frown. "My memory doesn't work quite as it used to. It's patchy, but I think they are questioning him and the pixie now. They've been trying to find you and Ellie. Time is ticking. Azalea is getting frustrated. Dirk did a clever thing when he cast the spell that hid your mother from scrying. He hid her house as well as her. That's why Azalea can't use magic to locate Ellie. They've been trying to get the address out of our boys, but so far, they've kept their mouths shut."

A door cranks open further up the hall, out of sight, towards the light. Shadows approach. The prickling, tickling sound of something slimy and slug like.

"You let me out of this cage, bogeyman. Unchain me and then we'll see who's tough," shouts a small angry voice.

She's never seen anything quite like the things that slither around the corner. They look as if someone with the world's nastiest cold had sneezed out a full-sized man. Legs replaced with a slimy blob of mucus. Bogeymen.

The pair drag a slumped figure down the steps. Her heart leaps. Dirk?

One blob removes a set of keys from within itself. They shimmer as it unlocks the cage on her left. It carries the figure inside and drops him to the floor. As it leaves, the other hangs a small bird cage containing an enraged Primrose from the ceiling. The pixie glares after them as they ooze back out of sight.

"Mark my words," he calls, gripping the bars of his cage and shaking a tiny fist. "You will get yours."

When they leave, the light from around the corner brightens, and she sees the fallen man's face.

Burt. Unconscious. His closed eyes swollen. Bruises cover his face. His lips are busted open and bleeding.

"Oh Burt," says Betty, sadly.

"Sadie," says Primrose, spotting her. "What are you doing here?"

"I followed the tall men." She looks down. "Where's Iron Bill?"

"I bought my feathered friend time to flee when they shot us down. I hope she is OK. At least we've found your husband."

A small hope rises inside. "Have you seen Dirk?"

"I'm seeing him right now." Primrose points into the shadowy cell on the other side. "Hey," he shouts. "Wake up, Dirk."

There's a familiar snort as someone draws in a sleepy breath. He's been here the whole time.

"What?" he splutters. Movement in the dark. "Sadie, is that you?"

He sits up into the light.

"Dirk?"

She doesn't know how to react. He's told so many lies. But the joy of seeing him overrides everything. She reaches through the gap in the bars towards him. "Are you OK?"

He pushes himself to stand. Hunched, favouring one side. His eyes screw shut for a moment of pain. Like Burt, bruises cover his face. He touches his ribs.

"I've been better." He tries to smile. Reaches for her fingers, but it looks like it causes him a lot of pain. His arm drops. "Why are you here?"

"I came to find you."

"How long has it been?" He leans his head against the bars.

"You said you'd come back Saturday. It's Wednesday."

"Five days." He closes his eyes and groans. "Where's Ellie?"

"I left her with Mum."

His eyes widen. He grips the cage bars with both hands. He rattles them, suddenly furious. "Your Mum?" Not furious, scared.

"It's OK. I've been lighting the candles. You said she would be OK."

He shakes his head. "No. No, it doesn't matter what I said before. She's not OK." Both hands press against his forehead as he paces. "She's not." He glares at her. "How could you do this?" He shouts it. It's not the first time he's ever raised his voice. They've never been the picture perfect couple. But it is the first time he's ever looked at her like that, like he hates her.

His face falls. Regret at his reaction?

Still, she comes back at him. "What do you mean me?" She lets it all out. Can't hold it in. Anger at him for leaving her. Anger at him for not coming back. Anger at him for trapping her in a life she's come to resent, maybe even hate. "You were the one who left us. What was I supposed to do? I have no friends. No other family. No one except you and Ellie." Her breath comes short and fast. Her head, light. "I had to come and find you. I can't raise her on my own. I needed you."

"Nothing is more important than that little girl right now." He says it as if something has changed to make it so, as if it hasn't always been true.

"Nothing has ever been more important," she claps back.

He prods himself in the chest and juts his head forward. An ugly, aggressive look on him. Not one he often displays, but she's seen it before. "Don't you think I know that?" He pauses. Turns away, then comes back. Frustrated. "These people, they're going to hu..." he gags on the words, "they are going to hurt her, and if you've left her with Be—"

"Why? What could they possibly want with our little girl?" She squints at him. Her jaw tightens. "Unless it's something you've done."

"I trapped him. It's my fault."

"Who?"

"Bergerberg." Dirk leans his head against the bars. All energy seeming to have left him at the mention of the name. "The demon inside your mother is more important than I made out." He sighs. "I was a cocky, stupid young man trying to impress a girl. And it's... it's come back to haunt me."

What did he mean by that?

"Who's Bergerberg?" She recognises the name.

"The ruler of Hell. He came to Earth to rule here too. The night we met, I tried to kill him, but something went wrong with the spell. His spirit fled, but his body stayed. I gave chase. But—"

"But it went into my mum."

He nods. "He used the seance your mum was conducting to get inside her. It was as if he knew she was there to use. As if he picked her."

"But what's that got to do with Ellie?"

"The firstborn of the vanquisher is the sacrifice required to return his strength," he says, as if repeating from a book. "I defeated him, and they need her to bring him back." He leans his weight against the bars.

"They want to sacrifice her?" Sadie's lips tremble. She bites them.

"And you left her with him." He stares at her across the gap. Was he really angry at her for something he'd done?

"Oh boy," says Primrose, frowning at Dirk. He shakes his head.

"I didn't know. How was I supposed to know?" She grits her teeth. "You lied to me about everything."

"I was trying to protect you. That's why…" he trails off. Bunches his fists.

"Why what?"

He can't meet her eye.

"You stayed with me to keep an eye on Mum, didn't you?"

"It's not like that…"

But it was. She can tell by the guilt on his face. By the way he continues to look away.

She shakes her head. Tears fall down her cheeks. She points an accusing finger. "You pretended to fall in love with me. You married me. You had a baby with me, just so you could keep track of this thing that you put inside my mother."

"No…" He holds up his hands towards her. "I was young. I've never been cool. And you don't meet many girls in my line of work. You were so amazing, and then when I stopped him, I was given an opportunity."

She folds her arms. "What are you talking about?"

Behind the bruises, his face is pale as bone. With the swelling, it doesn't look like him. Makes it easier for her to stay furious.

"When Bergerberg invaded with his army, it went against the treaty between Hell and Earth. Hell made Betty and me and Burt cover it up. It wasn't the right thing to do, but it was the easiest. Lots of people who fought for us didn't make it. The rest we cast a spell on to change their memory. Made them believe a disease killed their friends, their families."

"That's why The Drake is so confused. That's why he thought there was a war, because there was."

He nods. "He's always continued to believe. I don't know why it didn't work on him."

"There are a few of us who still have memories," says Primrose.

Dirk glances up at him, then continues. "But most forgot about what me and Burt did, forgot about Bergerberg. And Hell said if I watched him then—"

"Why are you working for Hell? I don't understand. I thought you were one of the good guys."

"I am." He points towards Burt, then Betty. "We are. It's complicated. Hell isn't intrinsically evil. Heaven isn't necessarily good. They are just two sides of the same coin. You need both for everything to function. Chaos and order. Torys and um... I don't know... probably not labour, maybe the greens? And The Bureau sits between. We worked in Hell Relations. Demons can be a bit tetchy so we have to deal with the fallout whenever there's a disagreement down there that threatens to spill over up here. And that's what happened with Bergerberg."

"So what was I? Some sort of witness protection perk?" Her rage blossoms. She is so bone-achingly tired she can't think straight, can't contain the anger that rises. Her whole body shakes. "You made a deal with Hell, and you used me." She can't believe it.

"I love you. I need you." His bloodshot eyes plead. "Are you really angry at me?"

She might not be, but the numbness that has built over the last five days, even over the last few years, makes it hard for her to think clearly. Had everything he'd ever said been a lie?

"You don't need me. You just need what I can do for you," she says. She feels as if her body has shut down. That she is just lips speaking words. "You just need me to cook your meals, clean your clothes, and... and..." she squeezes her eyes shut. She feels dirty. "You used me. You used me and went off gallivanting around with this..." she points to Burt, "...putting our lives in danger while I gave up mine for you."

"I should have told you. I've been selfish." He looks down. Doesn't reply for a moment. Takes a deep breath then looks her in the eye. The drip of water echoes in the dark room. Betty sighs. "We don't matter right now," he says finally. "This thing..." he points between them, "...doesn't matter. It has to wait. Ellie is in danger right now. Azalea has the horn from our unit. She can use it to call Bergerberg to them, and he will come. We have to do something, but if we hurry, we might still have time."

At least they agree on something. This *thing* doesn't matter.

"Come on, you two," says Primrose. "We need to work together to get out. We can still save the little one."

Sadie dips her hand into her pocket. Finds the little jar that had somehow made its way through this entire journey with her.

"I have an idea." She bangs a fist on the bars. "Hey," she shouts as loudly as she can. "You snotty buggers. I demand to speak to a lawyer."

"What are you doing?" says Dirk, shrinking away from the bars. "They'll only hurt you."

A shadow crosses the light, turning it a translucent and ghostly green.

"Baaarrrggg," it says, sounding much like an obese sloth on anaesthetic gas and air. It slobs towards them, inching its way down the hall at a snail's pace. "Whaaaat dooooo yooooou blooooody waaaaaantttttt—t?"

"I need to pee." Sadie crosses her legs, hoping to convince her captor.

"Gooooo innn the coooorrrneeer like everyyyybboooodddyyy eelllsssse." It oozes right up to the bars of her cage. Presses its horrific goop of a face through the gap between them, pulling its cheeks taught and squeezing its bugging eyes out of its skull as if it means to watch. Strings of yellow mucus drip from its mouth.

She looks it in the eye and eases open the jar in her pocket.

"Oh, like to watch, do you, big boy?"

The bogeyman nods, flicking tendrils of slime from its face.

With two fingers, she coats both palms in a liberal dose of vapour rub.

"Whaaattssaaat smeeelllll?"

Before it can back away, she claps her hands on either side of its jelly-like face and pulls it towards her. Its mouth gapes wide in pain, jaw dropping like a cartoon dog spotting a beautiful woman in a bikini. A piercing scream erupts from the quivering orifice, blowing stinking, slime filled air into her face as it tries to shake itself free. Despite its frantic motion, it can't escape her grip, the sides of its face having crystallised against her palms.

"Where are the keys?" she screams, as it wrenches her forward against the bars in its bid to get away. She grips harder with her fingers, ignoring the screams of the hardening horror before her. Hating it with every fibre of her being. "Unlock this cell."

"Sadie, wait," says Betty.

A clicking gasp comes from the creature's mouth as it reaches inward with one limb. It pulls the keys from inside and stabs one into the lock. They shimmer as they did before and the door clicks open. She wrenches her hands free, peeling the two sides of its face away.

All structure from the creature disappears and it melts into a sticky puddle on the floor.

"Oh, ho ho!" laughs Primrose. "I told him. I told him he would get his. Marvellous!"

Dirk stares at her through the bars, his mouth agape. "That was amaz—"

"Don't," she says, holding up a crust coated finger. "You and I are not OK, but..." His Adam's apple bobs. "We will talk about us later."

"But—"

"No." She steps out and throws him the keys. "We save Ellie. Then we save us."

He rattles them in the lock as she reaches up to bring Primrose down. His cage is bolted shut with a complex bar, which she manages to undo.

"I want to tell you something, Sadie," the pixie says as he climbs on to her hand and she places him on her shoulder.

Dirk rushes through the ring of keys to find the right one.

Primrose leans towards her ear. "All this morning I've watched those bastard blobs beat this man and his friend black and blue." He points at Dirk. "There was not one second where I thought he would give you and your daughter up. Mortal men fear death more than any other thing. Many would boast otherwise, but those are just words. When faced with death, men crack." He looks up at Dirk with something close to admiration. "But some, the very lucky ones, have a love so deep that they would see themselves die before they gave it up. They know that living, having had that love taken, would be worse than any death. It doesn't matter how things between you began, he loves you Sadie, and he loves your child. He would not be without you." He takes a breath, which has the faintest hint of a tremble. "It is an inspiring thing. Makes a pixie want to hang up his saddle and settle down."

She looks at Dirk. His swollen lips tighten into a smile.

"Dirk..." says Betty as he returns to wrestling with the keys.

His eyes move to her, then back to Sadie.

"I know. I know," he says. He brings the keys up to his lips and mumbles something to them.

"You know that won't work," says Betty.

"I have to try," he says, jamming the keys in the lock once more.

She shakes her head, and, gripping the bars of her cage for support, pulls herself to stand.

"What's the matter?" Sadie looks between them. She feels like she's done something wrong.

"There's an enchantment on the locks." Betty points at the keys with a shaking, long-nailed finger. "They won't unlock for any of us. Only that one." She nods to the puddle of mucus on the floor. "A fail safe."

"What about the other bogeyman." Sadie takes the keys from the lock. Studies them as if she'd know an enchantment when she saw one. "We could get him in here and make him do it." She takes the pot of vapour rub from her pocket.

Betty shakes her head. "You acted too fast."

Dirk sighs. He rubs a hand firmly over his face. "It's OK, Sadie. You didn't know."

"But—"

"Listen," he says, gripping her hand through the bars. His touch is electric. She holds on tightly. "You need to go." He leans his head against the metal. "You need to get Ellie. Take her far away. Hide somewhere." He gazes into her eyes from his cell. "Don't ever look back."

"There might be another key." Her voice rises. She feels so stupid. Has she really doomed them? "We just—"

He touches her chin with his other hand. Holds it still to keep her eyes on his. "This isn't your fault. You can do this. You just need to hurry."

"No..." Her breath shudders. She presses her lips together. "When I found you," she says, "when you came crashing through that window into my life, I thought having a... a warrior husband was right for me." She holds her position. "Someone like my dad, a soldier, a provider, someone who could take care of us." Her breath hitches in her throat. "*You* were supposed to protect *us*. I need you..."

He smiles. Almost laughs. "You don't need me. I just hang on to you." He looks down at his own fumbling fingers. Dried blood cakes his hands. His. He looks nervous. It hurts her to see him like this. "You make everything I do possible. Look how far you've come without me. You don't need me. I need you."

She throws her hands around his waist, draws him against the bars. Lets her cheek crash against his chest. He's bony in her hold. He's lost weight already, and he sways slightly before regaining his balance. "I've missed you. I've missed you so much."

He groans in pain, but his arms wrap down around her shoulders, stopping her from letting go. "You just have to get Ellie away," he says into her ear. The rasp of his stubble welcome against her forehead. "That's all. I love you."

"I love you too." She can't breathe. Her heart is ice in her chest.

"Maaaaaarrrrtiiiin? Wheeeeredyoouuuu goooo?" The second bogeyman slithers around the corner. It stops under the lamp on the wall. Its translucent body gleams in the light like a huge and molten, yellow gummy bear.

"Martin's dead snotbag," shouts Primrose. Using the drawstring of her hoody, he abseils down Sadie's body to the pocket, then removes the open pot of vapour rub. He jumps to the floor. "Fear Lady Sadie's magic pot of nose stuff." He scoops six handfuls of Vicks and slathers himself. "Time I got violent."

The beast shrinks back and blubbers a wet hiss. "Issss thaaat Vicckkkksssss?"

Before it can retreat, Primrose charges head first through its blob of a stomach. It screams as steam hisses out of its mouth and ears. Its face goes slack as Primrose swims up and out of its mouth, covered in gleaming slime. Just like the other bogeyman, its structure liquifies and splashes all over the stone floor.

Primrose bodysurfs the goo back down to the ground at Sadie's feet, then punches a fist in the air. "No one picks on a pixie."

"You are a stone-cold killer, Primrose," says Dirk. "Look after my girls, would you?"

"You have my word, Dirk."

"I don't know where I am. I have no car," Sadie says. "How will we even get back?"

"The witch's vehicle was out front," says Primrose. "I will lead you. Maybe find my blasted bird."

Dirk gazes into her eyes. She can tell he doesn't want her to go. "It's the best chance we have of keeping Ellie safe." His lips tighten as he removes her hand from his. "We'll get out. I'll find you."

She doesn't think she believes him, but he pushes the small of her back gently, guiding her towards the stairs. And though she hates herself for it, she goes. Looking back until she can't see him anymore.

The stairs from the prison lead back up into the corridor she'd found herself running around only hours before. This time the paintings are empty. A dark void left where that loathsome face had been.

"It's this way," says Primrose, moving towards the steps leading back down to the room with all the boxes.

She lifts him to her shoulder and hurries down the steps as he points ahead. The bright fluorescents hurt her eyes as she enters the stone storage room. The boxes are still there. Lids open. Contents gone.

Where were the kids? And what was the witch planning to do with them? She couldn't hope to answer.

The truck is also gone. A cool evening breeze blows through the open archway.

"Out there," says Primrose. "It's the way I came in. Then the witch got me caught up in her infinite corridor, before her tall men came for me. Iron Bill got away."

Sadie crosses to the exit and jumps down to an area of grass that runs between the side of the building and a huge hedge of laurel. She looks back. The building stands four-storeys high. A mansion with walls of sand-coloured stone. It's still not quite the haunted house she'd expected when she'd first set out on her quest, but it's close.

Darkened windows framed with curtains overlook the path, so she keeps close to the wall and sneaks to the left towards where the grass meets a tarmac driveway. It cuts a sweeping black line out across a long green lawn dotted with brightly coloured bushes of blooming azaleas. The flowers are stunning shades of pink and scarlet and purple.

Primrose surveys the heavens. "Where is that bird?"

The night is coming in. The grey, clouded sky above gives the air an ominous dead weight, like all life has been sucked from it.

Parked out front is the black mustang.

A breeze blows in off the lawn.

"What if the keys aren't inside?"

"Let's find out."

It's the only way back to civilisation. Of getting to Ellie as quickly as she can. Of making sure Dirk's sacrifice isn't in vain.

A serious motherly part of her wonders if it has isofix.

She eases out onto the drive. Tiptoes to the car. Tries the handle. It opens. The keys are still in the ignition.

"Seems our luck is in," says Primrose.

She can tell he's talking for her. Trying to stay bright to keep her going.

She looks up at the house. A sand-coloured gravestone looming under dead skies. The black windows, ghostly eyes and mouths.

She places the pixie on the passenger seat and climbs in. Slams the door and starts the engine with a growl. Well, more a primal, motherly yell. And shoots up the path, away from the witch's mansion, away from her husband.

# INNOCENT LITTLE SPONGES

When Sadie arrives at Mum's, she all but batters down the door.

"Once I caught a fish alive..." sings a low growl from upstairs.

"Mum? Ellie?"

A cough. "Er...we're upstairs." It sounds like Mum is putting on a silly woman's voice.

A giggle. A splash. The squeak of a little bottom in the bath.

She sighs. The tension she'd been holding in her shoulders for the whole drive eases. They are safe, for now.

Gripping the bannister, Sadie pulls herself up the stairs two at a time. Primrose lags behind. She tears through the bathroom door.

Mum is on her knees with a beard of bubbles on her face and a flannel in hand gently scrubbing Ellie's back. Ellie holds the measuring jug from the kitchen, happily tipping soapy water all over the place. The floor is flooded. The walls are wet. The door is dripping. They both look to be having the best time.

Sadie can't hold back a laugh. A release of absolute relief mixed with a little mania.

"Did you find him?" asks Mum, pressing herself to stand. Still that voice, like a pantomime dame.

Sadie steps forward, brushing her out of the way.

"What's going on?" Mum frowns.

"I don't have time to explain, Mum." Tears roll down her cheeks. "I need to take Ellie. Away from here. Away from you."

Mum's face falls. But not in the way she might expect. Not in the way you'd expect a granny to react when told she couldn't see her granddaughter. She frowns, confused rather than sad.

"I don't understand. She's safe here with me." She folds her arms.

Sadie grabs a towel from the rack and scoops Ellie out of the water. She wriggles like a fish, unhappy to finish her game so suddenly.

"Something's happened to you, Mum. It's not your fault. It's no one's fault."

"Um..." Mum wrinkles her nose, then looks away, sheepish. She waves a hand. "I'm sure whatever it is, we can fix it. You guys are safe here with me." She holds an arm out. "Why don't we just go have a little cup of tea and chat about this? You can have a whole biscuit this time. Ellie could have a biscuit. I'll have a biscuit. Biscuits for everyone." She squints into the middle distance. "Biscuit? Is that a word?"

Sadie shakes her head. "You're not well, Mum. I've got to take her somewhere else. Somewhere no one can hurt her." With Ellie in her arms, Sadie turns to leave. She has no idea where they'll go, just somewhere else. Somewhere far away.

Primrose finally reaches the top step and hurries across the landing. As if blown by a great wind, the bathroom door slams between them, shutting her and Ellie in and him out. She glances back. Ellie squirms in her grasp. Sadie's hugging her too tight.

Mum's head shakes rapidly back and forth. Her shoulders twitch and wriggle independently of one another.

Terrified, Sadie wrestles with the door handle, but it won't budge.

Mum's sporadic movements abruptly cease, and she opens her eyes with pin-prick pupils. Her voice loses that pantomime dame hoot and drops into a low Cockney-twinged growl as if she has, in the past millisecond, drunk a lifetime's worth of cigar-and-whiskey smoothies, with a little engine oil to spark it up a bit.

"Chill the eff out, Sadie, mate." Mum holds up a warning finger.

Sadie puts Ellie down and stands between them. "Mum?"

Mum scowls. "Naa. 'Sme. Bergerberg."

Sadie's legs turn to jelly. She props herself against the wall to keep from falling.

He puts his hands up. "Woah, woah, woah. Ain't nothin' to be scared of. I ain't gonna hurt ya. Or the little one."

"But...but you're...they're going to sacrifice her to bring you back."

Bergerberg rolls his eyes. Tuts. "It's Azalea, ain't it?" He clenches his fists. "She's an effin' prick, mate. Could never take no for an answer."

He sniffs, runs a thumb under his nose, and spits a globule of something black and revolting into the bath. It floats there, steaming, before sinking into the bubbly depths with a hiss. He ducks down and waves to Ellie between Sadie's legs. Sticks a long, black tongue out.

Ellie giggles. "Beebee."

Sadie finally gets it. "You're Beebee?"

"Thought maybe Bergerberg was a bit of a mouthful."

"You'd be surprised." She hears herself say as if on autopilot. "Her vocabulary is quite advanced..." She cups a hand over her mouth to stop herself from partaking in the baby race.

He smiles. Not Mum's smile. Somehow pointier, as if the mouth expects to have more and sharper teeth in it than it does. "I'd never let 'em hurt the little one. Yeah, sure, back when your boy Dirk killed me, I'd've eaten a thousand kids just for a laugh." He shrugs and blows an amused raspberry. "I did...but turns out it wasn't that funny. I was just angry. I've changed, turned over a new leaf, innit. She's a good influence, your Mum. Helped me find the real me."

"What have you done with her? Where's Mum?"

"Don't get your knickers in a twist," he says, wobbling his head from side to side as if she's being silly. He jabs a thumb over his shoulder. "I've just popped her to the back for a moment. She just blacks out."

Sadie's brain threatens to pour itself out of her ears as a hot frothy soup. "Have I been talking to you the whole time?"

"Most of the time I let her deal with you. She likes to see you. And I still don't really get this place well enough. But we've had a few convos."

She rubs a hand to her forehead. "But what about Dirk's candles?"

"Yeah," he says with a wrinkle of Mum's nose. "Those stopped working a while ago." He wags a finger. "If you came over more, you'd probably be able to tell."

She scratches her ear and looks away. Is a demon from the pits of Hell really telling her off for not going to see her mother often enough? And right after admitting to eating a thousand kids?

She sighs. It's an accurate accusation.

"You do right to act a little sheepish." His finger wagging continues, then he scratches his chin. "Either way, it's lucky for you I can pop in and out whenever I want. You'da been dog food if I hadn't come to check on you the other night."

Sadie frowns. Then her mouth falls open.

"That was you who saved us? You with the gun."

Bergerberg looks proudly off to one side. A ghostly breeze ruffles his hair as if he were standing atop a mountain. "Guilty as charged. I know Dirk's into some dangerous shizznit, so when he's away, I sometimes come and check in on you. Think of me as your guardian demon." He grins.

"But how do you know how to shoot? And why did you bring a gun? You can't have been expecting trouble."

"I know everything your mum knows, and your dad taught her everything he knew. Lovely memories, those."

Sadie shakes her head and smiles. Still so much she doesn't know about her parents.

"And I brought the gun cus there're loads of rats round your way." He holds up Mum's hands as if aiming a rifle. "Can't get good rat in Tesco's, and sometimes I fancy a little treat, so I have to make do."

She curls her lip. Poor Mum. "So we're safe then? If you don't want to hurt Ellie, then that woman isn't going to find her."

Bergerberg shakes his head gravely. "I wouldn't say that. Azalea and her crew are fuckin' nuts."

"Fuckin' nuts," says Ellie with gusto.

"Oops." The corners of Bergerberg's lips tighten downwards.

Sadie gives him a look.

Bergerberg rolls his eyes so far backwards that they pop back up from the bottom. "Oh, don't give me that. I've been trying to cut down on the swears. Do you know how ingrained swears are in Demonese? You can't say good morning to someone down there without effin' this and jeffin' that. Isn't the weather effin' chilly today, Lucifer? Sure as jeff it is, Berg, you effin' jeff. You should be proud. I hardly ever say cu—"

"Bup-bup-bup," hisses Sadie, widening her eyes and holding up a finger in warning.

Bergerberg laughs. "You know, if you'd have bup-bup-bupped me ten or fifteen years ago, I'd've frozen that tongue in your head and pulled it out. Click o' me fingers." He sighs and looks inward, sadly. "What were we talking about?"

"You were saying how crazy that witch is?"

"Witch? Oh, she's more than that." He rubs the back of his neck. His turn to look sheepish. "She's my ex. She'll stop at nothing to bring me back to life." He wrinkles his nose. "She likes the idea of being the mother of the next Antichrist. She wants to punish all men for their sins. She's an effin' psycho. Livin' in the past. Looking to relive the old days." His face hardens, but his shoulders sag. He blows a bitter sigh through his nose and seems to shrink. "She's nostalgic. Loved it when I took her to work with me and she could stick red-hot pokers up people's noses or find new holes to stuff snails in, but when I look back — I mean, properly look back — it was all just a bit immature. It's easy to be nasty to someone, but it never feels good, and they never learn from it." He glances at Ellie a moment and all the distress leaves his face. "When I look at Ellie here, and see what you humans start off like, I can see it's not your fault you sometimes go bad. It's because something or someone effed you up. When I see what some of you go through, when I learn the full story, it's impossible not to love you. You're all just innocent little sponges, soaking up your surroundings. You get broken by circumstance or biology or nurture. We shouldn't be punishing you for that. Back then, I was just going through the motions because that's what they expected of me." He jiggles his head and adopts a well-to-do voice. "Ooo, big prince of Hell, I bet he loves a-torturin'." Then drops the voice and falls into a sullen pout. "Hell was a pretty toxic work environment."

"But some people are just bad, right? What about Azalea?"

"Her family was killed by witch hunters back in the 1700s. Her mummy, her daddy, her sister. Hung up and burnt right in front of her when she was a little girl. All in the name of Heaven and God." He spins a finger around his ear. "Turned her a bit loopy." He shrugs, then ticks off one finger and holds up the next. "And I expect those witch hunters' mums beat 'em with rolling pins when they were little, and that mum's dad probably did something horrible, all the way back to someone's gran getting trod on by a mammoth or something unfortunate. It takes a big person to stop the cycle." He sniffs. "Still, we've got to stop her. Some people are too far gone. Their actions just breed more hate, more hurt. You just have to squish 'em like a black fly on your broad beans."

He pauses. Sadie doesn't know what to say, so she just stares, holding Ellie behind her.

"Azalea loved all that torture," he continues, then pats himself on the chest. "Not once did she let me take a step back and say, is torturing poor souls to within an inch of their sanity what Bergerberg wants? Is it right for me? Maybe if I'd had the chance, I'd have found something I like more…" His face brightens. "Like crochet. Crochet is the effin' biz, mate." He grins. "I made you a little something to go with your wand. It's in the shed. I'll show you in a minute."

"Err, thanks." Sadie thinks back to that crimson snarl of wool she'd seen on Mum's side table in the lounge. "But what can Azalea do now? If she resurrects you, you'll just be like this, but in your old body, right?"

Bergerberg clicks his tongue and shakes his head. "'Fraid not. My old brain, my demon brain, wherever that is, is a little different to a human's. Different wiring, different pathways of thought. Bit less complex. Bit more primal. I've learnt so much using your mum's brain." He taps his head. "But you stick my spirit in that old body, who knows if I'll remember any of it? I sure won't be able to think the same way. It'll be like sticking a supercomputer in a chainsaw. I'll be in there somewhere, deep inside, but unless you can get through to me, chances are I'll be like a big child throwing a tantrum. I'll kill. I'll maim. Do a bit of flailing." He flicks his hand at the wrist as if miming a tennis shot. "And, the first thing I'll do when I'm back in my body," he nods towards Ellie, "is eat her to get myself to full strength."

Sadie's skin prickles. "Then what can I do?"

"They're gonna need me and your mum, Ellie, and my body together in the same place. I don't know how they plan to evict me, though. I don't think Azalea is powerful enough to do what's needed, but—"

"They've been kidnapping kids from the Hanley Estate."

"What's that?"

"They are all natural magic users."

"Eff!" Bergerberg groans. "Azalea is powerful enough to make a whole group of people do exactly as she commands. Maybe one of those kids has a talent for removing spirits and putting them in different bodies. Or maybe..." His brow lowers and his lips tighten for a moment of concern. "...maybe she wants to reopen the gateway. The one I came through. That'd take a lot of power." Then he shakes his head and mumbles something to himself. "They need to find us first, right?"

"Dirk said they could call to you using the blue horn?"

"That only works if I'm willing. And I ain't willing." The door behind Sadie clicks open and Bergerberg moves to pass. "Where's Dirk now? We could do with his help."

"He's..." She bites the corner of her mouth to keep from sobbing. "Back at her mansion. I couldn't free him." She picks Ellie up, wrapping her in the towel.

"Hm. OK." Bergerberg opens the door.

Primrose stands on the other side, fist raised to knock.

"I've been knocking. Didn't you hear me?"

She hadn't.

"What the eff is that?" Bergerberg curls his lip.

"I'm Primrose Applewhistle. You must be Sadie's mother." The pixie removes his hat, kicks out his heel, and bows. "It is a pleasure to meet you, Miss..."

Bergerberg raises Mum's eyebrows. "Na. 'Sme, Bergerberg." He crosses the hall towards Sadie's old room.

"What?" says Primrose, hurrying after them both. He reaches for his missing swords.

"It's OK, Primrose. He's on our side." Sadie trails after Bergerberg. "Dirk's not who I thought he was," she says, picking back up on their conversation.

Bergerberg frowns as he opens her old bedroom door. Ellie's pyjamas are placed neatly on the bed, next to a hot water bottle to warm them up. "Who did you think he was?"

Sadie shakes her head. She doesn't know. She buries her face in her daughter's hair. Breathes it in. "He might be better than I thought he was."

"And after all this, have you realised *you're* better than you thought you was?"

She doesn't know how to answer that.

Bergerberg offers her a gentle smile. "I've watched you from in here." He taps Mum's forehead. "Watched how proud your mother is of you. You've done good, Sadie. And Dirk, he does his best. He's always popping by to check on your mum. I don't think it's just because of you know what..." He jabs both thumbs towards himself. "He's always making sure she's got what she needs. A lovely boy, she calls him, and I reluctantly agree, and only reluctantly because he killed me that one time." Bergerberg considers this. "Changed my life, though, dying, so can't say a bad word about the guy."

She looks down. How could she have just left him?

Bergerberg gently grips her arm. "Don't worry. We'll fix this. Maybe not everything is how you expected it was. Maybe he's made some mistakes in the past. But it's how we move on that matters." He smiles. Then points at himself again. "If we couldn't move on from our mistakes, yours truly would be pretty fu—"

She raises an eyebrow. His lips remain parted as his eyes swivel to Ellie, who watches him in awe.

"—nky." He wrinkles his nose at her.

Sadie feels movement on her shoulder. Primrose stands there clutching a six-inch splinter of wood. "You give me the word, and I'll jam this right in his eye, and we'll make a run for it."

She gingerly removes it from his grasp while balancing Ellie on her hip. "Thanks, but for now I think we're OK."

Bergerberg chuckles. "I like him." He takes Ellie from Sadie's arms and whooshes her through the air to stand by the bed. Crouches to her height. Ruffles her hair with the towel, then bops her on the nose. "Boop."

Ellie grins. A smile so natural and all-encompassing, so happily oblivious, it feels like someone is squeezing Sadie's heart in their fist.

Through the open window in her bedroom she can hear the low steady chug of several large engines, but is too engrossed watching the peaceful play between her tiny daughter and the prince of Hell trapped in her mother's body to notice.

"She's so good for you." Sadie crouches. Bedtimes with Ellie were often akin to trying to hold still a breakdance champion winding up for the big serve.

Bergerberg shrugs. Pulls Ellie's top down over her head. "We're not so different, her and me. Two square pegs living in a round hole world."

Sadie gazes at her beautiful, smiling daughter and her eyes begin to tingle.

A knock comes from downstairs. The rhythmical clatter of a fist on glass. Then a smash and a creak as the door opens.

"Sadie?" Kayder's voice. Thumping footsteps rush up the stairs. "You really shouldn't have taken Betty's car."

# THE LEECH

Bergerberg picks up Ellie and shoves her into Sadie's arms.

"Out the window. Like you used to."

She doesn't have time to question how Mum knows about that. Bergerberg's hands are on her back, guiding her around the bed. Then he rushes back to slam the bedroom door.

Primrose still grips her shoulder. "It's a bit of a way to jump," he says, looking down. "I mean, for you: pixies don't take fall damage."

"There's a trellis. I'm going to need your help."

"You shall have it."

Ellie wriggles in her arms.

"Mummy? Where we going today?"

"For a walk, honey."

Sadie looks out at Mum's old hydrangea trellis. Would it hold? The climb had been risky when she was a sprightly teenager. It's damn near impossible with an extra couple of stone and one arm.

While she weighs up the options, Bergerberg scrapes her old bed across the room and in front of the door just in time. The handle rattles. It shakes on its hinges.

"You don't think a door is going to hold us back, do you?" It's Kayder.

"Go," hisses Bergerberg. "I'll do what I can."

She nods. Looks Ellie in the eyes. "We're going to do a piggy back. Like you do with Daddy. But I need you to hold on yourself, OK? I can't support you."

"Like a game."

Sadie nods. It's hard to breathe. Tries to smile as the door shakes again. "The 'hold on as long as you can' game. You can do it."

Ellie grins, so Sadie throws her around onto her back. Those little hands wrap tightly around her neck and she presses down on them with her chin. Little feet with cold toes tuck into the top of her jeans for a foothold.

"Well done, baby." She hunches her back, giving Ellie more of a level platform.

"I'm brave and strong."

Sadie glances to Primrose. "You make sure she doesn't fall."

Primrose nods, then grips Ellie's fingers with his left hands and Sadie's hoody with each of his rights. Then she steps out, gripping the trellis. Blooming hydrangeas scratch against her face. The wood groans and leans back ever so slightly on the worn screws Dad had attached it with at least twenty years ago.

She takes another step lower. Her eye line drops below the sill as the sound of splintering wood comes from the room.

"I've told Azalea, it's bloody over," comes Bergerberg's voice through her mother's vocal cords. "She should just get over it. Go out with somebody else."

"Oh, she's over it," says Kayder. "Where's the child?"

Sadie's handhold snaps, shooting sharp splinters into her palm. She slips. Catches a branch that seems solid. "Hold on, baby."

"But…" Someone else's voice. They sound confused. "If he's in there, and—"

"It's not for us to worry about. She said this might happen," Kayder says. "Said he might be unwilling. This human body has messed him up. Seize him. As soon as we have him back in that stinking carcass, he won't remember any of this."

Sadie searches for another foothold. It's impossible to find something horizontal to step on in the overgrown bush of winding branches and flowers. Ellie's fingers slide along to her shoulders.

"Mummy, can we stop the game?"

"No," she tries not to shout. "Hold her, Primrose."

She has to move faster.

"The window," says Kayder.

His wolflike face leers over the ledge above. He smiles. "Evenin'."

Ellie slips and Primrose loses his grip on Sadie's hoody, toppling from her shoulder. He lands with a soft thump in the grass below. Sadie throws an arm around Ellie's back to catch her, gripping the branch with only her injured hand. Warm, wet blood oozes between her fingers. She jumps the last four feet, hoping not to land on the pixie, but not having much choice if she does. He's lost somewhere in the overgrown shrubs below. She bends at the knee to take the edge off the drop on to Mum's back lawn.

Skulking moving figures converge on her from the gloom of the garden. Slender forms loom out of the shadows like dimmed street lamps in fog.

"You got her, lads?" calls Kayder, with a clawed thumbs up from the window.

They are all around her. One grips her arm. Ellie screams as they tear her from Sadie's grip.

"No." Sadie tries to force her arm free, but they are too strong. She struggles as they lift her off the ground.

"Mummy!" Ellie screams again, but she's out of sight.

In her frantic struggle to locate her, Sadie catches the eye of her faceless captor. Her vision blurs. Her rage cools to numb apathy. Confronted with such horror, she is poisoned. A small rodent, frozen in the face of a cobra. Her body loses all energy. Her arms and legs fall limp as a tall man flops her over his shoulder and carries her around to the front of the house. Two others follow. They appear almost invisible in the shadow cast by Mum's house and in the soft glow of the orange streetlights, like they've evolved to blend in to the suburbs at night.

She tries to lift her upper body to look back, to see Ellie, but she can't move. Can't see the street she is being taken to where the sound of truck engines rumble. Someone shouts over the noise. Orders she can't quite catch.

Then Bergerberg/Mum is carried out of the front door on Kayder's shoulder. "Get the eff off me, dog boy. If you're a loyal follower of Bergerberg, you'll put me down."

Kayder laughs. "I don't follow you. I did. But you ain't all that anymore."

Bergerberg growls, then spots her. "Sadie? Ah, shit." He struggles, but Mum's body isn't strong enough. "I don't want to hurt the child."

Kayder scoffs. "Do you think I got up the other day and thought, let's just kill a kid?" he says. "I'm not like you, demon. It's the only way. And unfortunately for you lot, I'm incentivised. This is my world, too, but my kind are forced to live in the shadows. Well, not anymore. Things are going to change." He spots Sadie and grins with those terrible sharp teeth. "It's not like she's a puppy or anything."

They carry her towards the garden gate, with Kayder and Bergerberg behind.

"Get the leech!" shouts Kayder to one of the tall men. He drops Bergerberg onto the lawn and straddles him, holding his fists above his head.

Bergerberg leers up in his face. His eyes burn with blue fury. "As soon as I'm back in my old body, I'm coming straight for you."

Kayder's unease at this is apparent in the momentary flash of his eyes, but he doesn't let Bergerberg up. "Where's that leech—" His voice cracks.

A tall man appears at his side and holds out the blob from Dirk's storage unit.

"Don't give it to me! Get it on the woman's head."

The tall man does as he's told, pulling the leech down over Mum's head like a bobble hat.

Bergerberg grimaces. "Get that thing—"

The leech stretches and draws itself further over Mum's face, cutting off Bergerberg's pleas and swallowing her head whole. It pulses rapidly. Mum's body stiffens and tremors and the leech puffs up like a swollen balloon. It slips off and lies on the grass, glowing a deep, swirling blue.

Mum's eyes are closed. Sadie can't tell if she's breathing or not.

"Is it done?" asks Kayder, stepping away from Mum's prone form. He regards the leech the way someone might a ticking bomb. Pokes it with his boot. "One of you pick it up." He points.

The tall man bends and does so.

"But be careful." Kayder takes a step back. "If it bursts, we're dead."

He glances at Sadie. A smile returns to his lips. "Did you think you'd really escaped? We let you go."

She can't speak.

"Leave her here and let's go," he says to the tall man carrying her. "Azalea's expecting us back within the hour. Not long left, fellas." He laughs. Checks his watch. "That was a close call."

The tall man carrying Sadie drops her next to her mother.

She lies on the damp grass, unable to move, while the dogs leave with her baby.

# CROCHET IS THE EFFIN' BIZ

Sadie lies shivering on her back in the cold, dewy grass, frozen in place, fighting to stay conscious. The whisper of wings cuts through the night above her. A flicker of feathers in the orange glow of the streetlights.

"Iron Bill?" says a small voice next to her head.

Sadie swivels her eyes. Primrose stands just by her right shoulder. She hadn't known he was there.

"Sadie, where's the little girl?" he asks.

She tries to speak but can't. Paralysed.

"Don't worry, I've got you." He runs off towards Iron Bill.

The grass rustles as the duck and the pixie draw towards each other.

He quickly returns. Flicks his arm over her face. Her vision fills with sparkling stars that drift lazily down, tickling her cheeks.

"Pixie dust," he says. "That'll get you going."

She takes a breath. The taste of sherbet on her tongue. Miniature explosions detonate in her brain. Supernovas of pink and blue and orange before her eyes. The bone-deep tiredness in her limbs evaporates.

She thaws immediately and sits bolt upright with an enraged scream, filled with thrumming energy. "Ellie!"

She rolls over and rushes to her mother, who still lies flat on her back in the grass. She's breathing, but there's a nasty red mark around her neck where the leech had gripped her by the throat.

Sadie clutches Mum's shoulder and gives her a shake. "Mum, wake up." She looks at Primrose. "More. More dust."

He nods, then takes another fistful of the glittering powder from a pouch on Iron Bill's saddle, hurries over and throws it over Mum's face.

Her eyelids flutter open. She stares past Sadie, straight up at the sky. She blinks, then drops back down to earth.

"Why am I outside?" she says.

Sadie eases a hand under her shoulders and lifts her to sit.

Mum puts a hand to her brow. "Sadie? I feel a bit woozy. Did I fall? I was—" Her eyes spring wide open. "Ellie's in the bath. I left her in the bath." She pushes herself up to stand. Stumbles. Sadie holds her up.

"No, Mum." A cold stone sits in her throat. Her skin prickles. "They've taken her."

Mum's lips tighten into a thin white line. Her nose twitches. Sadie has never seen this look on her face before. Maybe the exchange between Mum and Bergerberg hadn't been one-sided. Maybe Mum had learnt a few things from him. "Then we get her back."

"Yeah?"

"We can't just do nothing."

Sadie leans back. Mum's look stirs her confidence.

"We have to prepare. We can't just go in; we'll need to fight."

"Look what IB's brought you," says Primrose, holding up the tentacle wand.

Sadie takes it. Turns it over in her hands. "Where did she get it?"

"She says..." he pauses. Looks questioningly at Iron Bill. The duck nods. "She says it found her. She said Dirk's still alive. Saw Azalea and her tall men walking him and the kids to the gate."

"What gate?"

"The Hell gate."

Bergerberg had mentioned something about a gate earlier.

"Do you know how to find it?"

"Iron Bill does."

"What is that?" says Mum, pointing at Primrose. "Is this your friend with a duck?"

"Primrose, meet Mum. Mum, meet Primrose."

"Janet," says Mum, holding out a pinched finger and thumb. The pair shake.

"An honour," says Primrose.

"We're going for that gate," says Sadie.

"Then that's three of us," says Primrose.

"Four," adds Mum.

A plan develops in Sadie's mind. A way to use what little she knows. "OK, Mum, we need as many thermos flasks as you've got. And plastic bottles." She pats her hands together in thought. "How about petrol?"

Mum leads them through the front door. "I have flasks in the kitchen. And Dirk might have filled some petrol canisters in your dad's shed for the lawn-mower."

"Boil water. As hot as you can get it. Fill the flasks. Get them ready in a bag." She pauses. "And a lighter."

Sadie leaves them in the kitchen and heads to the back door.

"The key is on the windowsill as you go out," Mum says, pointing as she fills the kettle. "Don't know what it's like. I don't go out there anymore."

Sadie takes it, throws open the back door, and hurries to Dad's workshop. She unlocks the padlock and opens the door. The warm, air-thickening odour of oil, solvents, and wood hits her. She fumbles for the piece of string that turns on the light.

Everything has been shoved to the sides. Stacked boxes, old paint tins, dust sheets, bits of wood that her father had always said might come in handy one day, assortments of screws and bolts and nails. It strikes her in that moment that a man's shed is the very definition of a fire hazard. Covering the floor are scraps of crimson wool. To her right, a washing line runs from one end of the shed to the other. Dangling from it, hung by their tails, are two enormous dead rats.

Something stands in the centre of the shed, covered in a dust sheet. It comes to her shoulder. It hadn't been here when Dad was alive.

When she takes a handful of the sheet, it crunches in her palm with old paint and turpentine. She pulls.

Mum's old wooden mannequin stands beneath. It had been in the attic since before Sadie was born. Draped over its shoulders is a crocheted crimson cloak.

Woven around the hem are several metal disks. Two more sit at the collar. They gleam with the sheen of oil on water.

"What's that?"

She turns. Mum and Primrose stand in the open doorway. Mum wears Dad's old army rucksack done up tight on her back. She has his rifle slung over her shoulder. His cap is on her head. Bullet bandoliers cross her torso. Primrose sits atop Iron Bill with Mum's neatly sawn-off knitting needles sheathed at his hips, and a steak knife strapped to his back.

"I was going to ask you." Sadie removes the cloak from the mannequin. The wool is thick. It's warm to the touch.

Sadie threads her arms into it. It comes down to her knees. She touches the metal rings that sit on her collarbones. They are freezing cold, yet have a comforting weight, like lead.

"Bergerberg's gift," she says.

"Who's Bergerberg?" says Mum. "The name's familiar. Old uni friend?"

"Yeah, something like that." Now wasn't the time.

"It looks good on you," says Primrose. "A real sorcerer's robe..."

She holds her arms out. It fits very well.

"It suits you," says Mum. She points. "Ah look, the petrol?"

Sadie follows her finger. Two small plastic canisters sit with her dad's old Flymo beneath a workbench as marked and worn as the one in Dirk's storage unit. She opens one. Gives it a sniff. Yep. Grabs the other. It's full.

"Have you got Dad's lighter?" Sadie asks.

Mum hands it over.

"And we'll need tape. And if Iron Bill is right about that gate, we're going to need some cold-weather gear."

She hopes she can do what she intends. If not, they'll likely all be dead before morning.

# Bergerberg Returns

Iron Bill leads the way, flying just ahead of Sadie's car, back towards Azalea's mansion, back the exact way she'd come earlier in Betty's mustang. They take a different road just before the entrance to the mansion's driveway. The winding country lane leads up through overhanging trees. A forest she presumes is on the land where the mansion is built.

As she drives, Sadie wonders if Azalea's house came with her previous body, or perhaps the one before that.

Her car whines as they take sharper and more precarious turns up the wooded hill. After the third, the spire of a church appears through the trees. It is jet black against the clouded night sky. It looks old and forgotten. Had Azalea built this here?

Staggered and leaning gravestones surround the building within a spike-tipped fence. She expects that if there were no forest, she could see Azalea's mansion from here, but a dense covering of spindly, spider-like trees tops the hill, obscuring her view of the surrounding landscape.

"Is this it?" asks Mum, as they pull up. She leans forward and peers up through the windscreen at the ghastly silhouette in front of them.

Sadie kills the engine and the lights. The building is all angles and points. Leering gargoyles loom on the two pillars either side of the opening where a gate may have once been. In the distance, thunder rumbles. On cue, the sky flashes with lightning.

"Oh, definitely." Sadie steps from the car as Iron Bill and Primrose come to land on top of it. They climb up on to her shoulders. Having them there, and wearing this robe, fills her with confidence.

She leads Mum through the gateway and stops behind a large gravestone.

"Look," she hisses.

Two tall men stand by the door.

"Leave them to me," says Primrose.

Iron Bill takes to the sky.

Moments later, the duck sweeps silently over one tall man's head, depositing a small grey blob, then jams her razor-sharp beak in the other's ear. Both topple to the ground like the last tenpins in a bowling alley.

She and Mum creep up the graveyard path.

"Good show," says Sadie, giving the pixie a thumbs up.

He is already saddled up, ready to go.

The door creaks open as she pushes it. The only light in the interior of the old church is that of the grey moon shining from behind the clouds and through broken stained-glass windows.

"Where do we—?" There's a faint glow of orange light at the far end of the nave. And now she's focusing that way, she can hear a rising vocal chant. A discordant scream of many voices, children's voices.

She hurries up the aisle towards the pulpit. Hidden behind the altar are steps leading down beneath the church. With Mum close behind, she descends directly into a huge open chamber.

She ducks behind a pillar that flanks the stairway. Mum does the same on the other side.

The chamber is a cavern cut beneath the earth, filled with the sound of an ungodly choir that shrieks and swells. A chorus of cacophony.

Above, the domed ceiling is daubed with disturbing images of demons fighting in some sort of hellish arena. Architectural spirals wrought of bone and stone curl in unnatural patterns around the paintings.

A huge rectangle of obsidian stands on a platform against the back wall. It's taller than a house and nearly as wide. The black frame is inscribed with unknown runes and decorated with skulls both human and other.

A crowd stands in a semi-circle before it, blasting it with the sound from their mouths, though she can see they are unwilling. The eyes she can see are wide with fear and their bodies blasted by a wind she does not feel. Cheeks pulled taut. Clothing whipped and pulled tight against their skin.

The choir comprises the kids from the estate. In their midst are horns, tails, wings. She can see Wren and the green-eyed boy. The Drake too. He is the oldest, by some way.

A glowing white light pours from them, feeding the frame, filling the space in its centre with energy that moves and ripples and bubbles like lava. The shapes of serpents, and skulls, and screaming faces writhe in the swirling mass that swells there.

A heavy weight presses down on Sadie's chest. In front of the frame, asleep on a small altar surrounded by burning candles, is Ellie.

With all this fire around her daughter, she will need to be careful.

Dressed in black robes, looming over Ellie with a knife in hand, is Azalea. She lifts her arms like a conductor, drawing the terrible sound from the crowd.

Several more tall men lurk nearby. Kayder is there holding the swollen leech.

Between them and the choir of kids is a huge black tarpaulin. It covers something. Something big.

To the side, standing frozen like statues, are Dirk, Burt, and Betty in Azalea's old body.

The witch lifts her arms, ripping one final dissonant chord from her unconsenting choir, and the swirling mass between the supports of the frame solidifies.

Now, beyond the frame of obsidian, is an open, icy plane. Grim and gloomy. Blanketed in fog. Grey clouds darken the expansive sky. Simmering flashes of silver lightning crackle above them. Mountains stand far in the distance, and great, dead husks of tree trunks break up the flat landscape, pointing to the sky like severed hands.

Dirty flakes of snow flit across the threshold like ash, spattering the floor with slowly melting grey.

"Hell," whispers Primrose. "She's opened the gate."

"Kayder," says Azalea, dropping her hands and placing the knife on the altar next to Ellie. She holds an upturned palm towards the tarpaulin. "Let's get this show on the road."

He tugs at the tarpaulin. Beneath is a hulking mass of matted navy fur, like some great bear. One door-sized paw covers its face. At its head is an enormous pair of sharp, light blue horns. One is broken.

Bergerberg's body drips with water and, now the tarpaulin has been removed, the stink of swamp permeates the air. Though, considering he's been dead for eight years, the body doesn't appear to have rotted away much, if at all, as if even bacteria were too scared to get involved with devouring this corpse.

Kayder passes a nervous look to Azalea.

"What are you waiting for?" she snaps.

"OK," says Sadie. "I'm going down there."

She passes Iron Bill the wand. She wants to appear unarmed in front of the witch; doesn't want Azalea to take the wand as she had before in the mansion. Sadie pulls down the sleeves of her robe. They only have one shot.

"We have to wait until Bergerberg is back inside his body."

Primrose clambers aboard Iron Bill and the pair float from her shoulder to the ground.

"Good luck, Lady Kilmore."

Down below, Kayder takes a deep breath, then pulls the leech down over Bergerberg's head. It flashes and bulges, and the bear's body jolts as if electrocuted.

Unarmed and unafraid, Sadie inches down the steps. Below, Kayder backs away from the monstrosity as its huge chest starts to rise and fall.

"He rises." Azalea clasps her hands together, her joy so mundane, as if she were referring to a perfect loaf of bread ready to be baked, and not the body of a demon who is also an ex-lover. "Isn't it wonderful how everything can come together at the last moment? Before long, he'll be up and the show can begin."

Sadie carries on, the choir of children masking her approach. She presses through until she's standing at the front of the crowd.

Azalea spots her first. She turns her head with a puzzled look on her face. "This is an interesting development."

"You know he's not going to hurt her, don't you?" Sadie says. "My Mum has changed him. He'll more likely kill you."

The tall men step forward, and Azalea holds up a finger. "Wait." Her voice snaps like a dry twig. She holds out a hand towards Sadie and closes her eyes. "You're unarmed? Why are you here?"

"I've come to ask you to return my husband and child. I'm going to ask nicely once, and then I'm going to take them."

Azalea lifts a black eyebrow. "Do you think I'm an idiot?"

"You must be, if you think I would spend eight years married to one of the world's greatest demon hunters without picking up a few tricks of my own." She grins, showing teeth. "Or maybe it was me who taught him everything he knows."

"She's bluffing," hisses Kayder. He licks his lips.

"Look at you." Sadie allows the contempt she feels for this woman to fill her voice. "Dressed in those stupid robes. Waving your hands around like some demented conductor." She scoffs. "Like who's even bothered enough to be evil anymore? You can get pretty much everything you want just by being nice. Being a dick is so passé. There're plenty of other hobbies you could have. Like crochet. Crochet, apparently, is the effin' biz. Why don't you ask your ex?"

Azalea glowers. "You know, when I took over Betty's body and received a residual of her memories, and I found out he had been with another woman all this time..." Her jaw tightens. Her cheeks dip and, in the light from the candles on Ellie's pedestal, her face resembles a skull. "It's safe to say I was a little peeved. It stung knowing he'd been up here all this time and had just been blanking me. If I'd have known where your mother lived back then, I'd have come straight round and done the both of them in, then and there." She gives Sadie a filthy, toothy grin. "But time heals. And you know what they say: best way to get over one demon is to get under another." There's a dangerous glint in her eye. "Bergerberg's brother is twice the demon. You'll see when Gyozarg takes the throne."

A scratch of claw on stone and Bergerberg's arm uncurls from beneath his body. A growled groan, then he lies still once more, breathing heavily.

"Why are you bringing him back if you've found somebody else? Why can't you just leave us alone?"

"It's not as simple as that, is it?"

"It could be."

Azalea's eyebrow twitches. Her pursed lips go white as they press together. "How is my revenge ever going to be wrought on the kingdom of Heaven if I do not control the most powerful beasts in the whole of Hell?" She moves away from the pedestal where Ellie lies, and closer to the top of the steps. "It was men who harmed me. Men who called themselves Christians. Men who called themselves good. Good men need to be wiped from the surface of this Earth. And then we shall turn our sights on Him up there. The real enemy." She points upwards. Then back into the desolate landscape on the far side of the doorway. "The regents in charge of Hell won't do anything, but if Gyozarg were ruler, then..." She smiles. "But he only gains his kingdom once he's fought and killed his brother for it. Until Bergerberg dies, he will never be number one. The battle must be fair, and to do that," she moves down the steps towards Bergerberg's body and gives it a good solid kick. "Hey, fatso, wake up, I've got snacks."

Sadie squeezes her fists and tries not to let anger get the better of her. "I'm going to count to five. If you haven't released my husband and child by the time I have, I'm going to kill you."

"Oh, you will?" Azalea raises an unbelieving eyebrow.

"One."

Azalea prods Bergerberg in his massive ribs. "Come on, lazybones. Up you get. If you're quick, you can eat the mother first."

"Two."

Azalea rolls her eyes with a shake of her head. "He used to be so ambitious. Used to leap out of bed with a spring in his step."

"Three."

Azalea leans right into Bergerberg's ear. "Still managed to mess up the invasion, though, didn't you? After everything I did to open the gate and let you through." She pokes him again. "Didn't you? Bet your brother wouldn't have buggered it up."

Sadie can see why Bergerberg dumped her.

"Four." She eases the lighter from her pocket.

Azalea turns and hitches up her robes, jumping up the steps two at a time.

"Four and a half."

"Oh, she's boring." The witch flicks a hand at her tall men. "One of you kill her, will you?"

As the tall men stalk forward, Sadie rolls up her sleeves and uses her opposite hands to undo the bottles taped to each arm.

"Five."

Iron Bill lands on her shoulder with wand in beak. Sadie takes it, and with all her focus on the oncoming tall men, flicks it through the air with her right hand whilst thumbing the lighter at its tip with her left.

"Petrol whip!"

A jet of petrol shoots from the two plastic bottles duct-taped to her wrists and ignites the flame with the lighter at the tip of the wand. A column of fire engulfs the three nearest tall men. The heat is almost unbearable, but Sadie doesn't blink. Azalea staggers back, her robes smoking.

A shot rings out from far behind. Another tall man drops.

Sadie focuses all of her energy on Azalea. "Move it!" she screams over the crackling flames.

Azalea raises a hand, deflecting the spell in a sphere of red around her. She says something and sends a bolt of red light back at Sadie. Sadie expects it to hurt, but the light just washes over her and nothing happens. The disks at her collar feel hot against her skin. For a split second, Azalea looks frightened at the lack of effect her spell has had. But then she shakes her head.

"Kayder. Get her."

He starts forward, a greedy gleam in his eye.

Sadie tears the plastic bottles from her wrists and throws them to the ground as tall men crackle and burn. The snap of a rifle sounds from the back of the chamber and two more tall men fall.

She pulls the thermos from a pocket in her robe, spins the cap off, and waves her wand at Kayder.

"Water whip."

A jet of hissing, steaming water shoots into his face and he falls to the ground, howling in pain.

Azalea lifts Ellie in front of herself like a shield. "She's right here!" she shouts at Bergerberg, stepping back towards the portal. "Take her. The first-born of the vanquisher."

To Sadie's right, Bergerberg growls, then presses himself to his feet. He removes the demon leech from his head and drops it to the floor with a wet splat. Though he stands hunched, he is still at least twelve feet tall. He lifts his burning blue eyes to gaze at Ellie with open hunger. He licks a black tongue over a grill of long, cutting fangs, then takes one step forward. He reaches out and picks her easily from Azalea's grasp.

"Your brother waits for you on the other side." Azalea grins. "You have fallen from Hell's grace and he calls you forth to fight. If he destroys you in battle, he will take your place as heir to the throne, but if you are the victor, your transgressions will be forgotten. Take the child. Devour her before him. Destroy him for your honour."

Bergerberg looks past her through the portal. He doesn't speak.

"No!" shouts Sadie. "Bergerberg, Beebee, remember who you are. Fight with us... Remember Ellie."

He turns to look at her. Those cold pupil-less eyes just burn. A murderous sneer crosses his face.

She'd been wrong. He isn't who he was.

"Go," cries Azalea, stepping out of his way.

Bergerberg lumbers forward on three limbs, carrying Ellie through the gate into the icy cold of Hell.

"Wait." Sadie doesn't know what else to say. She looks past Azalea through the portal as that great blue shape disappears into the bleak landscape with her daughter.

"Stop whining and kill her," says Azalea, snapping her fingers at Kayder as his face steams.

The wolf stands. His hairless head is red and swollen. Without speaking, he draws the hook from his jacket and slides it ceremoniously between his fingers, closing his hand around the grip.

Sadie wrestles with the lid of another thermos, but he is too close.

"Few get away from me as many times as you," he says.

Sadie steps back, trying to ready a 'Move It' spell, but it's hard to focus with everything going on.

He lifts his arm. "But no one ever escapes."

Something drops from above, landing between his ears.

"This is for Daisy Butterdew." The pixie lifts his blood-stained knitting needles high and shoves them into Kayder's scorched ears.

Sadie takes the opening. Her magic doesn't seem to work on Azalea, but she's got to try something. She dives forward and kicks her right in the arse as hard as she can.

"Oof," says Azalea, falling to her knees, gripping her cheeks in pain.

At the same time, the kids from the estate start to murmur, and Dirk, Burt, and Betty fall to the ground. Azalea's concentration, and the spell she held over them all, is broken.

A tall man looms forward, grabs Sadie by the hair, and drags her away from his mistress. A swish of wings and something short and brown impales his chest. Iron Bill rips out his still-beating heart and spits it to the ground. She quacks and swoops away towards another tall man.

"You're too late." Azalea ascends several feet into the air, surrounded by a red bubble of energy. With a wave of her hands, she flips and flies through the gate in pursuit of Bergerberg. Her red bubble marks her as a retreating glow in the hazy grey and snow-covered landscape.

The crack of a shot. "Bugger," says Mum from halfway down the steps.

Sadie rushes to Dirk, who is already standing. She helps him. "Bergerberg has taken Ellie."

His eyes widen.

"We have to go after her," he says, moving to help Betty.

"Bergerberg can't be allowed to regain his full strength." Burt eases himself up. His gaze travels quickly between Sadie and Dirk and his face tightens into a guilty smile. "And of course we can't let him eat your child."

"One of these days, Burt, I am going to smack you," says Sadie.

Dirk stares past them both at the landscape through the gate.

Mum throws down her rucksack and pulls out the contents of a winter sports catalogue. "We've got coats, gloves, hats, scarfs, long johns."

"Oh, nice one, Mrs. Bennet," says Burt.

Sadie, Dirk, and Burt wrestle them on. Mum is already dressed in a large coat and thermal trousers.

While they dress, Betty shuffles away towards the tarpaulin under which Bergerberg had been. She bends with difficulty and picks up the leech.

"You don't have to come, Mum," says Sadie. "You've done enough."

Mum tuts. "Like you could stop me."

Dirk moves closer to the doorway. "I know what they're going to do. We have time if we hurry."

The Drake emerges from the awakening members of Azalea's choir. "I will come with you," he says, his eyes, set like stones, staring beyond the gate. "These people killed my boy."

Dirk touches his arm. Looks at the gathering crowd of kids behind him. "I need you here to look after these kids, and to close the gate if we don't make it back."

He shakes his head. "I don't know h—"

Dirk cuts him off. "You've done it before." He holds a hand out. "Sadie, pass me your wand."

She does.

Dirk looks to the ceiling a moment as if remembering. "It's been a while since I've used this one, but I think it's..." He flicks his wrist. "Oh, where's my bag?" A satchel appears on his shoulder. Then he points his wand at Burt. "Oh, where's Burt's bag?" And another satchel appears on Burt's shoulder.

Dirk hands her back her wand, then removes a book from his bag and presses it into the Drake's hand.

"With this, you can do it again."

The Drake shakes his head with pursed lips. "It was all true, wasn't it? The war. I wasn't making it up."

Dirk meets his eye and nods. "I'm sorry, my friend. I will explain, but just know that we did what we did to keep everyone safe."

The Drake lets out an exasperated breath then nods. "How long should I give you?" he asks, stiffening and readjusting his beret.

Dirk stares out through the gate. His lips work. Calculating. "If we're not back in four hours, we're not coming back, and curious things are going to start coming through."

"OK." The Drake claps his hands and calls to the kids. "I want the youngest of you at the back. Those of you who have trained offensive spells with me form a line at the front."

The kids split into two groups. The eldest gather around him as he gives orders.

Betty returns with the leech. She turns the blob over in her hands. "I want to come with you," she says.

Burt fusses. "Who knows what that cold will do to you? You should stay here. "

She rolls her eyes at him. "Not like this, Burty." She holds up the leech with liver-spotted hands.

He shakes his head. "No, no. You don't know what it'll be like in there."

"I know it can't be much worse." Her body sags. "This isn't me, Burt. I'm through there." She nods past him through the Hell gate. "Help me."

Burt glances at Dirk. Dirk shrugs as if to say he can't argue with her.

"Alright. But let me help you." Burt takes the leech from his sister, and moves around her back. "Are you sure?"

"Yes. Just make sure you get me back in soon. Can't imagine that old crone has been keeping up with my squats. I'm going to have lost all my gains."

Burt gives them all a worried look over her shoulder, then places the leech on her head.

It pulses and throbs the same way it had when they'd taken Bergerberg from Mum, and Azalea's old body goes limp. Burt catches it as it falls to the ground.

He removes the leech with the same care one might carry a newborn, then places it into his satchel.

The four of them, Mum, Burt, Dirk Kilmore: Demon Hunter, and his wife, Lady Sadie the Sorcerer, stand on the threshold of the gate into Hell. Iron Bill lands on Sadie's shoulder with Primrose. A wet slurry of snow spatters against their coats.

"I hate the cold," says Burt, rubbing his hands together.

"Keep on your toes," Dirk says, as he steps through the portal. The sky is a swirling mist of grey where dark shadows swoop and dive. "If I'm right about where they're going, then we can expect nasties at every turn."

# To The Cold Pits of Hell

The cold leaches into Sadie's bones like a weight, sapping her energy. Her coat is thick, but it's as if the ice and snow want to get at her flesh, creeping up the gaps in her winter armour like a living thing with intent to do harm as she shlocks through the inches-thick ice in shoes barely capable of keeping out a light drizzle.

Behind them, the portal stands open in the grey mist of sleet, a gradually disappearing oasis of warm light in an otherwise desolate landscape through which she can see the Drake and the kids preparing for whatever may come.

Dirk charges ahead. A relentless black shape trudging through the snow, wand drawn, following what little remains of Bergerberg's tracks. Keeping pace with him is pummelling. Sadie glances back to check on her mother, but she appears to be happily engaged in an energetic conversation with Burt regarding the weather.

Just above, the dark silhouette of Iron Bill and Primrose circles.

Ahead, blurred by the thick fuzz of fog or smog that hangs across the plains, a huge mountain range breaks up the horizon. It could be near or far. It's impossible to tell in the light. Lightning flickers. Red bolts fork down from the blackened sky, illuminating the jet-black mountains in stark, crimson relief. And beyond, great tentacle-like things stretch up to the clouds and sway in the flashing light.

She guesses they are heading to the mountains. They could have at least put the portal a bit closer...whoever 'they' are.

Just ahead of the great, rocky range, two giant geometric shapes of what appear to be featureless stone hang suspended high in the air. One zips away, reappearing in an instant far in the distance to their right. The other just hovers there. It emanates a sense of intrigue, like a slight and curious turn of the head to examine the oncoming newcomers — as if it's alive.

Above them, high above Primrose and Iron Bill, creatures swoop and squawk in the bleak winter skies — terrible black-winged shapes that only ever emerge for a split second from the bulbous grey clouds.

Here and there, breaking up the flat plains, cyclopean columns of stone rise up, disappearing into the dense cloud as if they hold up some great ceiling miles above everything here.

Could Hell be a tangible, reachable place, deep beneath the Earth's crust?

"Dirk!" she calls. "Wait."

The snow that covers the ground, a thick dirty slurry of grey-brown, deadens all sound. Even the thud of her footsteps crunching beneath her seems distant.

He glances back. Slows so they can draw level with his eyes pointed to the sky.

"We're lucky," he says. "Bergerberg must have spooked the nightfliers." He points his wand up. "Otherwise, they'd be down here after us by now. We don't have much time 'til they realise we're not with him and so good for eating."

She glances up at those dark, dancing shadows.

"I need you to help me understand," she says. She feels more lost now than she has over the last week. "Where is he taking her? Who is he, really?"

Burt and Mum continue their conversation behind. They've moved on to the correct amount of yeast to use in the perfect loaf.

"What's happening here?" she says. "And what do you have to do with some war?"

"Before I met you, Bergerberg was the ruler of Hell. Took over when his father, Beelzebub, renounced the throne. Then he invaded Earth with an army. Azalea's followers opened that gate we just came through, and his demon horde poured through. I guess they didn't expect much resistance. But, by God, we resisted. The war wasn't long — Burt and I saw to that when we took him out — but I messed it up. We killed his body, but his soul escaped."

"That happened the night we met." It's not a question, but a confirmation.

He smiles at her. "The night I met you, everything about my life changed for the better." He scans the heavens, his brow furrowed. "When he was defeated,

Bergerberg's army fell apart. We cut off the head, and the body died. The ones that could, fell back through the gate. Then we closed it behind them. It's why she needed the kids — to reopen it."

"Why wasn't it guarded?"

"It was." He presses his lips together. "Kayder and his pack."

"I see. But what I don't understand is why everyone is so confused? No one at the Bureau knows who you are."

He glances back to Burt and lowers his voice. "As Bergerberg never truly died, his brother couldn't take his place as ruler, and a group of demons calling themselves Hell's Regent Parliament seized control. Bergerberg's invasion broke the treaty Hell had with Earth. The regents wanted to know where Bergerberg was so they could incapacitate him and continue their reign, and I wasn't going to tell them. So instead, Betty, Burty, and I made a deal with them. We'd cover it up so that Him upstairs never found out. And they wouldn't murder us for knowing. We made everyone forget. Chalked up the loss of life to a disease." He grimaces and wipes stray snow from his face. "But it seems Azalea never forgot."

"Why didn't you try and finish him off if you knew where he was? Or tell those bigwigs in Hell?"

"I didn't know how to do it without hurting your mum, and Hell wouldn't have cared. They'd have carted her off like that." His gloved fingers make no sound when he clicks them. "Locked her up in Hell."

"You risked the fate of the world because you didn't want to hurt my mother?"

"I'd do anything for you."

"Except tell me the truth." She raises an eyebrow. "We could have talked about this. Dealt with it together."

He stops and takes her hand. Burt almost careers straight into his back, instead swerving and falling into a slimy snow drift with a baffled, "woah".

"I'm sorry. I should have told you." He grabs Burt's hand and pulls him up, then starts marching again. "I just didn't want you to worry. I guess I was too confident. I didn't think any of this could happen."

She carries on after him, watching him side on. His eyes are fixed on the horizon with grim determination. He looks different beneath the bruises. It's a side of him she's never witnessed. The unrelenting warrior. He's not just the man she knows at home: the father, the provider, the husband. He's a demon hunter. It's as much a part of him as those other titles. More deeply ingrained because it has been there longer.

"Bergerberg says his old body will change him back."

"Yes, he has reverted to his old self. But we can fix it. He's still in there somewhere. We just have to communicate with that part of him. Cut through that relentless demonic anger to the area of his brain that can reason." He looks at her with a meaning she can't decipher. "Gyozarg will want a fair fight against his brother, so he will wait until Bergerberg is at full strength. Demons are also massive show-offs, so he'll make sure there's an audience to watch him win. That means Ellie has time. We have time to save her."

"But then what?" Dirk's words aren't filling her with hope. "We get there, and get our baby back in front of an entire army of hellions looking for a show. What then?"

"There are two ways for Bergerberg to attain full strength." He swallows hard. "You know the first. The second is this." Without slowing, he dips into his satchel and draws a sword. The same sword he'd been wielding when he'd smashed through Mum's window. "This is what I killed him with the first time. His strength is stored inside. If we can get through to him and give him this, then he has a chance of winning. And if he can kill Gyozarg, then he'll be in charge again. Maybe he'll let us leave."

"Maybe?"

"All I've got is maybe." He gives her that look again, like somehow she'll know what to do. "I'm hoping between us we can figure it out."

A warning quack comes from above. Dirk aims his wand to the sky and, with a flick of his wrist, shouts "Infernus!"

Something explodes above, and a flaming, shrieking ball of writhing limbs drops straight for them. Sadie's life flashes before her eyes, but her wand arm flicks as if on autopilot. "Move It!" she shouts, and the burning creature is caught and thrown to the snowy ground several metres away.

"Nice one," says Burt, then to Dirk: "Took us a month to get 'Move It' down."

Mum takes a deep breath. "How much further?"

"The amphitheatre is just up that nearest mountain. We need to get there before Bergerberg's brother." He looks up once more. "And before any more nightfliers spot us."

They trudge on in silence until they step into the shadow of the strange geometry of stone suspended high above. It regards them from the sky, tipping down slightly to face them.

"I'm not the only one who thinks it's looking at us, right?" Sadie gazes up, blinking the falling snow from her eyelashes.

"It is. It's a watcher, I think," says Dirk, without stopping. "It shouldn't hurt us."

"No, they just like to watch," adds Burt.

Dirk leads them to the foot of the mountain. Amidst the grey husks of ancient trees, which despite the absence of sun still seem to cling like unwanted nostril hairs to the nose of the mountain, a series of craggy steps rise up the side to what looks like a plateau roughly fifty feet above. The steps are each over a metre tall.

"Before Bergerberg's invasion," says Dirk, "to settle their differences, Hell and Earth would send a champion here."

"Were you a...a champion?"

"No. This was before my time. The last time Hell bested one of our champions was in 1939." He pulls himself up the first step and offers her a hand. "They demanded a gift of souls, so Earth's leaders gave them one. Six years of war. Unofficially, six years, six months, and six days."

"Why do they get to make demands?"

"Souls are like a currency down here to be spent and traded. Demons used to come up and take them, but Heaven saw Hell becoming too powerful. They changed the rules. Now, every fifty years Hell's ruler gets to make a demand for more from Earth. And Earth get to put up a fight. One champion against the ruler of Hell."

She scrambles up the frozen stone behind him, feet slipping on the slurry-covered rock. Then he and Burt help her mother.

"Every fifty years? But there wasn't a great war in 1989?"

"We won that one." Dirk continues up the mountain. "A champion from Earth came forward. But this time, they weren't a natural magic user, as others had been before. She was a powerful sorceress. Someone who'd learnt spells like Burt and me." He looks at the wand Sadie still holds in her hand. "That belonged to her. I learnt that, long after I found it, when I started working for the Bureau. She defeated Bergerberg's father, Beelzebub. Humiliated him so utterly that Bergerberg, in his fury, and with Azalea goading him, raised an army."

Something makes a sound in the trees to their right. Dirk trains his wand, but whatever it is retreats screeching into the grey.

"Nearly three decades later," he continues, as the steps shorten, making the going easier, "when he was sure no one was watching, Azalea's cultists opened the gate, and he came through to avenge his father. It had been the first time an army had invaded Earth in centuries. Broke all the treaties. Magic users from all areas of the world were called forward to stop it. The fighting lasted ten days." He looks down and listens. "Hear that?"

Somewhere above, over the shriek of the wind and the click and rustle of the trees, she can hear the hiss of an audience. A gathering of many, many baying voices.

"Despite the brevity of the fighting," continues Dirk, "we lost a lot of good people. A lot. Burt and I got to Bergerberg the night I met you. I was supposed to use that wand to stop him. I tried to use the spell that our last champion used in the arena, but it didn't work."

"You messed it up, you mean," says Burt; not nastily, more as a boyish rib.

Dirk gives him a narrow-eyed look. "I didn't mess it up." He traces a shape in the air with his wand. "I've gone over that moment hundreds and hundreds of times. Gone over the sigil. I didn't mess it up. I just...I just must have not been in the right frame of mind or something. Thoughts count with spells. Who you are counts." His eyes go vacant as he pulls himself up to the next step. "And now Bergerberg's brother has the opportunity to take over the family business by killing him properly. Who knows what that'll mean for us?"

They climb up onto a platform. Iron Bill and Primrose already wait at the threshold of a dark tunnel into the mountain.

"Down here, I should think," says Primrose.

With a flick of his wand, Burt creates a bulb of white light. "This way then, I suppose."

They quicken their pace. The sound of the crowd grows louder. Up ahead, the light of many blazing fires ripples through the archway at the end of the tunnel.

They break through into a vast room deep within the mountain to the sound of rapturous applause.

"It looks like Earth's champions have all finally arrived," blasts a charismatic male voice from nowhere. "It's been thirty-four years since Earth's champion humiliated the great Beelzebub in the arena, and here we are back again for a one-off, special edition, no guts no glory, bro against bro, battle to the deeeeeeeeeath."

The crowd cheer.

"Thirty-four years, Ted? I can remember it like it was yesterday," comes a similar female voice. "So, who do we have here? Burt Phoenix and Dirk Kilmore. Both seasoned sorcerers. Rumour has it they were the ones who stopped Bergerberg's army when he invaded Earth eight years ago."

"The less said about that, the better. What a disgrace to his father's name, and the whole of Hell, Cassandra."

"Couldn't agree more, Ted. Couldn't agree more."

"And that looks like Janet Bennet. Strange: she doesn't seem to have any magical abilities whatsoever, but they do say talent skips a generation or two. According to my notes, she's housed Bergerberg's soul since Dirk booted him from his body."

Cassandra lets out an impressed whistle. "She must have something going for her if she didn't succumb to his dark desires, Ted."

"Absolutely, Cassandra. And rumour has it, she's impressed quite a bit on the big fella."

"And is that a duck?"

"Not just any duck. That's Iron Bill of the Beaky Blinders with pixie knight, Primrose Applewhistle."

"My goodness, you can hardly recognise the Butcher of Winchester. He must have been working out, Ted. We are in for a show."

"And last, but certainly not least, the one we've all been itching to see. Sadie Kilmore. She has the wand. Jury's still out on whether she has the talent."

# Enter Gyozarg

The arena is the size of a football pitch and surrounded by a huge, filthy stone wall. Beyond that are the stalls filled with the shrieking and dancing denizens of Hell. Creatures of all shapes and sizes and colours and substances. Sadie daren't look too long into the crowd for fear that she might go insane. There are tentacles, and horns, and beasts with more eyes than it's possible to count. She glimpses something that appears to consist solely of floppy, slavering tongues.

It's as if these are the practice goes. The things a young God might try out before perfecting his art and making something beautiful like the creatures of Earth. The scrap bits, discarded and lost under the workbench of evolution, coming together to form something unnatural and unneeded.

"Dude..." says Burt, with a tone that expresses her feelings exactly.

"Dude indeed," confirms Dirk.

"Is that a commentator?" Sadie points to the ceiling.

"Sounds like it."

"What did he mean about them all itching to see me?"

"I have no idea." Dirk shakes his head, continuing to glare ahead to the middle of the pit.

The ground here is soft, sandy earth. Black and volcanic, like the beaches of Tenerife, broken here and there by shanks of sharp rock stabbing through the sand. The whole arena is lit by huge, swinging bowls of fire suspended from the ceiling.

Bergerberg stands in the centre.

"There she is."

Sadie follows Dirk's gaze.

"It's nice to see Bergerberg back, Ted, despite everything he's done. He always was a showdemon."

"He definitely has a charisma about him. If he's held on to that, we'll be in for an interesting fight tonight. And the crowd has always had a soft spot for him...despite everything."

"Despite everything."

Bergerberg stands dead centre, holding Ellie above his head in one clawed hand. The crowd cheers.

"Let's see how he feels when his brother emerges. He's grown a little in the last eight years."

"With this sacrifice!" bellows Bergerberg to the crowds, "I will rule once more."

They scream and pump their fists, tentacles, whatever they have, with a maddening intensity.

A huge metal portcullis, at least double the height of Bergerberg, stands in the wall on the far side of the arena. Sadie glances back to the entrance they've just come through. It's tiny in comparison. How must those human champions coming here alone to fight for the Earth have felt surrounded by this madness?

With a clanking of chains, the sound of the crowd drops into the jittering, tittering hush of the insane. Mad, gleeful eyes watch the portcullis as it ascends.

"Looks like Gyozarg is on his way, Cassandra. I wonder who he'll pick for his team. I expect Azalea will be there. They've fought alongside each other before, and now she's got that hot new bod."

Sadie starts towards Bergerberg. Primrose kicks his heels and Iron Bill takes to the sky, swooping just ahead as she runs. That maternal force within overcomes any fear she might have. Dirk is with her. They charge together. He's always been quick on his feet, but she keeps pace.

"Any ideas how we talk a demon down from eating our baby?" he says.

"I have one," she says, through gasped breaths.

She stops several metres from the giant blue bear and begins waving her arms. "Hey. Hey you!" she shouts. "Beebee."

Dirk gives her a frown. Mouths the word *Beebee*?

She waves him down. "Trust me." Then clears her throat.

"Looks like the Kilmores are trying something, Cassandra."

"Well, it is their child, after all, Ted. I hear most humans regard their infants as pretty important so they won't want to see it sacrificed, even if it does mean their team mate will regain his demon strength."

"All eyes are on them now."

Sadie tunes out the commentators as Bergerberg turns his navy, pupil-less eyes upon her. Beneath that cold gaze, she is an ant in a game of stares with an anteater.

Ellie sleeps in his enclosed hand. Unharmed as far as Sadie can tell. There's no sign that Bergerberg recognises her. No sign of what was once there remaining.

What had he said in Mum's bathroom? That he'd be like a big child throwing a tantrum.

Lucky she's done the first lesson of an internet course...

She takes a tentative step forward. Goes over the instructions in her head. How best to do this?

She holds out a hand. "Beebee, I know you're angry."

He bends low and roars — she can taste the stink of eight years of cold stagnation from here — but she perseveres. He'll have to try a little harder than that if he's going to top the primal fury of Ellie in full strop.

"It's OK to be angry, but you can't hurt Ellie," she says. "You don't want to. We have to be gentle. We have to be kind. Would you like to do crochet or would you like to face your brother in mortal combat using the sword my husband stole your strength with?" It's the best she can think of at such short notice.

Dirk raises the sword, ready for action. She waves a gentle arm to suggest he lower it. He does.

A growl comes from deep within the tunnel on the other side of the portcullis. A small shape hovers forward, glowing red in the depths. It's Azalea, followed by something big.

Bergerberg ignores his brother's approach and drops to three of his four limbs. He charges towards Sadie and Dirk. Iron Bill bristles and hisses.

"Woah," says Primrose, trying to wrangle her into stillness.

Sadie's heart beats hard in her chest, but she holds her position. Dirk shifts his stance nervously by her side, but he doesn't leave her.

This has to work or they're all dead.

She looks into those big, dark eyes. Tries her best stern voice. "Beebee, I know you're angry, and it's OK to be angry, but you can't hurt Ellie. You don't want to. We have to be gentle. We have to be kind. Would you like to do crochet or would you like to face your brother in mortal combat using the sword Dirk stole your strength with?"

Dirk turns the sword around and holds it forward. "I don't know why you have to point out it was me who stole his strength," he says out of the corner of his mouth.

"Well, you didn't leave me many options here," she says out of the corner of hers. "And maybe if you'd done the course as well, like I said to, you'd be able to come up with something better…"

"I know you're angry," she starts again. And Bergerberg hesitates. She takes the sword from Dirk and offers it. "And it's OK to be angry, but you can't hurt Ellie."

Bergerberg slows to a trot, then stands up on his hind legs. Looks down at Ellie in his palm. He takes a deep breath and his eyebrows knit together, confused at what lies there.

"I don't want to?" he says, his voice an unsure rumble.

"Oh, this is interesting, Cassandra."

"That's right." Sadie takes a step forward. "We have to be kind." She dips her head, drops her voice a little. "Come on now, big guy. Is torturing souls to within an inch of their sanity right for you? Is that right for Bergerberg?"

He growls low in his throat. "It…" His huge chest lifts and falls with slowing breaths. His eyes move to the side as he considers the question.

The crowd noise drops to the silence of a thousand held breaths.

Sweat sticks Sadie's top to her back inside her winter coat.

"No. It's not." Bergberg's voice is a low rumble.

Nearby, in the crowd, a group of four fat slug-like things dressed in jewelled robes start jeering. Bergerberg zeroes in on them, and with a method not too dissimilar to an experienced comedian silencing a heckler, snatches a head-sized rock from the ground and launches it across the auditorium. It crunches into the face of one monstrosity, exploding its splattered brains all over its friends. The others quickly shut up.

"And there we have Hell's Regent Parliament with their usual two cents," says Cassandra. "Looks like they'll be out of a job by the end of the night."

"Well, at least Festeroth will be, he no longer has a face," adds Ted.

"Can't say I'm upset about it, Ted. Bunch o' dicks."

Sadie steps forward with the sword. "Dirk says if you take this, it'll give you your strength back and you won't need to hurt Ellie."

Dirk gives Bergerberg a nervous wave.

"Well I never, Ted."

Bergerberg glances down at Dirk, then reaches for the sword. Sadie holds it back just out of reach, and the twelve-foot-tall bear-demon recoils as if stung.

"You need to share." She holds a hand forward. "Ellie for the sword."

"Risky move, Ted. Will it play out as she hopes?" The female commentator's voice is low, engrossed by the proceedings in the centre of the arena.

If possible, the crowd sound drops even more.

"Ellie?" Bergerberg says, looking down at the sleeping shape in his hand. His whole face changes when he sees her there. A bright, cheerful smile filled with scimitar teeth longer than she is. "Ellie."

She holds her breath. Shakes her raised open hand. "Ellie first."

Bergerberg nods, then places Ellie at her feet on the soft black sand.

Sadie places the sword on the ground and scoops up her child. Hugs her close to her chest.

"She's done it, Cassandra. Never before have we seen such an interesting development in advance of a battle."

"We all love and benefit greatly from a child sacrifice here at Hell Bowl, Ted, but this is just as exciting. A human has talked a demon into not feasting upon her child. Unprecedented."

"Unprecedented."

Dirk rushes to her and throws his arms around them both. For the tiniest of moments, Sadie closes her eyes. Home. Then she lets go and studies Ellie's face.

"Oh, she's cold, Dirk."

"I know." He removes his wand, and with a wave over Ellie's body, says, "Air calesco."

The surrounding air suddenly warms.

"That should do it for a while."

"What's the matter with her? Why doesn't she wake up?" Sadie can hear the panic in her own voice as she brushes the loose hair from Ellie's cheek.

"It's OK." Dirk touches a hand to Ellie's brow. "It's a sleeping spell. I can undo it. But we'll wait until we're safe. The more of this she sleeps through, the better."

"What's happening?" says Bergerberg, looking around. "Why are we here?"

The floor rumbles.

"Oh, look, Hell's champion has finally arrived," says Ted, as several multi-jointed spider-like legs extend from the blackness beneath the gate. "Fiends and freaks, demons, demis, and demonettes. Hell is proud to present your champion. The one, the only, Gyoooooo-zaaaaaarg!!"

The arena erupts as a black scorpion body stoops to fit beneath the portcullis. Its face is white, human and emotionless, like a porcelain mask, and sits at the end of a long black neck that snakes from between its shoulders. It's taller than Bergerberg, by some way. Azalea hovers over its shoulder, glowing red and cackling like a harpy.

"And there's his little pet, Azalea." Sadie can sense the eye-roll in Cassandra's tone.

"I'm not a pet!" shouts Azalea, her voice small and petulant compared to the enormity of the crowd. "I'm not a pet."

"You have to ask yourself, Ted, what's the sex like?"

"Two questions spring to mind, Cassandra. How, and why?"

"You've hit the nail square on the head. Why put yourself through that...for either of them?"

"The sword!" shouts Dirk, pointing it out to Bergerberg.

Sadie snaps back from trying to envision an answer to Cassandra's question with a confusing and descending cascade of images that gets worse the more she thinks about it.

"Wait," she says, "you said they'd want a fair fight. That they would only fight if Bergerberg was at full strength. What if he just doesn't get to full strength? Will the fight be off?"

"Um…" Dirk pauses a moment. "Um," he says again. "I'd not thought of that."

"No one leaves until one side is dead," says Burt from behind. He and Mum are together there.

"OK, scratch that idea," says Sadie.

"Good to see you're thinking outside the box, though," says Bergerberg as he snatches the blade from the ground. It looks like a butter knife in his hand. He turns to face his brother.

"What the eff am I suppo — woaaaah!" Two jets of bright blue light shoot out of the sword like the fields around a magnet, swallowing Bergerberg in their glow. His eyes crackle with ultramarine fire as the light coalesces and runs down his throat.

The thick fur all over his body ripples as if blown by a gale-force wind that shrieks and wails around him. His back straightens, then arches as he is lifted off the ground.

"My strength returns," he growls, and he grins widely before landing super-hero style. He stands and bellows into the air. This time, the roar is deafening; crushing in its intensity.

"I hope you both know what you're doing!" shouts Burt over the sound. He lifts his wand and backs off a few steps.

"We don't," Sadie says in perfect synchronisation with her husband. It's nice to start and end sentences with him again.

Mum lifts her rifle to her shoulder. "That other one is coming. What do we do?"

"We let them fight it out," says Dirk, ushering them all back towards the arch. "Let's get back to the portal. Whatever the outcome here, we'll deal with it on our own turf with Ellie somewhere safe."

As they approach the exit, the bricks around the arch grow across, blocking them in.

"Seems like they've forgotten the prime rule here at Hell Bowl, Ted. If your team leave the arena before a winner is announced, you forfeit the match."

"What does she mean by team?" Sadie looks between Burt and Dirk.

"Er..." Dirk looks unsure. "Burt? You've read more about this bit than me." Sadie scoffs. Like Burt reads.

"I have a sneaking suspicion they think we're on a team with Bergerberg and—"

They turn back to face the centre. On the other side of the arena, the space beneath the portcullis remains wide open. Five things stand behind Gyozarg and Azalea.

"What the hell are those?" says Dirk. He counts off on his fingers, ending at seven.

Burt raises his palm to his brow to block out nothing. "I can't see from here, but it looks like it's one of them for each of us, including the duck and the pixie separately, if you count Azalea and Gyozarg."

Gyozarg's bone-white masked face hovers roughly a metre over his brother. "Bergerberg, brother, where have you been?" His voice is felt as much as it is heard. It rumbles the walls and shakes the sand beneath their feet.

"Chilling out on Earth." Bergerberg shrugs. "It's actually pretty cool there. They've got this game called tennis—"

"Kill him!" shrieks Azalea, waving her arms around like a mad thing, and the whole of the amphitheatre strikes up like a band.

A Queen-style arena stomp accompanies their chant. Stamp, stamp, "Kill." Stamp, stamp, "Kill." It's very disconcerting.

Gyozarg crouches low, ready to pounce, and Bergerberg raises his butter-knife sword.

"We don't have to do this," he says, hopefully. "Let's talk."

"Scared?" says Gyozarg with the hint of a laugh. "How the mighty have fallen. The great Bergerberg, defiler of the enslaved, devourer of children, torturer of souls, takes a vacation on Earth and returns with less backbone than a pathetic human." He rocks from side to side on his eight legs. "Not once has one of Earth's champions tried to battle with words. And never shall we let them."

Gyozarg lifts two appendages to the crowd. They cheer.

"Fine," says Bergerberg, taking the opening and throwing himself forward into a charge.

A collective and somewhat surprised "Oooh" rises from the crowd as he closes the gap in moments. He brings the sword around like a shot-putter as his brother flourishes his stinger-tipped tail. Bergerberg ducks beneath it and hacks off one of Gyozarg's legs.

"Aaaah," coos the delighted audience, as if watching a particularly lovely firework show at a local school's Guy Fawkes night.

Gyozarg stumbles forward, dragged by the weight of his own swinging stinger, but quickly recovers. He kicks out with one of his other seven legs and boots Bergerberg several metres back towards the middle of the arena. Then he advances, snapping his pincers at his brother.

Azalea cackles, swooping high above her boyf like a glowing red fly.

"How likely is he to win?" asks Sadie, as Bergerberg pushes himself back up to his feet and ducks a swing of a claw.

Dirk shakes his head. Despite the cold, sweat stands out on his brow. "I don't know."

"Can we help him?"

Maybe they can even up the fight.

"We're going to have to deal with those other things first." He points across at the figures beneath the portcullis, who are yet to move.

Bergerberg is too slow to duck the second pincer and is whacked once more across the arena. He lands with a massive thud against one wall. Several demons in the stands rush forward to the edge of the crowd area to wave vuvuzelas and what look like burnt rats on sticks at him.

He swipes them away and presses himself to stand. Slower this time.

Dirk looks past the fight to the five creatures that stand motionless on the other side of the pit. "I thought it had to be one on one, but it looks like it's seven on seven."

The things begin their charge across the sand towards them.

Burt raises his wand, draws a knife from his bag, and once again precisely condenses Sadie's feelings into a single word.

"Balls!"

# HELL BOWL

"Things are really hotting up down here in Hell Bowl, aren't they, Ted?"

"Sure are, Cassandra," Ted chuckles. "I was a little worried the teammates weren't going to get involved, but looks like Gyozarg's minions have begun their move and are — wooooah, my goodness! Did you see that, Cassandra?"

"I certainly did, Ted. Janet Bennet has just blasted the heads off of Dint the Mischievous aaaand Percy the Bitter."

"Were those their heads? I always thought that was their...um." Ted chuckles again. "I had no idea. Those things are odd, even by our standards."

"Who knows, Ted, but Dint and Percy are out of this match as quickly as they came in."

"That has to be some sort of record, doesn't it?"

"Has to be. Maybe some of that talent didn't skip her after all."

With the two shots from Mum's rifle still ringing in her ears, Sadie readies her next thermos. "What are those things?" she shouts.

"Nuckelavees," says Dirk. He gives Mum a thumbs up. "Nice work, Janet."

The things charging them down look like horses, but they have no flesh, just bleeding muscle stretched over their bones and sinews. Growing up from the centre of their backs is the torso of a person, skin-less also, and rocking from side to side, lifeless with the galloping movement. Overly long human arms flop all the way to the ground. Sharpened, black claws drag along with a hiss through the sand.

"They are gross, is what they are," says Burt, waving his dagger in the shape of a great infinity symbol in front of himself. Lightning crackles within the shape. "Get behind this."

"We've not fought them before," says Dirk, Sadie assumes for her benefit. "Don't know what spells kill them, if any." He ducks around Burt's lightning shield and fires off an infernus spell. The rider on the back of one horse throws up their gangly arms, deflecting the spell, which forms a sizzling crater in the sand to its right.

"But bullets seem to work, right?" says Sadie. "Try again, Mum."

Mum readies her rifle, but up above Azalea closes in. The witch flicks her fingers, and the gun is ripped from Mum's hands. Trying to retain her grip, Mum is pulled to her knees. Azalea laughs as the rifle bends itself into a knot before her, then drops uselessly to the ground.

"Bottoms," Mum says, pushing herself back up to stand. She dumps the pack on her back and throws off her parka.

She sifts through her bag. Pulls out her biggest kitchen knife and a wok. The pan handles have been removed and two bungee cords are wrapped around it. She slides the wok over her arm like a bracer and brandishes the knife, glaring threateningly at Azalea from her position next to Burt.

"For Daisy!" shouts Primrose, and Iron Bill launches up from the ground and swoops into the air towards Azalea, who feints to the side. They circle each other, Azalea firing off spell after spell, deftly dodged by the duck while she tries to get close enough to deposit her deadly rider or impale the witch on her metal beak.

"Infernal bird!" shrieks Azalea, as she turns tail.

"Keep her body alive!" calls Burt, resting his hand on his satchel where Betty resides inside the leech.

Azalea flees over the area where Bergerberg is now up and grappling against Gyozarg's pincers.

The sound of the brothers' battle pounds in Sadie's ears. Two great beasts pitted against each other in mortal combat, throwing up fountains of sand into the crowd, to the audience's absolute joy.

The nuckelavees close the distance.

Sadie waggles her wand. "Move It." But once more the creature swipes a claw and deflects the spell, kicking up a wave of black sand some metres away.

Dirk gives her a '*nice try, hun*' look. "They're using their own spells to deflect ours."

"Had to find out demons could do that the hard way," adds Burt.

"Then what can we do? Is there a bullet spell?"

The sound of hooves and scraping claws on the dirt announces their imminent arrival.

"Not one I know." Dirk swipes his wand through the air and shouts something Latin-y. A huge spiky outcrop of brown stone stabs up from the ground just in front of the creatures. There's a satisfying crash and a shocked whinny from the other side as the nuckelavees slam into the surprise wall of rock.

"Ooof. Dirk Kilmore there with some sort of 'create rock' spell," says Ted. "The nuckelavees did *not* see that coming."

"I really like it when the Earth champions manipulate the environment to their advantage, knowing their offensive spells might not be effective."

"Come on!" Dirk shouts, leading them into a position to put the battling brothers between them and the horse-things. "We need to come up with a plan."

"We could try the old Ivanhoe Gambit," suggests Burt, holding the dagger aloft, giving them a sort of lightning umbrella in case Azalea attacks them from the air, although at present, the pixie and duck have her on the run.

"You can't time travel in Hell, Burt. It's all the same moment."

"Uh...Wall of Death?"

"Nah! What about Defenders of the Bridge?"

"You guys don't sound so sure." Sadie has not run this much since before Ellie was born. And never carrying a heavy, sleeping child. She doesn't know how much more she can take.

Burt considers this a moment. "Defenders of the Bridge might work. Just pound spells at the one in front until we find something that'll get through?"

"And if that doesn't work?" pants Sadie. She doesn't like to be a Negative Nancy, but they have to be realistic.

Burt jerks his head at Mum. "Then we take a leaf out of Janet's book." He pats his satchel.

"Move to melee range." Dirk nods, but he doesn't look happy about it. "You take the right. I'll take the left."

The duo skid to a halt as the creatures appear around the wall of rock and charge them once more.

Sadie stops beside her mum, just behind them.

Mum grits her teeth like an angry Amazonian warrior with her wok shield and knife.

"Are you OK, Mum?"

"Never been more afraid in my life." She clangs the knife against the wok menacingly. "But dare one of those little horse oiks come at my Ellie."

Dirk and Burt lift their wands in one synchronised motion. Two walls of rock rise from beneath the sand, creating a funnel, hemming the beasts in. The creatures trip and fall in line, still aiming straight for them.

"Water whip!" shouts Sadie, slinging her arm forward. The water from her thermos shoots out. Even the droplets of sweat from her forehead are sucked off towards the end of her wand. The jet of boiling water jettisons towards the beasts as they charge, spattering the lead. It hisses in pain as steam rises from its flesh, but it does not slow.

"Maybe with more water?" says Burt.

"I thought you said there was lots down here?" Sadie looks at Dirk.

"Outside, maybe," he says.

Burt looks up and around. "I guess they used a dehumidifier or something."

"Anything to make it difficult for us." Dirk waves his wand. "Crystalos." A spike of frozen ice launches towards the riders. It shatters on impact, but doesn't slow them. "Ah, balls!"

"Acid ball!" shouts Burt, and a green globule of sizzling goop fires down the gauntlet, splashing ineffectually over its targets. "Nothing's working," he says, panic edging into his voice.

Dirk looks to Sadie with Ellie in her arms. His face hardens. "Then suit up, Burt. We're going in."

"I thought you'd never ask," says Burt, with a face that suggests he hoped he'd never ask.

"It's time to show Hell who runs the show."

"Darn tootin'."

"Heck yep."

"Boom town."

She senses they are stalling, so tries to boost morale. "Um, are you two being excessively cool because I'm here?" She smiles at them.

"Number one rule of Monster Bashers Inc," says Burt. "Always be cool in front of chicks."

Dirk winces.

"*Chicks?*" says Sadie.

"That's mainly Burt's rule," says Dirk, then adds. "But is it working?"

She gives him a sultry half-smile. "Maybe."

It is...

Dirk grins, then lets out a nervous breath and nods at Burt. As one, the pair dig hands into their satchels, each pulling out a sort of skullcap. In perfect Power Ranger-style unison, they slap them atop their heads. Their bodies are instantly cocooned from head to toe in a thin, semi-translucent, latex-like layer of rubbery light.

"Burt the Mysterious — ready for action."

"Dirk the Unstoppable — ready for action."

Sadie lifts an eyebrow at the two "members" of Monster Bashers Inc. "You look like—"

"I know what we look like, Sadie Janet Bennet," says Dirk, before she can finish, using her full maiden name as he so often does when he's doing something silly and doesn't want to admit it. He wobbles his head from side to side to emphasise his annoyance (annoyance that, she expects, is aimed predominantly at himself).

Burt puts a hand to his head and shakes it. "It's condom-covered penises, isn't it?" He slaps Dirk on the arm, shooting out a shower of sparks. "You said armour of light would look cool."

"We are cool, Burty. We're demon hunters. Now, let's hunt some demons."

They dip their hands into their satchels again, and like a pair of Mary Poppinses prepping for battle, Dirk draws a set of samurai swords that are way too big for the bag, and Burt a gnarly-looking hammer.

With swords held by his sides, Dirk rushes to Sadie and kisses her hard on the lips. The light armour tingles, warm against her cheeks.

"I love you," he says, then looks at Ellie with a bittersweet sparkle in his eye. "Both of you. More than anything has ever loved anything. We'll get out of this." He turns to Burt. "Two men enter..." He holds out a sword.

Burt taps it with his hammer. "...no demons leave."

And they charge.

She can't take her eyes from her husband as he and his friend collide headlong with the first nuckelavee. It swipes a claw, knocking Burt against the wall of rock in a shower of sparks from his armour. Dirk swings a sword, but the creature ducks out of the way.

"We should help them," says Mum, taking a few steps ahead of Sadie.

"Mum, you said yourself you weren't one for fisticuffs. What can we do?" Sadie hugs Ellie close to her chest with one arm. Looks down at the wand in her hand. There's really nothing they can do...is there?

As her husband fights for their lives, she scans the arena.

Above them Azalea and Primrose continue to circle and dodge like dogfighting spitfires, ducking left and right between the crackling bowls of fire that light the arena. A searing ball of lightning, shot from Azalea's fingertips, connects with Iron Bill, and with a strangled quack she and Primrose fall from the sky.

Gyozarg now has Bergerberg pinned on his back. Bergerberg ducks as the stinger stabs towards his head, lodging itself into the sand behind him. He grips the tail, holding it in place, but things don't look good for him.

"There's no use fighting any longer, brother," booms Gyozarg with a mocking leer. "Once you and your team are finished, I'll sacrifice the child and gain all of your strength. Then I will be unstoppable, and Azalea and I will take Earth. We will finally accomplish what you never could."

Bergerberg shakes his head. "She's using you, brother."

"So, while it looks like this battle will shortly be coming to an end, Ted, let's recap for the fans at home a little of the last Hell Bowl."

"Absolutely, Cassandra. Beelzebub demanded souls from Earth, as he is wont to do, and Earth searched for a champion to deny his demand, as they are wont to do. Textbook negotiation."

"And who they found wasn't the usual sort, was she, Ted?"

"No, Cassandra. It is said that after Earth's previous hero was damned to an eternity of torture and pain upon losing, as is tradition, no one came forward. And as it is written, the champion must be a volunteer. The people of Earth were at a loose end. But then a shining beacon in the form of an old woman came forward. Joan Bennet offered herself as champion."

Sadie looks at Mum. And Mum looks at Sadie.

"Ah, remember how we all laughed when she stepped through the archway? That frail old thing with that little tentacle stick."

Sadie looks at the wand in her hand.

"She wiped the smile off our faces, though, didn't she?"

"She certainly did. Well, until we found out that Beelzebub hadn't been obliterated into dust; he'd just been sent straight to bed. That was flipping hilarious. What a humiliation."

Cassandra laughs. "What an absolute embarrassment."

They both cackle.

"I wonder why a human hasn't tried to use a similar spell to win Hell Bowl before, Cassandra."

"Well, we had Hell's best look into the spell, Ted, and rumour has it only a mother at the very end of her tether can perform such a piece of magic."

"There's power in the love of a mother."

"Indeed."

Sadie frowns at her mum. "Is this...?"

Mum's mouth hangs agape. "It doesn't make sense."

"Oh, look at that, Ted. Something's clicked in the Bennet women's brains. I wonder..." She sounds surprised. "Perhaps they didn't know."

"It was Granny Joan," Mum says. "The last champion was our Granny Joan."

"And she just cast the spell she used to send Grandma to bed to kick Beelze-bub out of the arena. And when he left, he forfeited the match, and she won." Sadie grips Mum by the shoulder. Searches her face. "What else did Grandma tell you about the spell?"

Mum shakes her head. "I don't know. All I know is when Granny Joan got really mad with them, she'd wave her wand, say 'Straight To Bed', and your grandma would end up in bed. Usually without any supper."

"There has to be a shape. A sigil." Sadie twirls the tip of the wand in the air to demonstrate.

"Dirk must know it," says Mum, looking up towards the valley of rock where he and Burt are still trading blows with the remaining trio of nuckelavees. "He said on the way here he tried to use the spell to send Bergerberg back."

"But Burt said he messed it up."

"He didn't mess it up. He just wasn't the right person for the job."

Something tingles in Sadie's pocket. A strange vibration in her hip, as if her phone is there and someone is calling. She pats herself down. Something flat there. Almost nothing. She digs her hand in and withdraws the card with the address for Dirk's unit.

She runs her finger over the edge. That pillow shape that Dirk so often doodled.

She lets out an excited yelp. "This is it!"

With shaking hands, she traces the shape with the tip of her wand.

She looks up when she hears Dirk let out a shout.

"Burt, look out!"

Burt lies on his back writhing in agony. Red lightning crackles over his body. He screams in pain.

Dirk leaps up into the air and, with a wild downswing of his sword, decap-itates the horse head of the leading nuckelavee. The thing goes down between him and the last two creatures, blocking their path.

He rushes to his friend.

Above them, Azalea hangs in mid-air. Crackling lightning zaps from her fingers, and though he tries to bring his wand up to deflect, Dirk is hit and knocked to the ground.

Iron Bill and Primrose lie smoking on the sand between Sadie and Mum, and Dirk, Burt, and the nuckelavees.

Azalea fires again. And the pair scream once more, pinned to the ground under her lightning bolt.

With wide, rolling, hungry eyes, the remaining nuckelavees try to scramble over the body of their fallen comrade to get to Dirk and Burt.

Sadie closes her eyes. She takes a deep breath and traces the shape again. She doubts herself. She glances at her mum standing by her side. She's going to throw up.

"You've got this," whispers Mum. "You're better than you think. You're brave and strong."

Gyozarg wrenches his tail stinger from Bergerberg's grasp.

With a flick of her wrist, Sadie traces in the air that pillow shape she's seen so often, and shouts, "Straight To Bed!"

Gyozarg blips into non-existence. Gone. Straight to bed without any supper.

"Oh, she's done it, Ted."

"I do not believe what I'm seeing, Cassandra."

"The audience might be a little miffed. They love a bloody finish, but don't we all just love the drama of the change? That'll be something to talk about over the water cooler on Monday."

"It is official, Gyozarg is no longer in the arena. He has forfeit the match."

Bergerberg springs to his feet. "Azalea!" he bellows in rage, then starts his charge towards the valley of rock where Burt and Dirk are pinned.

With as much care as she can in the hurry that she's in, Sadie shoves Ellie into her mother's arms and runs parallel to the twelve-foot-tall demon-bear. She sprints across the sand with everything she has towards her tortured husband. Strengthened by anger. Powered by love.

Azalea turns to her and raises her clawed, outstretched fingers. She shrieks something inhuman and red lightning shoots out of her fingertips towards Sadie.

But once again, nothing happens.

Sadie looks down as her winter coat dissolves around her, whipping away with the speed of her run, revealing Bergerberg's robe. The bolts of lightning crackle between the disks weaved into it, then dissipate.

"No!" shouts Azalea as she tries again. "Why won't you die?"

Bergerberg claws his way to the top of the pillar of stone that stands behind Azalea and leaps into the air. He crashes into his unsuspecting ex, drawing another delighted "ooo" from the audience. He drags her down to the ground and, with a smack of his paw, knocks her unconscious.

The scarlet lightning travelling over Dirk and Burt's bodies fizzles to nothing and the pair flop back against the sand.

"Wait," Burt wheezes as the demon lifts a claw to finish Azalea. He tears the leech from his satchel and scrambles painfully across the ground towards his sister's body. The demon steps back. "Don't hurt her. Betty's inside the leech."

He reaches her and places the leech over her head.

Just a few metres away, Dirk tries to push himself up, but his arms give way beneath him. He looks exhausted.

Behind, the final two nuckelavees are closing.

Primrose waves an arm from the ground between them as Sadie closes the distance. She scoops up the fallen duck and pixie like a pro-rugby player might a fumbled pass.

"You alright?" she asks.

The duck looks a little singed around the feathers. A little dazed too. Smoking, but still conscious. She quacks. It sounds positive.

"Just need a hand to get back in the air," splutters Primrose.

"No problem. Hold on tight."

Sadie holds the duck up over her shoulder like a dart as, with a frantic kicking of their strong, bloody legs, the nuckelavees finally trample over the dead body of their fallen comrade and clamber forward to get to where Dirk lies. Their mad black and yellow eyes stare as they jag forward with their lifeless human torsos flopping from side to side. The first rears up on to its hind legs over her husband and shrieks.

Sadie draws Iron Bill back and throws. The duck beats her powerful wings to gain speed, then pulls them in like a peregrine and spears head first through the neck of the first nuckelavee, carving out a red tunnel of flesh. As its dying body drops to the ground, she loops around with a barrel roll, flicking droplets of blood all over the surrounding rock, the sand, Dirk, basically everything, before coming straight back down to land on the other galloping nuckelavee's head.

Primrose jumps off and raises his steak knife as if baiting the audience, then plunges it down through the horse's skull, showering himself with high-pressure brains and cerebral fluid like a drill striking oil.

The crowd erupts. The noise is deafening.

"Oh, what a show!" Ted sounds truly delighted.

"That is what the devils have been waiting for, isn't it, Ted? My goodness."

"We'll have to get those two back, Cassandra. The crowd just love them."

"They don't call him the Butcher of Winchester for nothing."

"What a duck."

"What a team."

"What a night."

# Straight To Bed

Sadie bolts upright, noticing how beautifully tucked in she had been, then runs to Ellie's room with Granny Joan's wand still tight in her hand. She feels a little woozy from the sudden increase in temperature, and having gone from standing upright in Hell's arena surrounded by the screaming of a thousand happy devils, to lying down in her own bed in the blink of an eye.

Dirk is already there, cradling Ellie over one shoulder in the dark of her room.

Orange streetlight shines through the holes in Ellie's blind, picking out the purple bruises on Dirk's face. He smiles with those still swollen lips when he sees her.

"Did you get Burt and Betty home OK?" he asks.

She tries to ignore the spatter of blood from the dog man and the bullet holes that mark the bedroom wall.

"Yeah, I think so. Did you wake her yet?" she asks, looking at Ellie's peaceful face over his shoulder.

Imagine being able to sleep through all of that. Most kids just snooze through a wedding or a movie, but Ellie had just slept through an entire arena-based battle to the death in Hell. Not only that, but one her parents had won. Would they tell her when she was older?

He nods. Whispers, "yeah, she's really asleep now. Not a spell."

Sadie holds out her hands and he passes her over, then wraps his arms around them both.

"You go back into our room," he says. "I'll move her cot in so you can get some rest. I'll call your mum and make sure she's OK. Then I should call Betty and Burt. I predict a lot of paperwork on the horizon at the Bureau, now Bergerberg is back where he belongs. We're going to have to reinstate their memories."

"Not right now, though, right?"

"Nah." He smiles. "It can wait."

Sadie's body relaxes, as if her tense and tired muscles are melting, warmed just by having him near. A feeling she had taken for granted before, or perhaps grown too used to. This is how it's supposed to be.

"Did you know?" she asks.

"Know what?"

"That it was Granny Joan's wand. My Granny Joan."

He shakes his head. "I had no idea. But everything is connected. Everything wants to be back where it belongs."

Sadie looks at the curved tentacle. It wriggles gently in her hand.

"It does."

She kisses his cheek and carries Ellie back to their room, while he does his best to manhandle the cot through Ellie's doorway and around their landing without making too much noise. It'll be a few months, at least, before Sadie can leave their baby alone in her room again.

She lies in bed next to her sleeping child. Strokes her cheek. Closes her eyes. God, she's tired.

Maybe she'll make pancakes in the morning. Or perhaps they'll just go out for breakfast.

# School's In

"There are a lot of ways we can use magic. Can you name a few?"

Nathan raises a hand. His green eyes gleam. "Fighting!"

Sadie tuts, which she knows is bad form. She doesn't want to be that sort of teacher. She wants to encourage, not quash. "Yes, defence. But that shouldn't be the first thing we go to, and that's not what First Level Spells is about. What else?"

A small elf raises her hand. "Removing pests safely from beetroot leaves and—"

Nathan scoffs, and the girl's cheeks redden.

Sadie nods and gives the girl a reassuring smile. "Go on, Epple."

"And repairing the leaf once you've moved the pest so the plant can continue to grow."

"Brilliant answer." She turns the pages of Granny Joan's book to the specific spell. "Granny Joan often used modifications of her own spells to look after her vegetable patch. The spell you're thinking of, Epple, is called um..." She smiles. Granny Joan had a sense of humour like Mum.

"Bugger out!" shouts Nathan.

The other kids laugh.

"That's the one. If only it worked on all the little pests." She raises her eyebrows pointedly at him and the kids laugh again.

"Today we're going to practise something that at first seems simple, but requires a lot of concentration to perfect. I'd like you to scroll to page 54."

The kids tap at their tablets. There's no Wi-Fi down here and the only thing loaded on them is a scanned copy of Granny Joan's spell book, so she knows they aren't messing around.

"You'll notice the pan and spoon on each of your desks. The spell is called 'Stir the Pot'. If you can get one going and we've got time before your next lesson, I'll put you into groups of two and you can practise keeping one stirring while you get another started. It's harder than you think."

She herself has only managed three at once, and according to the Drake, she's a natural for an unnatural. She chalks up the page number, sigil, and spell name on the board while the kids begin.

"Granny Joan could cook a whole three-course meal without lifting a finger, except to touch her wand," she adds over her shoulder.

Nathan and the boy next to him start their spoons fencing in mid-air between them.

"Hey," she says, placing her hands on her hips, "there'll be plenty of time for that in Mr. Kilmore's defence lesson. Fifteen minutes and you can do all the sword play you like."

Epple shifts in her seat as her spoon spins around the inside of the pan. Sadie doesn't like to pick her out in front of everyone. She gets easily embarrassed and kids can be cruel even without meaning to be. But she gives her a wink and a smile, garnering a cheerful grin from the girl.

A tendril of jelly swings down from above and touches her neck.

*Dirk's here.*

*Thanks, Bloc.*

Toph's son has moved in and does a great job of both ceiling for the school and floor for Wren's house above. As he's still a young cube and has a smaller build than his father, the Drake has added a flight of stairs to the back of the room to get everyone down.

Together, the local community have made some improvements to the Drake's underground classroom. The walls are no longer bare earth. Instead, they are bricked and plastered with three magical windows conjured up by one of the other estate residents. They show actual views of stunning locations all over the world: the Himalayas, Milford Sound, Machu Picchu.

The mixture of light through the panes is beautiful. The classroom is the perfect place to daydream. It's her second favourite place to be.

While the kids are busy, she opens her desk drawer and checks her phone. No messages from Mum, which is fine. Ellie should be having lunch about now.

It's been four months since the arena, a month since she started lessons down here, and things are really coming together.

Azalea is back in her old body in jail at the bureau, Gyozarg still hasn't emerged from his bed chambers, and Sadie is teaching. Actually teaching lessons in magic from Granny Joan's book.

For her, the book still holds a great deal of mystery. Where did it come from? How was it lost?

Although she still finds it difficult to believe he reads, Burt has researched in depth the subject of magic books and wands and seems to think Granny Joan's book was a gift from a powerful magical creature. The spells inside are her own creations. Finch's explanation of them being like cheat codes holds true. Dirk and Burt think of them like hot keys. The combination of wand movement, sound, and thought unlocks something in the physical page that somehow makes the written word real.

Maybe, one day, she'll be able to add her own spells.

The natural talent of the kids she teaches means they can connect directly with the magic contained within the pages without the use of a wand or a sound. Granny Joan's spells are a guide to what they can achieve, allowing the children to make their own imagined effects real. As they learn from Granny Joan's book, the connection between the power inside them and what is possible coalesces and refines.

They've set up five classes so far: Her First Level Spells class and Dirk's defence. Burt teaches magical history, because, surprisingly, he's a bit of a swot when it comes to that. The Drake teaches business. And every other Wednesday afternoon Bergerberg takes a break from ruling Hell and logs in on Zoom to teach Hell Studies.

They have twenty children from the estate. It's about all they can handle with the space.

The plan is to renovate and take over the local community centre, with a view to getting more teachers in from the Bureau. With Betty back in charge of HR, and memories restored thanks to Bergerberg's reinstatement as Lord of Hell, the estate now has a lot more support. Twenty kids will become forty. Eventually, they might start teaching those without innate magical abilities.

She looks forward to a time when Ellie will be able to come and learn with the others.

The stairs at the back of the room squeak as Dirk descends. He wears a tweed jacket and a tie. She has no idea why. He says it's more "teachery". She tries to hide her laugh. It's so out of character.

"Mr. Kilmore!" shouts Nathan. The boy always seems to shout. "What we learning today?"

Dirk swallows and touches his collar. "Um…I thought we'd try light armour." He glances up at Sadie. There's a gleam of sweat on his brow. His Adam's apple bobs. "But you concentrate on whatever it is Mrs. Kilmore has you doing."

He approaches from the back of the room.

She lets his hand touch hers. Takes it and squeezes it, down low, so the kids don't see.

"You do know what he's going to say as soon as you put that thing on, right?"

His beard is neatly shaven with a hint of salt in all that glorious pepper. Though he has a scar on his lip and over his right eyebrow from the things the bogeymen and Azalea did to him, he's never looked more dashing.

"Uh, I…I know." He leans closer to her ear. "I've faced werewolves, vampires, and the worst Hell has to offer, and nothing makes me more nervous than standing up in front of these kids. How do you do it?"

She smiles and dabs his brow with her cuff. Straightens his tie. "Because there's nothing they can say that'll derail me. Because I know I'm perfect as I am." She boops him on the nose. "And so, Mr. Kilmore, are you."

# Hello!

Thank you for reading my book 'The Demon Hunter's Wife'. I hope you enjoyed it. I'd be eternally grateful if you could take two minutes to leave an honest review on Amazon and Goodreads. Even if it's just a few words. As an indie author reviews and ratings really help!

For updates on new releases, freebies, and offers on other books please sign up to my mailing list at my website - https://cjpowellauthor.com/tdhw – When you sign up you'll receive a playlist of songs that helped influence me in the writing of this book. Music I used as a soundtrack while sitting in the dark sipping chamomile tea and tapping at my laptop. They are all total bangers so worth signing up for! And don't worry I won't spam you.

Scan this QR code to go
straight there.

Please get in touch to let me know if you enjoyed the book - I'd love to hear your feedback. And feel free to recommend it to some friends!!

You can also find me on Instagram, Facebook, and Tik Tok by searching C J Powell Author.

Thanks again!!

Chris x

# Also By C J Powell

## There's Something Wrong With The Cats

If you enjoyed 'The Demon Hunter's Wife', then you'll love 'There's Something Wrong With The Cats'.

**Curiosity didn't kill the cat, it mutated it into a vigilante crime fighter.**

Dan's cats are acting weird. One has grown into a strength powerhouse, the other wants to communicate... verbally. And now other kitties have begun to go missing from his quiet suburban street. Could the man in the parka that haunts a nearby industrial estate have answers? Or perhaps it's something to do with the strange disappearing woman in the woods? Can our hero figure out the conspiracy before it turns into a catastrophe?

**There's Something Wrong With The Cats** is a fun science fiction mystery. If you like zeroes becoming heroes and twists that keep you guessing, you'll love this fun standalone novel.

Available from amazon or to order from all good indie book stores.

"Part science fiction, part cosy crime, and part thriller... completely fun — and a terrific read. I loved it!" - **Loree Westron - Author of Missing Words**
"completely original and very funny. You'll want to read it in one sitting" - **Alain Elliot - Author of Home Sweet Home**

"An absolute blast... I'm staying a dog person. Very funny. Totally recommended." - **Onia Fox - Author of Listless in Turkey**

"another amazingly unique story from promising young writer C.J.Powell." - **Amazon.fr review**

# Also By C J Powell

## A More Perfect Human

**Two high-profile celebrities found dead in an alley. Another missing. Can a recently widowed bodyguard keep his new client alive when the assassins turn their sights on him?**

Nige Davies just wants to reconnect with his family. Hoping for a little extra cash, the club bouncer takes a security job for the world's oldest man. But his client isn't your usual 135-year-old. He's tanned, toned, and works as a health guru for the world's biggest food company. Everyone's heard of him. Everyone loves him.

But when other influencers turn up dead, the pair are forced to flee across a near-future London. With assassins hot on their heals, Nige soon discovers his client is hiding something. Something that will change the world forever. Something that an evil organisation will stop at nothing to keep hidden.

Can he reveal the truth, or will the Earth-shattering secret of the world's most beloved centenarian die with him?

**A More Perfect Human** is the fast-paced first book in the Chrysalis science fiction series. If you like action-packed thrills, witty dialogue, and unexpected twists and turns, then you'll love C J Powell's darkly humorous manhunt.

Available from Amazon or to order from all good indie book stores.

"A perfect balance of tension and comedy..." - **DK Pike (Author of Fauxville)**

"A wonderful cast that literally jump off the page..." - **Amazon Review**

"One of the best books I've read..." - **Goodreads Review**

"I truly am stunned to see that this is this young author's first book because it really is a masterful work of fiction" - **Amazon.fr Review**

# Coming Soon...

## I Eat Mushrooms For Breakfast

**An abandoned colony, a host of abominable creatures, and a space pirate with a tequila induced hangover trying desperately not to vomit inside his respirator helmet.**

Mark just wants to be a hero. A Star Sailor. Jetting across the galaxy saving colonists and giving aliens what for. All he needs is a little bit of cash to cover the training. So when he's offered the biggest score of his life, he knows he has to take it. Stick up a fancy hotel yacht. Rob a bunch of wealthy executives. Make off with the cash. What could be simpler? But when the yacht unexpectedly self destructs, his only choice is to take an escape pod to a nearby colony planet along with the yacht's guests and crew. Awkward... Upon arrival they find the colony abandoned. Strange flower gardens hide even stranger creatures. Can Mark get himself and the other survivors to safety or will the mysteries of Rosen-54 swallow them whole?

**I Eat Mushrooms For Breakfast** is a fun space adventure. If you love weird alien creatures and unlikely heroes stepping up when they have to, then you'll love this action packed sci-fi story.

# About The Author

Hi, I'm Chris. I'm a wedding band musician from the south of the UK. I'm also now an author :)

This book is dedicated to my wife and daughter. I don't know what to write in about the author pages, but the software I have to format my books suggests I put one in. I like board games, mushrooms, and board games about mushrooms.

Get to know me by knowing the things I like...

Top four films: Alien, Fifth Element, Blues Brothers, Trolls: Band Together.

Top four games: Half-Life, Dungeon Keeper, Streets of Rage, Goldeneye.

Top four bands: Fink, M83, Kishi Bashi, Foals – although this changes on a daily basis.

Uuuuuuuuuum! So... thanks for reading! So loooooooong!

Milton Keynes UK
Ingram Content Group UK Ltd.
UKHW030855051124
450766UK00005B/552

9 781739 209834